There Falls No Shadow

By

David E Crossley

ISBN-10-1-905562-01-2

ISBN-13-978-1-905562-01-5

ISBN-978-1-291-25758-8

Acknowledgements

I would like to thank the many people who assisted me in the production and editing of this novel. Their participation helped it to become a work I can hope everyone will enjoy.

I particularly want to thank Jenny Hewitt of the Jacqui Bennett Writers Bureau http://www.jbwb.co.uk/jacqui.html for her eagle-eyed editing, incisive suggestions and constant, friendly, professional encouragement.

And of course I cannot miss out my wife Patricia, for her encouragement and patience during long hours of my being squirreled away pounding the keyboard, and disturbed nights when I was up at 3 a.m. fighting to find that elusive piece of dialogue or technical detail.

Thank you all.

In soft deluding lies let fools delight.
A Shadow marks our days; which end in Night.

How slow the Shadow creeps: but when 'tis past
How fast the Shadows fall. How fast! How fast!

Loss, and Possession, Death and Life are one.

There falls no shadow where there shines no sun.

- Hilaire Belloc (1870–1953) On a Sundial

Index

Prelude	5
Awakening	7
Encounters	27
Pest Control	40
Gathering	59
Settling	76
Contact	103
Directions	134
Flames	155
Neighbours	184
Hunters	212
Workers and Queens	237
Wind and Tears	261
Postscript	286
About the author	292

Prelude

After the twin towers fell in New York, America declared war on terrorism. First they struck at Afghanistan and then Iraq. Other nations joined in. The terrorists fought back with brutal effectiveness, but were met by such overwhelming retaliation that even their commitment eventually waned. Politicians hailed the lull as proof that terror could not win. For years then it seemed we stood a chance of peace but the terrorists were playing a waiting game; changing their strategy, building their resources.

Then they struck at London. A lorry full of explosives surrounded by radioactive waste exploded in the heart of the city's business district. It wasn't a nuclear explosion, but the blast took hundreds of lives, destroyed or contaminated countless buildings and the shock waves from it shook the financial foundations of the world. It was only the beginning.

In Brussels, a car left running in the car park spewed out blister-agent gas through its exhaust, killing, blinding or maiming politicians and workers at the European parliament complex. In the Hong Kong stock exchange, a computer technician uploaded a new virus. First it collapsed the market, and then it spread its tendrils throughout the global financial structure, causing chaos. In the Middle East, Israeli intelligence discovered a plot to sail a nuclear bomb into a major port in America. The US navy and Coast Guard boarded and searched every cargo ship at the three-mile line for four months. They found nothing.

Again the terrorists rested. Long enough this time for their victims to believe life might be returning to normal. Then they struck again. Not from the sea but from the air. Four cargo aircraft, each carrying a nuclear device, detonated at over thirty-thousand feet above Washington, Bonn, Tokyo, and New Delhi. The bombs killed no one except the crews but the electro-magnetic pulses generated by the blasts surged like a flood through thousands of square miles of power and communication systems. The effects were more catastrophic for technologically dependent nations than a ground burst could ever have been. Circuits, transistors and relays blew. Large tracts of the supposedly nuclear-attack-proof Internet evaporated as the unhardened commercial servers, support centres, and telephone networks running it died. Mutually dependent, time-sensitive, industrial, commercial and financial systems fell apart.

People panicked. Shortages became commonplace. Riots were now a regular feature of the news. Most people tried to get on with their lives as best they could but everyone knew, there must be more to come. Ever more aggressive restrictions were imposed on the freedoms people had believed were their rights. The world was demoralised and confused, frantic to replace the technology on which it relied so heavily. It was in no state to defend itself against another blow. And this time, the terrorists were not going to wait.

Awakening

Emma Gordon slammed down the phone. Growling in frustration, she swept away the tears from her eyes. Bloody men! The world was falling apart and all her fiancé could talk about was oil flow and his bonus.

Damn, Robert infuriated her at times! But she was missing him and it would be three weeks before he was home again. She needed him here, now. So many things were going wrong and the 'flu' epidemic worried her and she thought she might have caught it and ….

Emma cursed silently as she stared out of the window. Their fight, before he left for Aberdeen to catch the helicopter flight back to the oilrig where he worked, nagged at her. She had been bitchy but she was desperate for him not to leave. He was dismissive. His job paid too well to risk it, he said, and the war in the Middle East meant the UK needed every drop of oil it could pump from the North Sea.

Last night when she wanted to call him the telephone had been dead again. Then at eleven o'clock the electricity had failed. She had boiled a pan of water on a single-burner camping stove and gone to bed with a whisky toddy. At least this morning the telephone was back on, even if the electricity wasn't. But while she sat winding up the internal dynamo of her Freeplay radio to listen to the news, the kitchen light flickered back to life. Emma looked up, her face brightening to match the light. The energy-saver bulb pulsed, dimmed then steadied to a full-force glow. She switched on the radio.

Over the low grind of the dynamo slowly winding down she heard a minister talking about the tightening of fuel rationing. Then the Chancellor, in his now-familiar dour tones, informed everyone that taxes would have to rise to pay for ensuring the security of the nation. The war between Israel and its neighbours rumbled on, with increasing fears that Israel would use nuclear weapons if things went against them. Some hospitals, in the larger English cities, were becoming overcrowded due to an increasing number of 'flu' cases. A footballer had been transferred for a new record fee.

Emma sipped her only cup of coffee of the day, savouring the taste and aroma. This month's ration was almost gone. Next months would be smaller, she had heard, and probably twice as expensive. As she sat fretting over the worsening world news Minx sprang into her lap, purring loudly. The purring deepened when she greeted the cat by stroking its coal black ears. Emma gazed distractedly through the drizzle running down the kitchen window, then was prompted into a smile by a whiskery nose rubbing under her chin.

She giggled and tickled the cat's head with her fingertips. "At least you know what's important, Minxy. Come on then, breakfast time."

Minx was joined at the food bowl by her patient, brown and white partner, Brian; the neutered tom she seemed to delight in tormenting at every opportunity. Brian licked the she-cat's face once then, without eating, mewled up at Emma. Water dribbled into the bowl Emma was holding under the kitchen tap and she groaned at the low pressure. It had been like this for three days, despite all the rain. It was because of the extra filtration processes they had put in, as a precaution against terrorist attack, the water company said. They were working on it, they said. She turned off the tap and put the half-filled bowl on the floor. Brian sniffed once at the chlorine saturated contents then stalked away in disgust.

Emma decided that if the water situation got any worse she would step naked into the garden, to shower in the rain. That way she might get washed and rinsed before the water ran out. Besides, old Mr Whitlam next door would enjoy the show. He was a good neighbour even if it did sometimes seem that he couldn't raise his eyes above her chest. The low water pressure wouldn't be so bad if they hadn't recently put up the charges for the third time. She might yet need the second water butt she had connected to a down pipe from her gutter. She shook her head. Her mind was wandering, she realised. The throbbing ache from her blocked sinuses was getting her down and she had not slept well.

Without thinking, Emma wiped the back of her hand across her forehead to smear away a sheen of perspiration. A car horn beeped a brief but cheerful tune from outside. That would be her lift to work. Emma grabbed her coat, keys, and the small daypack that served as her handbag, shopping bag, even weekend bag, told the cats to be good, then dashed out of the house and down the path to the waiting BMW.

Her neighbour, Malcolm, smiled as she climbed into the passenger seat. "Morning, Emma." Then he frowned in concern. "Are you okay?"

Emma smiled back and then sniffed. "Just this damn cold … and another argument with Robert."

Malcolm winked. "I've told you before; he isn't good enough for you. You should dump him and come to live with me."

"Oh, yes! And what would Pamela have to say about that?"

Malcolm chuckled as he accelerated away from the curb. "That might be a slight problem, I suppose."

Emma had not lived in the village for long but already Malcolm and Pamela were becoming her friends. Despite his joking, she knew how devoted he was to Pamela. Not surprising really, considering some of the things Pamela had confided to her over their second bottle of wine one evening while Malcolm was away at a conference. The 'Friday night' outfits Emma had been shown might help too.

Suddenly, Emma realised that Malcolm was talking to her.

" … did they say it would take to fix your car?"

"Sorry, Malcolm, I was miles away, what was that?"

"How long, to mend your car?"

Emma scowled. "They didn't know. They're having delays getting parts. I'm just grateful you go into Aberdeen too."

"No problem. With the cost of petrol these days I'm glad to share. We should do it even after your car is fixed."

Emma nodded but didn't answer. It might come to that, especially with the talk about reduced fuel allowances, but she liked the independence having her car available gave her. It was reassuring to have the offer though, in case things did get worse.

As they rounded a bend on the approach to the city, Emma drew her identity card from her pocket and plucked Malcolm's card from where it was tucked under a rubber band on the sun visor. Malcolm slowed the car, then his eyes widened in surprise and he flashed a look at Emma, who was staring back at him, equally perplexed. Traffic was sparse but flowing freely past a point where they usually had to queue at a roadblock.

"What, no police checks today?" Malcolm questioned.

Emma shook her head. "Strange, they must all be off on leave or something."

Malcolm frowned. "Well, let's not knock it. We'll be in work early for once."

Aberdeen was bustling with bicycles, electric mopeds, and still quite a few cars as always at this time in the morning, but the traffic was noticeably lighter than usual.

"I think it's the flu," Malcolm said. "We had almost half the staff at our office off sick yesterday. I think Pam and I might be coming down with it too."

Emma nodded in understanding. "We have a few missing as well. It isn't too bad, because we haven't been getting anything like as many calls for help as usual, but I'm worried about some of our overseas volunteers. I haven't heard from them either."

Malcolm snorted. "If the telephone systems are as bad as they are here, is it any wonder? Some of your people work in pretty remote places, don't they?"

Malcolm pulled into the kerb by Emma's office and she twisted to face him as she released her seat belt.

"That's true. None of the satellite phones work since the EMP and the normal landline systems in some of the countries we deal with weren't very reliable in the first place." She leaned across and kissed him briefly on the cheek. "Thanks, Malcolm."

Emma climbed out of the car, pulled her daypack from the back seat and then crouched by the front door before shutting it. "Five o'clock as usual?"

He frowned in thought. "About then but don't be surprised if I'm a bit late. We have an emergency meeting this afternoon. I think one of our subsidiary companies might be about to go down."

"Okay. I'll wait. Good luck with your company."

She waved as he drove away, then she dashed across the gravel-covered forecourt to the converted Georgian house that held the offices of the refugee charity for which she worked.

#

General Sir Roger McArdle took a deep breath. Reluctantly he swivelled his chair away from the spectacular view over the Firth of Forth and its famous Railway Bridge. He was dying. So were most of the people in the world. The difference was, he knew it.

At sixty-four he wasn't ready to die, he wasn't even ready to retire. His mind was as acute as ever and he still passed the

Service's physical fitness test every year, even though it hadn't been a requirement for him for the past nine years. But within the week he would be dead. His lips twitched in a rueful smile. His blood showed none of the natural antibodies that would prevent it, unlike the blood of the man sitting on the opposite side of the desk.

McArdle took another breath and tried to ignore the sharp stab of pain it brought to his chest. "We believe the woman is somewhere in the northeast, Aberdeen or Inverness perhaps. The man is under surveillance in Glasgow. If he doesn't contact her within the next twelve hours he'll be picked up and we'll try more direct methods to find out where she is."

His subordinate nodded as he memorised the photographs he was holding but his face remained impassive. McArdle had given him every scrap of information available on the UK and world situation. The operative's mission was to find and eliminate any of the terrorists who had brought the plague to the UK, if he or they survived. Of all the members of the Service, and of the Special Forces who had also been tested, he was the only one who had shown the immunity that could give him a chance to live through the current pandemic.

Except that information from America suggested that a second, completely different but equally lethal infection was also taking hold there. McArdle had briefed his man about that too. If the terrorists in the UK might have access to that second disease, it would give him an added incentive to complete his mission, whatever else happened.

The general surveyed his operative carefully. If he could have chosen whom to entrust with this mission he could not have picked better. The man was a natural hunter, with the tenacity of a hound with a fox in its sight. The only problem was that they weren't even sure where the vixen in the northeast had her den.

McArdle shuddered and wiped the sweat from his forehead. "Find her, Sean! We'll take care of the man in Glasgow and give you whatever information we can but you find that bitch and kill her, before there's no one left."

Sean Applegarth nodded again but said nothing.

"You've got access to all the equipment and supply caches, whatever weapons, transport and other gear you can use. Take what you want, but for now get out of here. Get yourself up north and hole up somewhere secure until we can give you more information. If you lose contact with us then operate independently. The mission remains in effect until completed. Find her!"

Sean stood up and extended his hand to the man who had been his commander for five years. He didn't expect he would see him again. "I'll get her, boss." He frowned, not sure what else to say.

McArdle stood, gripped Sean's hand and shook it briefly then turned away to look out of the window. Only when he heard the door close behind him did he give in to the spasm of coughing that left his handkerchief stained crimson.

#

It was mid afternoon when Emma left her director's office, closed the door behind her and then leaned against it and shut her eyes. Her head ached. He had felt no better than she did. Across the hall in the reception office Agnes Whitlock had her head in her hands, rubbing her face, but she straightened as she heard Emma close the door.

"You okay, Agnes?" Emma asked.

"Not really, Em. I think I might have to go home."

"Why don't you? Put the phones through to my office, Lachlan won't mind."

"I might do that. I'll see. Maybe in a little while."

Emma pushed herself upright and plodded up the two flights of stairs to her own office, slumped at her desk and stared at the telephone. It had not rung once today. Normally, she struggled to keep up with the settlement or relief requests from the refugees it was her job to help. At first, as the pandemic hit, there had been a flood of calls begging for advice on where to get medical care but not any longer. The calls from other aid workers, pleading for help to get home, had stopped too.

Emma wiped her nose, then frowned in annoyance at the smear of red staining the crumpled white paper. She stuck out her bottom lip and puffed at the strand of hair clinging wetly to her forehead. Damn the power conservation regulations, she needed a fan. Mentally, she kicked herself for complaining. Others were worse off. She rubbed at her eyes and temples to ease the ache that was growing there, shivered, blinked rapidly and shook her head to clear it. With a start, she realised that her vision was becoming clouded and narrowed.

Emma swivelled in the wheeled typing chair, aiming to toss the soiled tissue into the bin. She threw but missed. A swirl of dizziness and nausea engulfed her. Her fingers whitened as she desperately grasped at the arms of her chair. Swallowing hard, she tried to take a deep breath. Her eyes widened in desperation. Her mind screamed. Her lungs refused to expand. Tilted by her tottering attempt to stand, the chair skidded from under her.

Emma pitched sideways to the floor. Rolling onto her front she struggled to push herself up but found no strength in her arms. Saliva trickled from the corners of her gaping mouth. Frantically she fought the encroaching darkness but her sight was failing, a terrifying blackness closing over her. Slowly her head sunk to the floor. Her last thought was to hope that someone would take care of Brian and Minx and her lips barely formed the word, 'Robert'.

#

On the evening after Emma collapsed, John McLean gently pulled a sheet over his youngest daughter's face. Some twenty-five miles northwest of Emma's office, in a small, whitewashed cottage, he blinked his weary eyes as he turned to look at his other daughter, Elizabeth. Her face was as pale as a waning moon and beaded with sweat. Her thin chest pulsed with each shallow gasp for breath. Only the day before, Elizabeth and her sister had been playing happily in the garden. Now her mother and sister were dead and John's throat clenched as he realised that Elizabeth would surely soon follow them.

Crossing to sit by the stricken child, John dragged a towel from the chair back and dabbed at her face. Elizabeth's eyelids flickered but didn't open. For a while he talked to her. He murmured soft, reassuring words he longed to be real but in which he could not believe. John was a countryman, had been a soldier. All his married life his family had relied on him for strength and reassurance. Now he felt useless. His skills, his strength, his confidence, what use were they now? The people he loved were dying and he could do nothing to help them. Nothing.

For hours Elizabeth lingered and then she stiffened. Her frail body gave a final shudder and with a long, sighing breath it was over. John closed his eyes and let the tears come. He sneered at his uselessness as his throat burned with his attempt to swallow. His beautiful girls were gone and all he suffered was a sore throat. Where was the fairness, the sense, in that? In anger and frustration he raised his face to the ceiling and the walls shook while he howled his agony at the universe

#

Hunched in a corner of a bedroom in a guesthouse in Aberdeen, not so very far away from Emma's office, Morag Rose knew exactly what was going to happen. She could hear the heavy tread of her tormentors as they climbed the stairs. They were going to do, and make her do, the things they had been doing ever since they caught her. And they would beat her again if she didn't get it right. They would probably beat her even if she did get it right. The one called Al seemed to enjoy seeing the marks his belt left on her thin back and legs. Her school friends had boasted about having sex but never about the things these men, Al and Jace, did to her.

Morag tried to wipe away the tears she knew would make them hit her even more but their footsteps had stopped outside the door now. Even above the pounding of her heart and the rattling of teeth she couldn't stop from chattering she could hear the scraping of the key as it entered the lock. The door began to open and Morag tucked her head in to her chest, squeezed her eyes tightly shut and tried to shrink into the corner, praying that she might disappear.

#

Sean Applegarth should have left the city immediately after the briefing but it was late, the chance of a final night with the girl he was seeing was too great a temptation and the delay shouldn't have been a problem. She died in the early hours of the morning. He spent the following day avoiding rioters and looters while he prepared and hunted for a way out of the city. The traffic jam that stalled him now was caused by panic that swept through Edinburgh during that night but which gave him the chance to escape. Accidents, breakdowns, dead drivers and no one to move any of them, then made this mess of vehicles inevitable.

He leaned to his left, to balance himself while he steered the Range Rover along an embankment. In front of him, the stationary queues of people trying to escape the city extended to the horizon, across all three lanes of the motorway and the hard shoulder. Finally he was forced to a halt by a motorway sign too wide to get around and an embankment too steep to navigate. He glanced to his right. The old Ford Escort hemming him in had been abandoned. The woman driver of the car in front of it was collapsed over the steering wheel. They could have been any of the ten thousand similar victims he had passed.

Sean sat, thinking. On the other side of the central divide, the carriageways leading into Edinburgh were virtually empty. No vehicle had passed that way for over an hour, but he had seen an army lorry abandoned about a mile back towards the city.

Within thirty minutes he had jogged to the lorry, dragged out the bodies of the driver and his mate, driven back to opposite where his Range Rover was parked and begun to transfer his gear and supplies. It was during his final trip with supplies that he made his mistake.

When he pushed past a saloon car, a small, yappy terrier jumped at the window, barking frantically. In a simple act of kindness, he opened the door as far as the car squeezed close to it allowed, then lifted the dog out, intending to set it free, to give it some chance of survival. In return, when he set it down, the dog whirled round and nipped his finger. While he was cursing and shaking his hand the dog slipped past, barked at him twice, then ran off. He could have sworn he heard it chuckle as it went.

Sean grinned. If that was the worst he got in this whole affair he wouldn't be doing badly. He wrenched the lorry into gear, released the handbrake, then drove off up the wrong side of the motorway, singing the tune to the Ride of the Valkyries as he went.

#

Emma blinked. For what could have been eternity she had been conscious of the carpet against her face and of her thirst, but moving seemed impossible. Even altering the position of her arm was beyond her strength. She lay still, listening. Thin, grey, February light filtered into the silence. The parched stickiness in her mouth, matched only by the burning in her throat, made swallowing a continuing part of the nightmare. Eventually even pain and weakness could no longer allow her to deny her body's unrelenting demand for water.

Groaning with the effort, she curled up and then rolled onto her knees. Her head swam and she closed her eyes as she rested her forehead against the floor but that made it worse so she forced them open again. Finally she lifted her head. Her gaze focused on the half-full bottle of water on her desk. Drinking became the only thing that was important and she crawled towards it.

The water was tepid, flat but wonderful. Rivulets ran down her chin as she poured it into her gaping mouth, spluttering with the effort to swallow. Emma stared at the empty bottle, shook it, tried to drain out the few remaining droplets, and then dropped it. Desperate for more she dug her fingers into the edge of the desk and dragged herself upright. She was about to call out when the smell and clinging discomfort below her waist hit her. Her face burned and bile rose in her throat. She took a deep breath then staggered towards the door. The washroom was only a few steps away down the hall. If only she could make it before she met anyone.

But the hall was empty; of people, of sound, of any light except the greyness seeping through the window of her office. Had they all gone home not realising she was still there? It wasn't unusual for her to work late but they should have seen she hadn't signed out. She shook her head. Thinking was too difficult. At least she needn't worry about any of her friends seeing her like this.

She pressed the washroom light switch. Nothing. It didn't matter; the light from the window was enough. Groggy but achingly grateful for privacy, she stripped then stepped into the small shower cubicle.

The gush of icy water against her flesh shocked Emma's body and mind into wakefulness. Using soap from the liquid dispenser she quickly but thoroughly scrubbed her goose-pimpled flesh until it was clean. When she was finished, mindful of the water shortage, she turned off the shower. It had been cold but at least the water had lasted long enough for her to cleanse herself. She drew back the shower curtain and reached for the towel, then glanced down and paused at the sight of her body.

Standing upright, Emma smoothed her hands down over her breasts, across her belly and sides, wiping away the clinging water droplets. Her ribs were beginning to show and her tummy was flat at last. She raised her gaze to the bathroom mirror. Her face, normally tanned from walking in the sun and wind, was pale except where dark bags hung under her eyes. She thought that she hadn't been this fit yet this worn since Kosovo. She took a deep breath, exhaled hard then shivered. Ducking her head she rapidly towelled dry her short, blonde hair.

Back in her office, Emma quickly pulled on the tracksuit bottoms and a tee-shirt she had brought for her lunchtime exercise but had felt too ill to use. She shook her trainers from a carrier bag, bundled up her soiled clothing and stuffed it into the bag in their place. The clothes could go straight into the washer when she got home, she decided. She tipped her chair back onto its wheels then quickly sat down and leaned back, breathing deeply to still a sudden bout of dizziness that threatened to fell her. When her head had cleared she carefully leant forward, laced on her trainers and then pushed herself unsteadily to her feet. Her legs shook and her head felt heavy but at least Emma felt awake as she set off down the gloomy, wood panelled corridor towards the stairs.

She glanced in as she passed the open door of the fundraiser's office and stopped in mid-pace.

"Janet? Are you okay?"

Janet's head rested on the desk and her eyes were open but she made no reply. Emma's hand trembled as she reached out to gently shake her colleague's shoulder. She received no response. Stroking aside the long, dark hair, she reached to feel for a pulse. Her hand jerked away as she touched cold, stiffened skin.

Emma had seen enough as a first aider to know that it had been a long time since she, or anyone else, could have done anything to help her friend. Summoning her nerve she closed Janet's eyes, brushed away the tears rolling down her own cheeks and left, quietly closing the door behind her. As the latch clicked into place, a spasm of trembling gripped her and she shivered as she ran towards the stairs.

At the bottom of the steps to the right was the reception office. For a moment Emma stood, frozen, overcome by confusion and disbelief. Agnes Whitlock lay face down beside her desk. A silent telephone receiver dangled near her hand. Moving at last, Emma crossed to the reception desk. Spinning the signing-in book the right way up, she saw four people, other than herself, had not signed out. Lachlan Ferris, the branch director, was one of those still here.

From habit and respect Emma rapped on the dark oak door and waited a moment before opening it. Lachlan was still in the enormous, brown leather, manager's chair. His eyes were closed, his mouth open as though in sleep but the familiar snore was absent, his chest still.

Emma found Edgar Forbes, the driver, spread out on a couch in the crew room. He had been a volunteer with the charity for nearly forty years and since retirement worked at the branch every day. For him at least this was the right place to die. Collapsing into one of the old armchairs, confused, exhausted and weak, Emma wept until eventually she slept again.

It was full light when she finally woke. A shudder coursed through Emma's aching body as her eyes focussed on Edgar but she took a deep breath and then forced herself to her feet. She had to get a grip of herself; she needed find out what was happening. This wasn't like her. If there had been anyone to see she would never have shown this lack of control. She had seen too much while working overseas with refugees to be thrown like this, far too much.

Shaking away the memories, she filled a plastic cup from the water cooler again and again until her mouth was finally clear. At the crew room sink she filled her cupped hands with cold water and rinsed her face until she felt properly awake. Feeling at least a little more in control she returned to reception.

The battery-driven clock and calendar on the reception wall had to be wrong. It was Thursday when she fell ill and according to the calendar it was now Sunday. Then Emma remembered the bodies. Four days? Had she really been ill for four days? And the others, if they hadn't come to help her they must all have fallen ill within a few hours. The country, everywhere in fact, had been in the grip of this cold or 'flu' epidemic for weeks. There had been reports of deaths among elderly people and infants. She had even heard that some hospitals had been restricted to quarantine cases only. Rumours had spread that the deaths were widespread in some other countries, but not here. But how could any disease have become fatal so fast among otherwise healthy people?

Fear of another kind seared through Emma's thoughts. What about Robert? Her fiancé was on an oilrig; maybe he would be protected there, isolated from infection. Then again, people had been ill before he went back for his current shift. He or any one of his workmates might have been carrying the disease. Fighting to control a rising panic, she crossed to the phone. Purposely not looking at Agnes, she replaced the handset briefly and then lifted it again. No dialling tone.

After running back to her office, Emma picked up her new mobile and switched it on. She had replaced her old phone after the EMP blasts wiped out so much of the network but this one was better anyway. The battery was still good but the signal indicator was at zero. What now? She would achieve nothing by staying here. She must get out, must find out what was happening and she needed to go home.

Emma's own car was in the garage for repairs she remembered and she couldn't call Malcolm. She would have to borrow one of the company cars. From the office window she could see the light-blue vehicles with their distinctive logo on the doors. She could choose from a Ford Escort estate car, a Sherpa mini bus or a Land Rover. All would have more than half a tank of fuel, everyone filled up before returning if it fell below that, or was supposed to, but she knew the Landie had not been out since she refuelled it on Monday. She would take that.

After hastily throwing a few personal belongings and her house keys into the small daypack, Emma stopped, wondering if she would ever come back here. Remembering the bodies downstairs she shuddered at the thought and ran from her office. She collected the Land Rover keys from the board in reception then signed out, entering her signature and the time in the relevant places in the register. The car park was at the back of the building and Emma was halfway to the door that led out to it before the futility of signing the register struck her.

She knew this place and the people who had been her friends so well. But her skin was tingling. Her body trembled. Cold sweat beaded her forehead. Her eyes darted to the doors along the gloomy corridor seeking out the shadows and ... what? Ghosts? Her friends rising to follow her? Nonsense! But the hairs on the back of her neck prickled and the echoes of her footsteps chased her as she headed for the door. Were the echoes gaining on her? Were they really echoes? Too afraid to look back, Emma tucked in her head, ran the last few steps and slammed the door behind her as soon as she was outside. Her eyes were wet as she scurried towards the Land Rover.

Aberdeen was quiet on a Sunday morning but never this quiet. The gulls were in full cry but she could hear no other noise and there was an eerie absence of traffic. Turning out of the back lane, Emma decided to drive through the town rather than along Great Northern Road. She believed she should find out more that way. She headed down Union Street and then onto King Street, past the neat grey buildings, some concrete, some granite but all so grey, past the hospital already strong with the smell of putrefaction. She detoured briefly to call at Malcolm's office but the BMW wasn't parked outside and the building was locked.

As she drove through the dank morning mist Emma watched, sickened but unable to look away, as excited gulls and crows rose squabbling over morsels from bodies lying on the pavements. Some cars had been abandoned with their doors open and others parked at odd angles to the pavement with their drivers or passengers still inside. She stopped, staring at a poster on a newsstand, which proclaimed, 'SUPER FLU - terrorist bug blamed - thousands die worldwide'. Studying it more closely, she saw it was for Friday's paper.

Emma was still trembling. The bodies, the lack of traffic, of bustling, living people. What had happened seemed obvious. What might happen, who, or what, was left, not knowing … Emma's throat tightened as she tried to swallow. Breath came in gasps. She wasn't the nervous type, she didn't scare easily, she reminded herself, but it was … not knowing. She closed her eyes, forced herself to breathe deeply and started a conscious relaxation exercise to regain control. Gradually the trembling eased and her breathing slowed.

She drove the length of King Street, seeing more gulls and crows, more bodies, and the inevitable pigeons. A bedraggled dog cowered in a doorway as she passed and now she noticed a few rats darting between cover and this unaccustomed glut of food. She drove on but she saw no living person. Emma stopped again, this time to enter the small general store where she regularly bought her lunch and daily paper. Its door was standing open. On the floor behind the counter lay the body of the elderly Indian woman who always served her and who was always ready to chat. Blood had congealed to a dark brown crust in the dead woman's white hair and on her face.

Emma leaned on the counter, closed her eyes and composed herself once more. This was all too much. She shook her head to clear it as she surveyed her surroundings. Spirits shelves stood empty, as did the open till. Food cans rolled on the floor, abandoned in haste perhaps.

Friday's newspapers were still neatly stacked on the racks, or at least those few that had been delivered for that day. The papers were thin and smaller than they used to be but still out every day. Until Friday.

Emma's stomach rumbled. She felt sickened but knew she was also weak from hunger. From the shelves she selected some chocolate biscuits and a bottle of water. She picked up an apple from a basket on the counter but quickly dropped it again at the sight of gnaw marks on one that had been beside it. It seemed pointless to pay but she hunted in her bag and found coins. They clattered as she slid them into the empty plastic drawer of the till, which she then pushed shut; whatever the situation, it didn't feel right to take things from here without paying.

The aluminium door of the old Land Rover Defender slammed behind her and she sat, trembling, breathing hard. By the time Emma had reached the lightless traffic lights at the bottom of the street she had seen enough. Pressing down on the accelerator she crossed the Bridge of Don and headed north then turned northwest towards home. She discovered no signs of life in any of the small villages on the way. On a bend two cars had collided blocking the road, their drivers slumped over the steering wheels. Emma took to the grass verge and gently, but determinedly, nudged one of out of the way, wincing as the metal scraped the paint from the Land Rover wing.

Her home village of Deerton boasted twenty-eight houses and a hotel. No one came to Emma's knock at any of them. Where the doors were unlocked she opened them and shouted but silence, and sometimes the smell, was the only answer. Mr Whitlam had died in his bathroom. Malcolm and Pamela were not at home and the BMW wasn't there either. At the Claymore and Targe the bar was open but empty except for the bodies of Ricky, the barman, still behind the counter and a man she had never seen before. The stranger lay on one of the long green bench seats, a forest of beer glasses and spirit bottles on the table in front of him. She found the owners, Tim and Gwen, curled up in bed together. Drawing the sheet over their heads, she left them to their final embrace.

Downstairs, Emma tried the phone but it was dead. Her mobile still showed no signal but then it never did in the village. Moving behind the bar, she stepped carefully around Ricky's still form and poured herself a large Macallan. She finished the whisky in two swift swallows, put down the glass and left. This time she didn't pay.

As Emma entered her cottage, Brian and Minx pranced over to greet her. They were both fine, seemingly glad to see her but otherwise unconcerned at her absence. Both had always been good hunters and only seemed to eat what she gave them as dessert to whatever they found for themselves. They would come and go through the cat flap as they wished and drink at the burn that ran past the bottom of the garden. They were country cats who lodged with her; happy for her company when it suited them but never reliant on her. The phone was dead here too and no messages on the answer machine. She tried a light switch, no power.

Emma flopped down on the sofa. She lived in the country and loved it but unlike her cats she was a town girl, used to all the modern conveniences. People considered her independent, she went backpacking in remote places for fun, but right now she didn't want to be independent. Right now she would give anything to hear Robert or a neighbour calling hello from her door.

In every war, every famine, every epidemic from which she helped refugees, some people always survived. Tears again ran down her face. She knew that, right now, she would give anything, more than anything, to know, really know, that she was not the only person left alive.

Encounters

John McLean sat motionless, except for his eyes. He slowly scanned left to right, right to left and back again, across the distance, then the middle distance and finally the ground close to him, missing nothing. His back rested against an old birch tree, at the edge of the wood, which covered the top of the hill above his home. He gazed down at his cottage, far below, and the wooden crosses that marked where he had buried his wife and two daughters.

This was one of his favourite places. He still felt dazed by the speed with which everything had changed. He had suffered no more than a sore throat and a cough, while he watched everyone around him die. Here at least, he could find some comfort, some sense of continuity and peace.

His family, his neighbours, his friends, the people in Keith, Huntly, Elgin and the villages around, were all gone. He had driven round them all but found no one left alive. He wasn't a deeply religious man, though as a child his parents took him to church every Sunday and he was still a believer, but from what he remembered, the world was not supposed to end like this.

A rabbit hopped out of the gorse patch, fifty yards below him. As slowly as a branch rising in the breeze, John lifted the .22 rifle that lay across his lap. Inch by inch he edged his body around so that he could use his knees to brace his elbows. As he exhaled, the dot in the centre of the cross hairs of the telescopic sight rose to settle on the rabbit's head, behind the eye. He moved his feet fractionally to shift his aim half an inch to the right to compensate for the breeze, breathed half in and then out again, stopped, released the safety catch and then gently squeezed the trigger.

The rifle barely moved. The rabbit did a backwards flip and landed on its back, its legs stiff and quivering. The crack of the high-velocity, hollow-point bullet echoed around the hills, seeming unnaturally loud for a .22. The sound had disappeared before he took another breath and lowered the rifle.

A week before he might have fitted a silencer, to avoid disturbing the young couple who had moved into the cottage next to his but that was no longer a concern; he'd buried them too. But they had been the last. After that there had been too many to bury. Too many even to count.

He worked the bolt to chamber a new round, set the safety catch to on, then picked up the ejected empty cartridge case and dropped it into his jacket pocket.

The quiet and the peace, they were the good things. He always liked the quiet of early morning on the hill. He had done many things in his forty-five years: farm labourer, gamekeeper, soldier, and pest controller among them. Outdoor life kept him fit, though his thick brown hair was greying at the temples. Now he owned a small roadside shop where he sold the walking sticks and leather goods he made for the tourists and the harness and shooting accessories that he made mainly for the locals. Tourists and customers - he wondered if either still existed, somewhere in the world.

He had most enjoyed his time as a gamekeeper, until death duties forced the estate to be split up and sold. He breathed deeply, stood up, and walked down the hill to retrieve his dinner, the rifle loose and comfortable in his right hand.

John finished cleaning the rabbit and was slitting one of its back legs between the bone and tendon, to hang it from the game loops on his jacket, when he raised his head, listening. It was still some way off yet but the whine of a Land Rover was too familiar to miss. It was coming down the A96 from the direction of Aberdeen and it was travelling fast.

He wasn't a man to rush things and nor was he desperate for company but there had been nothing but static on the radio since last Saturday, even on shortwave. He guessed that the radio breakdown could be an after-effect of the EMP bombs or perhaps some new technological attack. Maybe things were not this bad everywhere after all. He had a brother in the borders who might still be alive in that case. He wiped the stained blade of the old, wooden-handled Opinel No8 knife on the rabbit skin, folded it and put it back in his pocket, picked up his rifle and loped down the hill, the rabbit dangling in his left hand.

#

Emma almost didn't see him. The weathered, green Barbour jacket and cap and the brown cord trousers he wore were natural camouflage against the trees by the road. As it was she had gone thirty yards past before she could stop. She looked back, still not sure she hadn't imagined the man, but there he was, standing by the road, head cocked to one side, watching her vehicle. She slammed the Land Rover into reverse, backed up and screeched to a halt beside him. The tyres kicked up a hail of gravel as she braked.

She stared at John through the side window, hardly able to believe he was there and he stood, waiting patiently. He seemed mildly interested but not really concerned, like one of her cats when she offered it a titbit from her plate after it had already eaten and it was trying to decide whether it was worth getting up. He was medium height, lean but fit, not thin, she thought, with the honest, weather-beaten, clean-shaven face of an outdoorsman. The corners of his dark green eyes bore deep wrinkles from squinting into sun and wind, and his mouth was firm, somehow giving the impression it should smile but did too rarely.

Then his lips twitched at one corner and he nodded to her. She stepped out of the Land Rover and stood looking at him across the bonnet. For the first time she noticed his rifle but it wasn't pointed at her and a rabbit dangled from his other hand. She felt no sense of threat from him, only a calm detachment. It seemed important that she didn't seem silly, for some reason she automatically wanted this man to like her, but she was nervous.

Still, she forced a small smile. "Hello."

He nodded again. "Fit like, quine, come far?"

His voice was deep and gentle, so relaxed it fit him. His greeting was so familiar to her, phrased as it was in her native Doric. It would have sounded odd translated into Standard English, as 'How are you, girl?' But here it would have been as strange for him to say anything different.

"From near Aberdeen, I'm heading for Forres. My parents stay there," Emma told him. She had to ask. "Have you seen anyone else around here?"

The man's eyes saddened and he shook his head slowly. "Nobody, though I haven't been further than Elgin. What about you – is it as bad down south?"

Emma swallowed and took a trembling breath. "You're the first person I've seen alive since I came to on Sunday."

His brow wrinkled. "You were ill then?"

"The last thing I remember, before I woke up, was being at my desk on Thursday. Then after I got back home I fell ill again, I've hardly been able to move for days. Weren't you ill?"

He shook his head. "Nothing to speak of."

Emma almost smiled for real. She didn't disbelieve him but she had the impression he was the sort who would refer to a near amputation as 'a bit of a scratch.'

Emma was torn now between the urge to go on, to find out about her parents, and the desperate need to hang on to this human contact.

Finally she asked: "Do you live near here?"

He twisted slightly and pointed the rifle in the direction of the shop behind him. "Aye, this is my place."

His name was on a neatly hand-painted board over the shop window: 'John McLean Highland Goods'.

"Would you mind if I come back, after I've been to Forres?" she asked. "Just to talk."

John considered. She was a bonnie lassie, her short blonde hair matched the high-cheeked round face and small mouth, and she was pleasant enough; nervous but not one to give in to it easily, he decided. "The kettle will be on. I'll no be far away. Stop by when you're ready," he invited, then started to walk towards the shop.

"I'm not sure how long I'll be. I'm Emma, by the way," she called.

He waved the hand clutching the rabbit and answered without turning. "I'll be here. If I'm not in the shop, come to the house. The door will be open."

Emma sighed with relief as she climbed back into the Land Rover. She wasn't the only one, and if two of them were alive, there would be others. As she accelerated through the gears she relaxed for the first time since she recovered consciousness. Forres was no more than half an hour away; whatever she found there, she could be back by afternoon.

#

Emma found her father's body in his shed. A half empty bottle of homemade rhubarb wine stood beside him. Next to it lay an empty container that had once held Mum's sleeping pills. Mum was on the sofa in the sitting room. A note for Emma was on the sitting room table.

She would never forget those words. 'Emma, love. I don't know if you will ever get to read this but if you do I want you to know how sorry I am. Your mum and I have been together for over thirty years and I can't leave her to go on her own wherever we go now. I'm sick anyway and I don't think it would be much longer. I'd rather go on my own terms. Take care, lassie. Whatever we leave is yours. We both love you very much, but you know that. All our love.' He had signed it, Mum and Dad.

Emma closed the small wallet of photographs and added it to the few other things she had collected from her parents' home. The note was carefully folded in with the photographs in her bag. Her gaze roamed around the sitting room, bringing back memories of all her happy times there and her head drooped as she blinked back impending tears and sniffed as the grief tightened within her chest.

Forcing her head back up, she glanced through the French windows. A pile of stones rose over the trench Dad had been digging for the foundations of a new rockery wall; a trench which, Emma had discovered, was wide and deep enough to take both him and Mum. It had been hard work but at least they were together now, as they would have wanted. The garden statue of an angel that she had positioned at one end of the burial mound would serve in place of a cross. They had loved the garden. The grass of the lawn would never have been allowed to grow this long but as yet its edges were still neat and the weeds didn't invade much of the flower beds. All that would change but the angel would show her the way, if she returned to visit them.

Emma left her house keys on the table in the hall and pulled the door shut behind her. For some time she sat in the Land Rover, not really thinking, simply sitting. She wanted to cry again, but she couldn't. She had already cried too much. Her lips tightened. What was she to do now?

She was alive; other people were alive. She had talked to John McLean and seen two people in Elgin, though they ran away when they saw the Land Rover and she hadn't been able to find them again. The electricity was still on in Elgin, even though it wasn't here in Forres or in Aberdeen. Plenty of food and other things were available in the shops but already a bad smell was starting to permeate the town. But she needed to be with other people. Things in the shops wouldn't last forever. She believed that if people were to survive they would have to come together, to work in unison and help one another. She shuddered at the memory of how she had felt when she thought she might be alone.

This was predominantly a farming area with thousands of cattle and sheep. She had passed a pig farm on the way here. It was February, so not many crops were showing in the fields but there must be seed somewhere for later. That was surely the only way they could survive; going forward by going back to the old ways.

"I have got to find people." The sound of her own voice startled Emma for a moment then she started the engine and drove towards Forres town centre.

From a camping shop Emma took a backpack that she loaded with a small tent and all the camping gear she thought she might need. Then she selected Ordnance Survey maps of the area and a compass. As an indulgence she added a full box of chocolate-covered nougat. To hell with the diet! From an optician's she took a good pair of binoculars, and at a small supermarket she loaded the Land Rover with a range of foods, bottled water, toilet paper, disposable lighters and other items. She had picked up a box of instant coffee, relieved that at least she no longer had to worry about rationing, when she heard the crunch of glass behind her.

He was a couple of inches taller than her, skinny, unshaven and unwashed. He was wearing a dinner suit with an Evil Dead tee-shirt under it and a pair of obviously new trainers. She guessed he would be in his late teens. He was also staggeringly drunk. Around his waist he wore a green webbing belt with a pistol holster attached. The pistol was in his right hand and a bottle of whisky in his left.

The youth's speech was slurred. "Wha' you doing in mah store?"

Emma's mouth dried. She was used to dealing with drunks in the pubs and clubs at weekends, but amorous drunks didn't carry guns, not even in Aberdeen. A cold tingle shuddered up her neck and her voice was shaky.

"I'm sorry, I was only getting some food; I didn't realise this was your store."

He took a step towards Emma, wobbling unsteadily and thrust his head forward glaring at her. "Well it is see, an' all this is mah stuff."

Emma put the box back on a shelf. "I'm sorry, I'll go somewhere else."

He leered as he blearily examined her figure. "Nay chance, bitch. This is mah place. You've taken stuff, now you're gain tae pay me fer it."

He attempted to push the pistol into its holster and missed, reached across to assist himself with the other hand and dropped the whisky in the process. He cursed and as he bent to recover the bottle, Emma swept the box of coffee jars off the shelf and brought it down on his back. The would-be rapist collapsed with a cry. Emma scooped up the pistol from where it had fallen, flung it across the store and ran out of the door.

In the vehicle she fumbled for the key, only to drop it by her feet among the pedals. Desperately she scrabbled to find it. Glancing back at the store she could see the drunk climbing to his feet, hunting around for his lost gun. Unable to find it, he raised his head to see where she had gone. Shaking himself, he focused on her face staring back at him from the Land Rover and started towards her, swearing under his breath.

As he reached the shop door, Emma's fingers found cold metal and she grabbed it. He was almost to her as she thrust the key into the ignition. The Land Rover started at the first try and she tore away, leaving him pointing after her, screaming words she would never hear.

She had planned to check the commune at the Findhorn Foundation and possibly go on to Inverness, now all she wanted to do was get away in a direction where she hadn't been threatened. She stopped to refuel at the Shell garage by the Elgin by-pass. The power was still on and to her relief the pumps still worked. The shelves held a selection of plastic cans and two 5-gallon metal cans, so she filled the larger ones and put those in the back of the vehicle, together with a flexible metal spout for refuelling from the cans. Emma hesitated, gazing towards the town. Should she drive through to see if she could find the people she had seen earlier? She shook her head in silent decision; no, not after Forres, not yet.

#

It was early evening by the time Emma drew up outside John McLean's shop but already it was getting dark. Light from a lantern in John's hand spilled across the tarmac to welcome her as he opened the door of the cottage. His Barbour jacket was missing but the checked shirt under an old green jumper was exactly what she would have expected in its place. After making sure she was alone, he stepped out fully from behind the door that had half concealed him. Emma could now see the shotgun he held in his other hand. She locked the Land Rover then walked to meet him.

"I was beginning to wonder if you'd changed your mind," he said. "Come on in."

She smiled gratefully. "It's good to see a friendly face."

John frowned at that but didn't reply, simply stood aside for her to enter.

John had been as good as his word; the kettle had been on when she arrived. Dinner was also well under way and she hadn't hesitated when he invited her to eat with him. With a large helping of rabbit casserole and half a glass of whisky inside her, Emma was starting to feel better. The comfortable old armchair in which she now sat wrapped around her like soft armour. The crackling log fire eased its heat through her to meld with the warmth of the whisky inside. She had kicked off her boots and socks, and her bare toes now played among the thick sheepskin of the rug. This was a good room, she decided. The low, oak-beamed ceiling and rough white walls hugged the warmth to themselves and those they surrounded. A gas lamp hissed quietly on the heavy wooden coffee table between her and John. The few decorations melted into their surroundings.

Emma smiled across at John, who was sitting in another armchair by the fire. His chair was as comfortable and worn as the one in which she sat but they didn't match, she noticed. For no reason she could fathom, that pleased her. It added to the sense of normality and safety, which was as warming as the fire and the whisky. After a moment she spoke, more than anything from a desire to hear his voice. It seemed so long since she had talked to anyone; anyone from whom she hadn't wanted to run.

"That was a wonderful meal, John. Thank you. I've been living off tinned food, biscuits and whatever I could find, anything that didn't look as if it might have been gnawed or crawled over or gone off. I wasn't sure what fresh stuff would be safe and what wouldn't."

John's nodded in understanding but he didn't speak.

Eventually Emma told him about her parents and her two encounters with other survivors. His face grew concerned as she recounted her experience in Forres.

"I suppose the shock of something like this, and the freedom, was bound to bring out the worst in some people," he said thoughtfully. "He must have got that pistol from one of the airbases, Kinloss or Lossiemouth. The guards were always armed."

"I hate guns!" Emma almost spat. "I've seen too much of the misery they caused for the people I used to work with."

John shook his head. "I grew up with them. On the farm and in the army they're a tool of the trade, something to be cared for, treated with respect and used when needed but not much different in most ways from a power saw or any other potentially dangerous tool. Same now, they provide me with food and help to control the pests." He frowned again. "It sounds as though there might be some bigger pests will need to be controlled, if they become a problem."

Despite everything, Emma found herself shocked at the idea. "Surely it needn't come to that!"

John smiled cynically. "Drink takes away people's inhibitions, Emma, but it doesn't alter their basic character. Do you really think that lad would have been much different if he'd been sober, except that he might have been more dangerous? Things may not have turned out as they did if he hadn't been so drunk."

Emma was quiet and reflective for a while. Suddenly her big idea of getting people together seemed much more dangerous than she had imagined. John sat, sipped his whisky and let her think her own thoughts.

Eventually she spoke. "I was thinking that people needed to gather together, so that we could co-operate in creating some sort of community. Now I'm not sure if that's a good idea. Where will you go, John, what will you do?"

He shrugged. "I won't go anywhere. This is my home."

"But what will you do, how will you live?" she asked. "There won't be any tourists to buy your walking sticks and sporrans now and the stuff in the shops won't last forever."

"No, neither are there council tax nor electricity or phone bills to pay." He explained. "Look, the meal you just ate. The rabbit was the one I shot this morning. The potatoes, carrots and onions came from last year's crop from my own garden. I cooked them on our Aga and when the oil runs out it will burn coke or wood. It heats water for the house too. The water comes from three reservoir tanks on the hill, which are fed by a spring. Waste water goes into a septic tank. All the farms and houses around here are the same.

"We have – had," he corrected, "mains electricity but no mains gas or water supply. There's plenty of game on the hill and sheep and cattle too. I've been letting stock out of barns and pens, and leaving gates between fields open as I went round. They'll have to fend for themselves and a lot won't make it but the strong ones will survive. About the only thing around us now that I need the shops for is the gas for this lamp," he raised his glass, "and the whisky."

Emma could see that this was a good place but the whisky was relaxing her and she had to push the point. "But what about the cartridges you use and matches and all the other things you don't make for yourself?"

John nodded. "Aye, I'll have to go into town and build up my stocks of some things but modern factory-made cartridges are well sealed. I used some military surplus .308 not so long ago that was made in the nineteen sixties and they were fine. They'll outlive me. I'd guess disposable lighters and matches are the same."

Emma thought for a few moments. "But what if you get sick or are injured?"

John took another sip of whisky. "That could be a problem. I'd have to do what I could for myself and if it wasn't enough … let nature take its course, I suppose."

It was nearly midnight by the time John commented that he hadn't talked as much in the last ten years as he had that evening. Emma realised she hadn't been invited to stay but the thought of leaving, of being on her own again, was almost too much to bear. She forced herself to her feet. "Well, it's getting late, I better be going."

He caught her hopeful look and shook his head. "You don't have to, Emma." He gave a small smile. "Besides, you've been drinking, you shouldn't drink and drive, you might lose your licence." His smile faded. "I'd offer you one of the girls' rooms but I haven't done anything in there since … Well, you're welcome to the sofa though."

Emma accepted gratefully. John showed her to the bathroom, fetched pillows and blankets for her and bade her good night. She was tired out but it was many hours before her mind quieted enough for her to sleep. So much had happened, she had so much to think about for the future and she wasn't at all sure what direction she should take. Maybe it would be clearer in the morning but whatever else, tomorrow she must make a decision on what she was going to do.

Pest Control

The whistling of a kettle awoke Emma the next morning. She stretched as John came in carrying two steaming mugs.

"Tea or coffee?" he asked.

"Coffee, please."

He smelled the steam from each mug then handed her the one in his left hand and put the other down on the hearth. He poked at the embers for a moment then added new logs. "Old oak, came down in the winds last autumn but it had been dead a while so it seasoned standing. It burns slowly so it usually lasts the night through." He went back to the kitchen and returned with a bowl of sugar, spoons and a jug of milk.

"Long-life milk, this," he explained. "There's a dairy herd at Mosshead but they haven't been milked in a while. I don't know how they'll be faring. Rannoch has a bull if any of them survive."

Emma discreetly studied him as he sat in his chair by the fire, staring into the flames while he sipped his tea. She wasn't sure whether he was thinking aloud or, perhaps unconsciously, giving her reasons to stay. The previous evening they had spent hours discussing her ideas of a community. His experience as a countryman had changed many of her conceptions and especially of how easy it would be to set up and make it work. Subsistence farming was totally different from the intensive agribusiness that had become the norm, but then so many of the modern advantages might not be available either.

During the conversation John had never come round to indicating that he would be a part of the community, or even that this would be the right place for it, but his explanations and points about her ideas had always been patient and positive. Never once had he mocked her for the townie she obviously was. Now he was offering up the idea of stock in the area that she could use.

She decided to ask outright. "John, would you have any objections to us settling in one of the farms here? If I do find people who want to come, I mean."

"It isn't my land, lassie, but I knew my neighbours and I reckon any of them would have sooner seen their land worked and beasts cared for than leave them to rot."

"But you wouldn't mind?" she probed.

He looked at her directly. "You've decided you're going to do it then."

Emma grinned. "I suppose I have. I'm going to give it a try anyway."

The corners of his mouth twitched upwards as he replied to her previous question. "Well, you've plenty of places to choose from. I reckon I could put up with you as a neighbour."

After a hot bath and breakfast, Emma loaded the Land Rover with her pack and a few other items she thought might be useful and left the rest in John's garage. She had decided to return to her cottage, to collect a few personal belongings and check on her cats. Then she would do another search of Aberdeen before widening her area to include other villages and towns. Even if no more than one in ten thousand people had survived, as seemed likely, twenty or so people could be left in the city. It was a big area to cover on your own but the obvious places would be shopping areas and supermarket complexes. John had said that he had some work to do and supplies to get in, so she took that as a hint that he wouldn't be coming with her.

As she was walking back to the house to say goodbye, John came out. He was carrying a shotgun opened over his arm and a box of cartridges in his hand.

He offered them to her. "I think you ought to take these."

Emma's mouth set and she shook her head. "Thank you, John, but for all you said about them only being tools, I still hate guns. I couldn't bring myself to use it anyway and if I didn't then someone would probably take it off me and then they would have a gun."

John frowned. "Remember Forres."

"I know, but I still don't want it. I'll be careful." She reached out and touched his arm, "but thank you."

He nodded. "Aye, well, stay safe then. I'll see you in a few days."

"Three or four," she promised, "no more."

He nodded again and walked back to the house.

#

The cats were not in the cottage when she got there but Minx arrived shortly afterwards and rubbed around her legs, purring. Emma put down the last of the cat food and scratched the black cat's head.

"You'll have to take care of yourself for a while, Minxy, and don't give Brian too much hassle. I'll be back to get you both when I get settled."

Minx purred in response, then tucked into the bowl of food.

Emma packed a holdall with the clothes and personal items she wanted to take. In the kitchen she picked up the Freeplay wind-up radio. For a few moments she considered. Was it worth taking it? She hadn't been able to find anyone transmitting, not in all the days since she had gone to work for that final time. Still, the Freeplay didn't need batteries or mains power and she could check occasionally to see if anyone had started to broadcast again. She put it into the bag. The wind-up torch that had come with it as a package might be more useful, so that went into the bag too. She looked around but couldn't see much else she would need, for a while. She tidied the house, then to avoid attracting rats, mice or insects, she put all of the food other than tins into a rubbish bag and dumped it in the dustbin. Satisfied she had done all that she wanted, she locked up and set off for Aberdeen.

Emma decided to take an alternative route into the city, to cover ground she had not been through before. She was passing the flats in the Woodside district, when an Asian boy, about ten years old, ran into the road in front of her waving desperately. Emma swerved and braked. The Land Rover came to a shuddering halt, several yards past the boy and she leapt out.

"Are you completely stupid? I nearly went right over you," she yelled.

The boy faced her, shivering and panting. He swallowed nervously. "Are you a ghost?"

Emma stared at him incredulously. "A ghost? No, I'm not a ghost. Who the hell are you?"

He swallowed again. "I'm Dan," he said.

Emma took a deep breath then puffed out hard to release her tension. "Well, Dan, I'm Emma and I promise you I'm not a ghost, okay?"

He considered her doubtfully then nodded his head.

Emma smiled at him. His face was clean but she didn't think he had bothered to wash his hair recently, nor his baggy jeans and sweatshirt. She stretched out her hand and took a pace towards him. "I'm sorry I shouted at you, Dan. I was just scared because I nearly knocked you down."

Dan started and hastily back-pedalled several steps. "Have you been sick?" he asked.

Emma dropped her hand. "Yes, I've been sick, have you?"

Dan nodded. "I was for a while, but I got better."

"So did I. Are you on your own?"

Dan's head drooped and his bottom lip started to quiver. "Mam died, the baby too, I went to look for Dad at the bank where he worked but he wasn't there. They were all dead as well."

Emma took another step towards him and this time he didn't back away. "Have you been on your own all this time?" she asked.

"Not quite. I met an old lady, she said she had been in her flat all the time because she had bad legs, but the home help didn't come and she hadn't heard anything. Then she saw me and shouted and I went to talk to her but soon she got sick and she died. But she was very old." He frowned in thought. "Probably thirty or something."

Emma coughed; she had been thirty last birthday.

"Well, I'm trying to gather a group of people and we're going to live on a farm and grow our own food and have lots of animals. Would you like to join us?"

Dan's eyes opened wide, almost as wide as his mouth. "Real animals, cows and sheep and horses and … cats and things?"

Emma chuckled. "Yes, all those, starting with cats, I've got two cats who live with me already."

Dan straightened his shoulders and lifted his chin. "All right then, but I have to make my own way. Dad always said it was important to make your own way in this world."

Emma stifled a chuckle. "Then we'll make sure that your way and mine are the same way, Dan."

She held out her hand again and the boy came forward to shake it. "That's a deal," he agreed.

They toured the city for some time. At places which showed any signs of there having been activity, Emma sounded the horn or they got out and called but they never received any answer.

It was early afternoon when Dan announced, "I'm hungry," and Emma realised that she was too.

From habit she parked neatly in a slot in the car park at the ASDA near the Kaimhill roundabout. They were surrounded by cars, some abandoned, some with their occupants still inside as if waiting for shoppers to return. They were still browsing the shelves when the man's voice came from behind them.

"Well now, what have we got ourselves here, Jace?"

Emma and Dan both spun towards the voice. The man was tall and powerfully built. His belly stretched his T-shirt and hung over the broad, thick, leather belt, which held up his jeans. His gut protruded through the open front of his leather jacket.

Another voice came from the direction in which they had been walking before the interruption. "Looks like a pair of chickens to me, Al, just ready for … plucking."

Emma and Dan both spun towards the second speaker. Jace was walking towards them. He was as tall and powerful as the one he had called Al but without the belly. He was grinning but there was no friendliness in it.

Al laughed. He had closed the distance between them but as Emma backed away Jace grabbed her arms from behind.

Dan leapt to her defence, yelling, "Leave her alone!" as he pounded at Jace's arm with his fists.

Al wrenched him away and swung a full forced punch into the boy's face. Dan careered backwards, bouncing off the shelving before he collapsed motionless among a cascade of tins and packets.

With anger searing away the fog of fear that had been billowing through her mind, Emma screeched her defiance while she tried to reach Dan. Jace swept his foot in front of her legs, tripping her, then slammed her down onto the tiled floor. Still gripping her arms, he pressed his knee painfully into her back. Her ears ringing from the impact of her face against the tiles, Emma felt him tying her hands behind her. Then they rolled her over. Seething, she shook from side to side, vainly wrenching at her bonds.

Jace wrapped his fist in her hair and banged her head sharply against the floor. Instantly Emma ceased her struggle and squeezed her eyes shut, nausea and pain now surging through her head.

Al knelt on her ankles, a sneer of triumphant lust contorting his face. "Now let's see what we've got."

He reached forward and ripped apart her down jacket, undid her belt and then dragged down her trousers and pants.

He laughed coarsely. "Well, well, a natural blonde."

Emma lay still, panting, her lips drawn back from her teeth, her eyes blazing with hatred. The numbness was seeping from her bruised cheek, becoming a throbbing ache and she could feel the flesh around her eye starting to swell.

From behind his back Al pulled a knife with a long curved blade and with a single cut, sliced apart the trousers and underwear that had been around her calves.

Freed of the restriction Emma pulled back her legs then lashed out, flailing desperately to kick him away. Jace grabbed her shoulders. Al fought down her legs, and then pushed the tip of his knife against her groin.

The fat thug glared at her, his teeth bared. "Try that again and I'll gut you like a fresh fish, then we'll have our fun with the boy."

Emma believed every word and lay still again, trembling. Al stood, unbuckled his belt and dropped his trousers. He was wearing no underpants and his penis fell free, hard, erect and huge, as Emma stared up at him, shaking in terror of what she knew was to come.

With tears pricking at her eyes and nausea rising, Emma tilted her head away from Al and stared at the ceiling, trying to force what was happening from her mind. Still she felt every movement of her clothing as Jace tore apart her shirt and produced a folding knife, which he opened with his thumb. The back of the serrated blade slipped coldly between her flesh and the front of her bra, then an upward jerk of the knife sliced it through the thin elastic, springing the cups apart.

Jace threw the knife aside. His big fingers began to maul her breasts while he pinched and pulled at her nipples.

"Nice," he leered. "Oh this is much better than that skinny little whore we caught the other day."

Al sneered back. "All the same in the dark, Jace boy, they've all got the same holes."

Jace laughed. "Yeah, but I like to look while I fuck and this one's worth looking at."

He let go of Emma's breasts, unzipped himself and pulled his penis from his trousers. Emma's teeth ached from the force with which she clenched them. Sickened, she turned away but Jace twisted her hair and lifted her head as he gripped her jaw and forced her face back towards him. Then he let go and slapped her hard before grasping her face again, his fingers and thumb pressing deep into her bruised cheeks.

"You bite me and I'll break out every one of your teeth, one by one, with a pair of pliers, you hear me?" he warned.

Emma tried to pull her jaw from his fingers but again he wrenched her face back and slapped her, this time even harder than before.

"I said, did you hear me?" he demanded loudly, his face so close to hers she could feel the heat of his breath.

Emma nodded. She was trying to appear defiant but she was near to tears and she knew he must be able to see it. The fear was gone. The anger was gone. Now she felt only a burning hatred and frustrated helplessness.

"Then open that pretty mouth and let's see how well you can use it," Jace

snarled at her.

He forced his member between her lips and Emma gagged at the bitter taste of urine and the stench of old sweat that invaded her senses. At the same time, she felt Al's fingers digging into her thighs as he forced them apart. Despite herself, to fight the pain as Al thrust himself into her vagina, she sucked hard on Jace's penis. He groaned in appreciation and loosened his grip on her hair.

Al came quickly and she lay still as Jace pulled himself from her mouth to take his turn at her. When they had finished they walked away, laughing and joking.

Al stopped at the end of the aisle and pointed at her. "Don't worry, girlie, we haven't done with you yet. We'll be back when we've loaded some stuff."

Emma curled up on her side, shaking in misery, aching with hurt and shame. Her face was smeared with tears and dust. As much as she hated Jace and Al, she hated herself for not being able to stop what had happened. Was there nothing she could have done? As much as she knew, logically, there wasn't, she could still not convince herself.

Once, when she rolled over, she saw Dan lying where he had fallen. He was still and silent but his thin chest rose and fell as he breathed. At least he was still alive.

She heard her attackers moving around, calling to one another. Eventually they came back to use her again. This time Jace said he preferred her back passage to Al's 'sloppy seconds' and, as if from far away, she heard herself scream with the pain as he forced himself into her anus.

Afterwards they stood discussing her. "This one isn't at all bad, you know, Al. I reckon with a bit of knocking about we could train her to be more active. We could take her with us."

"What and wake up with your throat cut? Have sense, Jace lad," Al scoffed. "No, there'll be plenty more where she came from and we can always find her again if we want."

Jace laughed. "Aye, if she doesn't come after us, begging for more."

Their footsteps gradually receded. Eventually even the echoes through the otherwise silent store had gone. Emma heard what sounded like the doors of a van slamming, before it drove away. She lay still for a long time, her mind numb, her body throbbing with torment. She heard Dan moan and move and she realised she had to get up. She couldn't let him see her like this. Rolling over, she climbed to her knees and then, by leaning against the shelves, unsteadily to her feet.

On the kitchen equipment racks she found a knife and began to saw through the rope binding her wrists. Blood trickled down her hands as the edge sliced thinly into her skin but she hardly felt it. She worked on until the rope finally parted. From the toiletries shelves she took some wipes and cleaned herself up as well as she could.

In the clothing area she stripped off the tatters that remained of what she had been wearing and dressed in new clothes. Only her socks and boots were wearable from what she had arrived in. The kitchen knife she had found to cut herself free had never been far from her hand and now she tucked it under the broad leather belt she had buckled on over the new trousers. In the distance Emma heard Dan weakly calling her name and she hurried back to where she had left him.

His face was covered in blood and he was clearly dazed but he was sitting up. When he saw her coming towards him he started to cry.

"I thought you'd gone," he sobbed. He peeked up at her face as she crouched beside him. "Did those men hurt you?"

Emma choked back the nausea that was rising in her throat and the unreasonable anger towards Dan that threatened to engulf her. "Don't you worry about that," she forced out. "Let's get you cleaned up and see what the damage is."

In the Chemists' next to the supermarket Emma found some tissues and took a bottle of water from the cooler cabinet. As she washed the blood from his face, Dan flinched whenever she got near his nose. Dark rings were forming around his eyes and his nose was flattened.

"I think you've got a broken nose, Dan," she told him softly. "You're going to have to get used to people thinking you are a boxer."

From the stock room she took some children's aspirin and the two items she had desperately hoped to find. Taking a swig from the bottle of water, she swallowed a 'morning after' contraceptive pill and two antibiotic tablets. She only hoped they would be enough if either of the men were diseased. She gave Dan some aspirin and then piled packets of the pills into a large cardboard box from behind the counter and added as many boxes as she could of different types of painkillers and other medical supplies. She would take a double dose of the antibiotics and to hell with any side effects.

Both Emma and Dan were quiet as they drove away from Aberdeen.

At one point Dan asked, "Are we going to search for other people now?"

Emma shook her head. "Not now, maybe later. We'll call in at my house then I'll take you to meet John."

They found both the cats in the cottage and Dan sat in the rear of the Land Rover, stroking them, as Emma drove back towards Huntly.

#

John was surprised by Emma's early return but, without hesitation, welcomed Dan. Emma didn't talk about what had happened in Aberdeen and John didn't push her but from her bruised face and the little Dan could tell him about the encounter in ASDA, he could guess. The first thing Emma did when she got back was to ask if it was okay for her to have a bath. He heard the water emptying and then the bath refilling, several times.

While Emma soaked and scrubbed herself, John stripped the beds in his daughters' rooms and made them up with fresh bedding. He tidied away some of the girls' personal belongings and emptied the wardrobes. He left their things in plastic bin liners in the rooms for the time being; there would be time enough to move them later if needed.

Emma was quieter than before and preoccupied but she wasn't totally withdrawn. They stayed up for a while after Dan had gone to bed, sitting in the armchairs by the fire sipping whisky but they didn't talk much. Occasionally John glanced over at her and down at the kitchen knife tucked under her belt.

As the fire settled to a glow Emma stood up. "I'm off to bed," she stated, but then wavered. "And thank you, John … for not asking and … well … thank you."

Then suddenly she could control herself no longer. She dissolved into tears and fell to her knees at the side of his chair.

He put his hand on her head and hugged it against the padded arm of the chair, then sat, stroking her hair while she cried.

After a long time she looked up and forced a tremulous smile. "Sorry," she whispered.

He shook his head, as he carefully wiped the tears from her cheeks with the back of his finger. "You've nothing to be sorry for, lassie. You go on up, and don't you worry, we shan't let it happen again."

She squeezed his arm once as she rose and then headed for her room. She peeped in at Dan as she passed; he was sleeping on his back, snoring quietly.

Emma changed into her warmest pyjamas, feeling the soft comforting fabric slide reassuringly against her skin, then slipped under the covers. She lay on her back staring at the ceiling, the horrendous events replaying over and over, wondering what she had done, what else she could have done. Eventually she could think no more. She had survived the 'flu', she would survive this, she decided. She would not give those bastards the victory of raping her mind, as well as her body.

She rolled over to block out her thoughts with sleep, snuggling against the softness of the feather pillow but beneath it, her hand rested on the smooth cold handle of the kitchen knife. It wasn't long before she slept but her dreams were haunted by images of terrible beasts from which she seemed powerless to run. She didn't hear John's Mitsubishi Shogun pull quietly away in the early hours.

#

After Emma had gone to bed, John sat for hours staring into the fire. Eventually he got up and walked through to his workshop.

He unlocked the gun cabinet and took out the .308 rifle he used for hunting deer.

Placing it on the rests on the workbench, he threaded a piece of cotton flannelette through the loop on a cleaning rod and carefully worked it through the barrel, to remove the preservative oil. From a safe under the bench he took the bolt and a box of twenty rounds of his hand-loaded ammunition. He slipped the bolt into the rifle and closed it, then removed the magazine, fed in five of the cartridges from the box, and then put it beside the other ammo.

The Schmidt & Bender telescopic sight that topped the rifle had been an unusually extravagant purchase for him but it had never let him down. The three tapered posts of the reticule gave him a clear aiming mark even in the misty light of dawn forests. Flipping off the 'scope lens covers, he aimed out of the window at a moonlit pine tree at the bottom of the garden, then gently pressed the trigger. The firing pin flew forward with a sharp click. He replaced the lens covers, clipped in the magazine, slipped the rifle into a padded gun bag, and then laid it on the bench.

From a hook on the wall John took his Barbour jacket and cap, then collected the rifle and box of ammunition, picked up his binoculars from the shelf and quietly left the house.

He let the Shogun roll to a stop several streets from the ASDA store in Aberdeen, switched off the engine and sat still and silent. While he waited for his senses to become attuned to the surroundings, he scanned the few yards he could see through the mist. Then, taking his rifle and other equipment, he left the vehicle, lifted the door handle and eased the door closed. It locked in place with barely a click. The mist closed around him, cold and damp on his face as he stood, listening.

The stench of rotting fish and rotting flesh was strong in the still air. Somewhere in the distance a dog barked angrily, then fell silent. Rats scuttled along the pavement, their claws skittering against the hard surface. All around him, his country-tuned senses detected the darting, stealthy night movements of small creatures. But nothing moved that need concern him.

Like a deer through beech woods, John wove his way among the gardens and houses. The only trace of his passing was a swirl in the mist that quickly closed in his wake. At last he found a garden with ornamental bushes, overlooking the shopping estate that was to be his hunting ground. After backing around the corner of the house, he lifted his cap and allowed the net that was sewn into it to drop over his face. Then, on hands and knees, he slipped among the shrubs and sat down to wait.

He had left the gun cover in the vehicle. The rifle's five-round magazine was loaded and the other ammunition was in his pocket. A round was ready in the breech. His rubber-armoured Bausch and Lomb Discoverer binoculars were slung around his neck under the jacket.

He knew that, when you are hunting, four places give the best chances of finding your quarry: where it sleeps, where it eats, where it drinks and on the routes in between. With so many easy pickings in this area he didn't think Emma's attackers would, as yet, be travelling far from their lair.

As the weak morning sun persuaded away the mist he spotted a movement in a garden, a few houses down the road from where he now sat. A young girl, quick but painfully thin, darted cautiously between patches of cover. After stopping for several minutes, she made a dash for the back of the store and entered through a small door by the main unloading bay.

Fifteen minutes later, she peered carefully around the door again and, when she was satisfied that it was safe, dashed back across the tarmac carrying two carrier bags. Halfway across, one of the handles gave way and some of her booty spilled from the bag. She wavered, peered nervously around and at the lost items, then bundled the bag up in her arms and ran for cover, leaving the tins and jars she had lost where they lay. Eventually she disappeared from sight among the houses.

About mid morning a white Ford Transit van drove past and turned in the direction of the city centre. An hour later it returned, to park in front of ASDA. Three men climbed out of the van, all carrying shotguns. Moving slowly and cupping his hands around the lenses at the front of the binoculars to avoid any chance of reflections from the sun, John carefully examined the men.

Two of them fitted the descriptions Dan had given of his attackers, the third was smaller and younger, thin-faced. He flinched when one of the men raised his hand as if to give him a back-handed slap, warning him to stay with the van. The youth clambered back into the cab while the other two went inside.

John took the lens covers from the telescopic sight and put them in his pocket. Then, staying low under the cover of bushes, hedges and walls, he crawled out of sight of the van. Stalking from car to car and bin to bush, using shadows where he could, he made his way to within twenty yards of the loading bay. After observing for any sign of movement, he crossed the open area at a run and slid in through the door he had seen the young girl use earlier.

Making his way through the stock area and then through another door he found himself in the bakery. The dusty, slightly sour smell of stale bread dried his nostrils but the floor was clear and clean, creating no hazard to his steady stalk to a place where he could see through the open-fronted area into the store. He found a suitable firing point behind one of the smaller ovens, well back from the open area. On top of it lay a folded apron, which provided a padded rest for his hand and above it a cupboard, giving him a gap of a few inches through which to observe and aim.

The men were moving through the store, each pushing a shopping trolley, loading anything that took their fancy. Jace had put his sawn-off side-by-side shotgun muzzle down in the trolley. Al's pump action rested across the trolley handle. John listened to them talking, his face hardening as they confirmed their identities.

"Hey, Al," called one, "that bint from yesterday has gone, the boy too. I thought you'd killed that little bastard."

Al laughed. "Don't worry, Jace boy, we'll find you something else to ass fuck. You said she was too tight anyway."

The hard edge of the oven pressed against the back of John's left wrist while he slowly adjusted his position. His chest fell and his shoulders relaxed as his already slowed and steady breathing stilled. Without clenching, the last three fingers of his right hand pressed against the pistol grip, pulling the stock firmly back into his shoulder.

The tip of the central post of the sight steadied, centred on Jace's face. With infinite care, John rested the first joint of his right forefinger against the front of the trigger and began to increase the pressure.

As Jace threw back his head and howled in laughter, a one hundred and sixty-five grain, .308-inch diameter bullet smashed through his bottom teeth. At a range of less than forty yards, it was still travelling at over two thousand seven hundred feet per second and the soft lead nose of the copper-jacketed projectile started to expand on impact. It tore through Jace's palate, the hydrostatic shock wave adding to the effect of the mushrooming metal, pulping bone, nerves and tissue where they left the top of his spine, spraying them in the direction of Al as the bullet exited the back of the skull. Jace was dead, his brain blanked out even before his head bounced from the floor.

The boom of the shot echoed around the otherwise silent building, horrendously loud in the confined space, overwhelming the sound of John working the bolt of his rifle to feed in another round. Al's hearing was not even starting to recover when a bullet seared through his groin, severing his penis, destroying his lower bowel and crashing out through the coccyx. He collapsed, screaming in agony and continued to scream as John worked the bolt once more, picked up the ejected cases and then slowly emerged from behind the oven. Carefully John made his way around the counter and walked towards the now whining man.

Before John reached his quarry, their accomplice ran in through the door shouting for Jace and Al. The young man was carrying a shotgun. As he saw John he made the fatal error of swinging it around to point at him. Had he been unarmed, or even if he had dropped the gun, John would have left him alive; Dan had made no mention of this man. As it was, John raised his rifle far quicker than the youth could ever have matched and shot him squarely through the heart. The youth's face instantly froze in astonishment. He dropped to his knees and then collapsed forwards.

John operated the rifle's bolt and stood looking down at Al, who now stared up at him in hatred and pain.

"Who the fuck are you?" Al grated, his face contorted and white with shock.

John pushed away Al's trolley, together with the shotgun still across its handle. He rested his rifle across his arm as he reloaded the magazine and clipped it back in place, before answering.

"You're vermin. I'm pest control," John told him.

Al sneered up at him, his teeth bared like a cornered dog. At first he cursed, then he curled in agony and peered up pleadingly. "Come on, man. Why us?"

John's hard stare gave him no comfort. Any hope he did have instantly disappeared as John told him, "You raped a friend of mine yesterday. I promised her it would never happen again."

Frightened now, Al began to beg, then, as John coldly raised the rifle, Al screamed a curse at him. "You fu…."

The room filled with the echoing boom of the shot as a neat hole appeared in Al's forehead and bright red blood mixed with pink-grey brain matter and fragments of gleaming white bone splattered across the tiles below him.

Slowly and deliberately, John again fed a new round into the chamber, applied the safety catch, picked up and pocketed the ejected case, slung the rifle across his back, and then took a deep breath to steady himself. One at a time, he dragged the bodies outside and propped them up against the wall. Using a cardboard tray from the shelves and a marker pen and string from the stationery section he made a sign, which he hung around Jace's neck. It contained one word, 'Rapists'. It took little time or effort and if it would make one other would-be miscreant think again before attacking someone, John considered it might be worthwhile.

He gathered up the shotguns then strode away from the store, towards where he had left his truck.

Drawn by the noise of gunfire, the young girl he had seen earlier peeked over the windowsill in the back of a parked car. Sliding out, she sidled between the other cars and stopped in front of the bodies. She stood staring down at the three corpses labelled by the sign and a smile lit up her face for the first time in days.

Morag Rose drew moisture into her mouth and spat down on the remains of Jace's face, then ran after the man she had seen place him against the wall.

Gathering

The four of them sat around the big, pine kitchen table. John had made a rich lamb and vegetable stew flavoured with fresh herbs and both Dan and Morag were on their second helping.

Emma had risen late, to find John already out and in the excitement of welcoming a new arrival when he got back, she hadn't found chance to talk to him in private. John had not spoken much at all since he returned. He and Morag had talked on the way back and she agreed not to discuss what had happened at the supermarket.

Morag was finding it difficult. She was already considering John to be something of a hero and was bursting to tell about what he had done. All the others knew, so far, was that John and Morag had met in Aberdeen. What he had been doing there remained a mystery.

Morag was, otherwise, talking enough for them all, so it wasn't long before they knew not only her story of coming through the deaths but the rest of her life history too. She was a bright and extrovert girl. Before the plague she had worked on the checkout in the same supermarket where she had seen John. He wasn't far out in his guess, she was in fact fifteen.

Morag gabbled on. "I got sick before most people and it was weeks before I came round in hospital. There was bodies everywhere, doctors, nurses, patients, they was all over the wards, in the corridors, everywhere. I run out of the hospital still in my nightdress and slippers, I didn't know where my clothes were. Then those two caught me.

"I was just wandering; I didn't know how to get home and everybody was dead. After they … it was two days before I could walk good enough, then I escaped while they were out of the house they took me to. After that I hid and got food from ASDA … then I saw John."

It was agreed that Morag should share a room with Emma that night but that the following day they must start preparing somewhere larger. John suggested a farm, a little way up the hill. The track to it left a minor road, which joined the A96 by his cottage.

"Knockside should suit you fine," he explained. "It's a big place – they were a big family in Bob's father's day, and it was extended a few years back. Ellen used to do B&B and a couple of the cottages were set up for self-catering holidays too. Bob and Ellen and their daughter-in-law went into Aberdeen, to the hospital, with their son Alistair. They never came back."

He glanced at Morag but she didn't seem to have been upset by his mention of the hospital. He sipped his tea before he continued; it gave him time to think.

"They only did B&B in the season and there weren't any visitors, so the place will be clean. There's a Rayburn, like my Aga but bigger. Water comes from the same reservoir tanks as mine. Bob was mainly into sheep, some main stock, some rare breeds; he was doing well with them. They had a couple of dogs but they were gone when I was last up there. I reckon they had a go at some of the sheep in one field on the way too, I had to shoot a few that were badly mauled.

"The cultivated fields have nothing but winter cabbage growing in them now but there's summer cabbage and winter sown oats planted. Plenty of land could be used for other crops. We'll take a walk up and have a look after dinner, if you like."

That evening, Morag and Dan ran around the Knockside farmhouse exploring while John showed Emma the various buildings. Emma watched him carefully but noted that, whenever they were alone, he kept up a commentary about the place, not giving a chance for her to start a conversation.

Fair enough, she decided; if he didn't want to talk about what he had been doing in Aberdeen that was his business. He hadn't pressed her about things she didn't want to discuss. She started to ask him questions about the house and the farm equipment and eventually he relaxed a little. By the end of the tour she was convinced, this was exactly the place for what she had in mind.

After they returned to the cottage, John laid out an airbed for Morag in Emma's room. It was past nine in the evening now and Dan was already in bed. Morag declared that she was tired and wanted to go up too.

John considered for a few moments and then told her, "There's a bag of clothes and things in your room, Morag. They belonged to my daughter, Elizabeth. She was a year younger than you but not far from the same size. You might find something to fit, if you need anything."

Morag thanked him and made to go. Before she passed him she stopped, bent down and quickly kissed his cheek. "Good night, both," she said, then ran off to the stairs.

Emma smiled at John; stroking Minx on her lap while Brian curled up by the fire, pretending not to notice. "That was kind, John, and it couldn't have been easy for you to say it. I think you have a fan."

John grunted and took a sip of his whisky.

"You were quiet up at Knockside," he said. "You don't have to move there if it doesn't suit you, you know. Or not yet, if you want to wait until we find more people."

Emma sighed gratefully. "It's exactly what I was thinking of but it's a big place for the three of us and I'm not sure I could cope with what needs to be done and those two as well." She took a sip of whisky. "I know the kids will help but it needs more people."

John nodded. "We'll start by seeing if we can't find those you saw in Elgin, an older woman and a young man, you said?"

"We?" Emma asked.

John glanced up. "I need to get one or two things in the town, and anyway, I'd prefer to come along, if you don't mind."

Emma bent and scratched Brian's ears, to hide the relief she felt. "No, I don't mind – come if you like."

Not long afterwards, Emma said good night and went up to bed. Morag was still awake, sorting through the bag of clothes and other items belonging to John's daughter.

"Anything that fits?" Emma asked.

Morag beamed. "Oh yes, and it's good gear too."

"Didn't you have anything to bring with you, Morag?"

Morag shook her head. "After I got away, I found some stuff to wear in a house and then in ASDA and then I just went back there to get food and things. I didn't dare go out much. I was scared that they might catch me again."

She started to cry, burying her face in the bag of clothing. "I'm glad he killed them. Bastards, bastards, bastards!" she sobbed.

Emma knelt by the weeping youngster and held her until she calmed down. She was sure of what she had heard but she had to be certain.

Suddenly Morag's head jerked up in alarm. "Oh God!" she whispered. "I promised him I wouldn't tell anybody. Don't tell him I told you, Emma, please don't tell him."

Emma smiled gently. "Don't worry, I won't."

"What I don't understand is that sign he put on them. How could he know what they did to me and, I know he's a good man," Morag said, blushing, "the best, but why should he bother for me anyway?"

It was Emma's turn to be confused. "What sign? Put on who?"

"After he shot them – Jace and Al and the other one, he dragged them outside, then he hung a sign round Jace's neck, Rapists, in big black letters."

Emma forced out the question: "Who did?"

"Well John of course, who else are we talking about?"

Tears ran down Emma's cheeks and she pulled Morag's head against her. "I don't think he did it for you, Mor, I think he did it for me," she whispered.

Morag pulled her head away, staring at Emma in astonishment. "You?"

Emma nodded. "You weren't the last one Al and Jace … attacked."

Morag's face fell, as her hero fantasy of John, abruptly deflated. "Oh, but I thought …"

She never finished the sentence. Emma rolled onto her bed facing the wall.

#

Next morning, Emma was up even before John. When he came down she already had a kettle boiled and breakfast cooking.

"Good morning," John greeted. "You're up bright and early."

Emma took a pace towards him, laid her hand on his shoulder and gently kissed his cheek.

John blinked in astonishment. "What was that for?"

Emma made no reply, simply returned to pouring water over the tea bag in his mug. "These are good eggs we collected at Knockside yesterday. Those hens must be good layers, John."

He shook his head, confused. "They are. Ellen used to give me a few eggs now and then in return for a couple of rabbits or pheasants, or after I'd spent a day keeping the pigeons off young shoots."

Emma laid a plate of eggs, tinned ham and tomatoes in front of him and then put his tea by the side of it.

"I wanted to get an early start if we could," she announced. "I'd like to go on to a couple of other places, as well as Elgin, if we have time. I'll go and wake the others."

John nodded, bemused. He stared after her as she left, then shook his head and tucked into his breakfast.

While the rest were washing and eating, John hitched up his trailer to the Shogun and checked both vehicles. He returned to the kitchen to find Dan clearing the table and Morag washing up.

Emma came down the stairs carrying her coat and dropped it over the back of the sofa. "Well, I'm ready when everyone else is," she announced.

"Shall we take both four-by-fours?" John asked.

She thought for a moment. "I don't see why. If we find other people who want to join us they'll probably have their own cars anyway."

"Fair enough," he agreed and went through to his workshop.

Dan and Morag were already in the vehicle and Emma was waiting by it when John came out. He had his rifle on a sling over his shoulder and was carrying the Jace's sawn-off side-by-side. He offered the opened shotgun to Emma.

Her face set and he thought she was going to refuse again but she surprised him. "Show me how to use it first," she demanded.

Warning Dan and Morag to stay in the vehicle, John took Emma a few yards off to one side, facing across the road. Within a few minutes he had shown her how to open and close the gun, load and unload it and use the safety catch. Then he had her go through the actions. Finally, he gave her a warning. "The barrels had been hacked back to fourteen inches but at least they left the stock alone. I've cleaned up the ends of the muzzles and the AYA is a good gun, so it's safe to use.

"The short barrels mean that it is going to make a hell of a noise when you fire it though. It will kick like a mule and not all of the powder will burn in the barrel but lack of choke will allow the shot to spread faster than from a normal gun. Which all means, that it will hit with less concentration, so less power and its effective range is shorter than it should be, no more than about twenty yards."

Emma frowned. "But I thought a sawn-off shotgun was supposed to be the .... sort of ... most powerful weapon you could have," she protested.

John snorted. "So the television and films would have you think. Don't expect anything you hit with this to fly backwards, or doors to fall down, or cars to blow up with a single shot. It just doesn't happen like that, as you'll see in a minute. The short barrels make it easier for you to carry around, especially in confined spaces. They also make it more convenient to get in and out of vehicles, or even use from the vehicle if you have to. Unfortunately, short barrels also make it easier to point in the wrong direction and the wrong direction is towards anything you don't want to shoot." He waited while she took that in.

"Okay, lecture over, let's have a go," John told her.

John showed her how to aim, by looking over the end of the barrels, pivoting the gun on her left hand as she brought the stock to her face. And he made sure she understood the importance of holding the butt firmly in her shoulder and leaning forwards to absorb the recoil. Then he hung a cardboard box on a fence post on the opposite side of the road about ten yards away and got her to load two cartridges and take a shot. The shotgun boomed ferociously but she managed the recoil well.

Four finger-sized holes appeared in the box but otherwise it hardly moved under the impact.

"Now bring the gun down and then try again with the other barrel," he instructed.

Emma went through the same procedure, less nervously this time, and five more holes appeared in the box.

"That was good," he complimented. "The cartridges you're firing are loaded with SG shot." He reached into his pocket and then held out his hand to show nine, dark grey, lead balls in his palm. Each ball was about the size of the head of a drawing pin. "That's nine lead balls, like these, in each cartridge. You may not knock an attacker back ten yards but if you hit with four or five of these at short range, anything or anyone you have to defend yourself against will definitely lose their interest in attacking you."

He watched Emma examining the shotgun with a renewed respect but far less trepidation than she had at first. Without prompting she turned the gun to the side, opened it and ejected the two spent cartridges.

"Very good," he said sincerely. "Now load two more cartridges, set the safety catch and let's be off."

As they drove away, Dan leaned forward. "John, will you teach me how to shoot too, please?"

Emma glanced at him sharply but John replied apparently without concern. "Aye, Dan. We'll start you off with an air rifle. I'll teach you and when you can regularly hit a two-pence piece at twenty-five yards you can start helping out by controlling any rats around the farm buildings. Then I'll take you out and teach you to stalk rabbits, so you can help to fill the pot. We'll pick up a rifle for you today."

Morag chimed in from the back seat. "Me too please, John."

John nodded.

Emma frowned. "Isn't Dan a bit young for that, John?"

John shook his head firmly. "He's going to be around guns; that's inevitable in this situation. The sooner he learns to be safe and to use them for a purpose the better. If he gets to use them, he won't want to play with them. Besides, if your community is going to work, everyone is going to have to contribute. Dan isn't very big yet but he's going to grow into a strong lad and the sooner he starts to learn things, to carry on as we get older, the better."

John sat quietly for a while as he drove. After the deaths of his family he had expected to carry on alone. He really hadn't thought about any long-term plans at all, hadn't even considered anything beyond survival for as long as it lasted. Without any intent it seemed he was going to become a member of this community, whether he liked it or not. Well, so be it. You do in life what needs to be done and if this was the plan for him, he would play his part and hope he could play it honestly and well. Out of the corner of his eye he glanced at Emma. I could have worse companions, he decided.

It was Morag who first spotted the smoke. "Look, over there on the left, there's smoke coming from behind that farm."

John slowed the vehicle to a stop.

"She's right," Emma confirmed, "and I think it's only just started."

John started the Shogun moving again. "We'll see who's there. Keep that shotgun handy."

Emma had the gun open across her lap. She checked that the two cartridges were still in place, snapped it closed and made sure the safety catch was on.

John turned past a sign that named the farm as Wester Cultain and drove up the track towards the buildings. He stopped in the large yard behind the farmhouse and he and Emma started to get out.

"Stay in the vehicle until we say it's okay," he told Dan and Morag, firmly.

A Sherpa van was parked in the yard, its back doors open. He lifted his rifle from the rack behind the front seats and stepped away from the Shogun, shutting the door behind him. As he walked around the front of the Sherpa, a woman came out of the farmhouse.

She was tall and broad, in her late forties or early fifties with neat, shoulder-length dark hair and her cheerful, chubby face lit up in welcome when she saw them.

"Well hello," she greeted them loudly. "It's a bit early for visitors – we've not even moved in properly yet."

Emma smiled back. "Hello, I'm Emma and this is John. Are you well?"

The woman nodded enthusiastically. "I'm well thanks. I came through pretty much unscathed. You?"

"I was ill, but it didn't have much effect on John," Emma confirmed.

"I'm Margaret Hilton and this," the woman announced, gesturing towards the farmhouse door, "is Tony."

Emma glanced towards the door as Tony edged around it, an over/under shotgun in his hands. He was tall and rather slim His thin-featured face was framed by long dark hair, tied in a ponytail. He was probably in his early twenties, she judged, and he seemed nervous.

Margaret glowered at him. "You can put that away now, Tony. I don't think you will need it for these good folk." She frowned and then pointed to his mouth. "And get rid of that!"

Tony awkwardly opened the gun, tucked it under his arm, then took the cigarette from his mouth and tossed it aside.

"Sorry about that," she apologised. "We had trouble with a pair of yobs in Elgin. You have to be so careful these days."

Emma realised that she too was still holding her shotgun in both hands. Self-consciously she slid the barrels into the crook of her left arm and cradled her right hand with her left. It was a more relaxed pose but it kept her hand on the small of the stock and her finger near the triggers.

Margaret followed John's gaze towards what he had thought was a bonfire but could now see was a funeral pyre. The shapes of human remains were clearly visible within the flames.

"The previous occupants, poor souls," Margaret explained. "A whole family, gone … but only a few of so many, I suppose."

John nodded but didn't speak.

"Did you say you were in Elgin?" Emma asked. "I think I might have seen you there a few days ago but you ran off when you saw my Land Rover. Are there only the two of you?"

"Ah, that was you, was it?" Margaret returned. "Those yobs had a Land Rover too, we thought it was them coming back. Yes, there's just Tony and me. We had to move out of the town. The smell is getting bad and we were seeing a lot more rats. I didn't think it was healthy to stay any longer. Where are you heading for?"

Emma explained about the community she was hoping to gather, told her about Knockside, without actually revealing the location, and called Morag and Dan from the Shogun, to introduce them. Then she asked if Margaret or Tony had seen anyone else apart from the yobs Margaret had mentioned.

Margaret shook her head. "No-one and we had a good wander around the town."

Emma sighed. "We want to pick up some things in Elgin and then we're going to look at a few other places. Are you happy to settle here or would consider joining us at Knockside, Margaret?"

Margaret hesitated for only a moment before she said, "Pack up our things again, Tony, we're moving to Knockside." Her lips tightened when he hesitated. "Well go on then, don't just stand there, get a move on!" she commanded.

Tony winced but hurried away to do as he had been told.

It was agreed that Emma and John would meet Margaret and Tony on the way back from searching some of the other villages and towns. Margaret offered to gather any supplies they had been intending to collect, to free up their time for searching for people. Emma gratefully accepted and gave her the list.

"The rats and mice are already getting into packets and bags," Margaret warned, "but tins, bottles and jars are still sound, and hardware items of course."

Emma agreed that would be fine but asked her to collect any of the things on the list if she considered them to be safe. At Knockside they could transfer soft packages into vermin-proof containers.

In Elgin, John emptied the gun shop, placing all the firearms and ammunition into the trailer together with reloading equipment and supplies and other items.

"I know we don't need this lot," he confirmed, "and I know the yobs will probably find what they want somewhere but there's no point making it easy for them."

They toured the local villages but found no one else alive. Once they thought they heard another vehicle in the distance but couldn't be sure how far away it was, or exactly in which direction.

They also called at the RAF camps at Kinloss and Lossiemouth. John collected those weapons that were in the ready use racks or on belts in the guard room and police offices, including self-loading rifles, pistols, sub machine guns and even a couple of belt-fed machine guns, all with the relevant ammunition and accessories.

"Heaven help us if anybody really decides to raid these places," he said, climbing back into the vehicle. "Lord knows what we might face. The military must have stepped up security towards the end. Some of this weaponry is heavier than they would normally have deployed for guard duties."

As they prepared to leave Kinloss, Emma noticed the huge wind turbine that provided power to the Findhorn Foundation.

"The Foundation is a little way up the road here," she reminded John. "Let's give it a try. There might be somebody there. It was a commune started to develop self-sufficient, environmentally friendly lifestyles. It might have attracted people after the epidemic."

When they neared the entrance to the foundation, the stench of decaying flesh became almost unbearable. John was reluctant to go in but Emma insisted they should investigate.

To their surprise, the further they drove into the commune area the less intolerable the smell became. Then, standing in the road wearing an inquisitive smile, and a loose, flowing dress and sandals despite the cold wind, they saw a petite, pretty woman. Emma guessed she would be in her twenties. Her waist-length hair was dyed silver and purple. They stopped the vehicle, got out and approached her.

"Welcome," the young woman greeted them. "Welcome to the Foundation. I am Sunflower. Are you well?"

"We are well," Emma said. "Are you?"

Sunflower inclined her head briefly. "I am recovering, thank you. You will have no need of those guns here, we wish no-one any harm."

She turned to a low building roofed with grass and called, "Leah, come and meet our visitors."

The young lady who emerged from the bungalow stopped Emma's breath. She was five feet nine, even in her flat-soled sandals. Her rich coffee-coloured skin and soft full lips were matched with eyes more like those of a doe than Emma could imagine. Venus would have envied her figure. The silky multi-coloured dress, which clung to her in the rising wind, seemed entirely designed to enhance the effect.

Leah placed her hands together and bowed her head. "Welcome."

Sunflower invited the visitors into their home for tea. John declined, saying that it had been a long time since he had visited the Foundation and would like to take a walk around. Dan decided to go with him.

The tea was a delicious herbal mix, which they drank while they exchanged their stories. Leah had been unaffected by the disease and had nursed Sunflower, the only other Foundation survivor, through her fever. Soon afterwards three motorcyclists, all of whom were carrying guns, visited them. Sunflower proclaimed that the bikers had a most aggressive dark aura, so she and Leah hid until they left. Afterwards, she and Leah moved all the bodies to the camping field by the entrance, to discourage visitors. They had been surprised when Emma and John drove through.

"I don't know why I was so determined to come here," said Emma, "but I somehow knew it was somewhere I had to check."

She explained about their gathering people for a community, while Sunflower and Leah looked at one another and smiled.

"Then you were drawn here to us by the fairies," Sunflower proclaimed. "We were going to have to leave soon anyway. The Foundation is not sustainable by only two of us and we seem to have attracted every rat in the area. Living creatures they may be, and entitled to life, but they are not ones we can live with in such numbers and survive the diseases they carry, even if they do not eat all our food supplies."

Emma explained that Sunflower and Leah would be welcome to join them but that she and the others they had gathered so far did not share all the philosophy of the Foundation. In fact, beyond a need to survive and find company, they had not really developed any philosophy at all as yet.

"You may come to share our beliefs," suggested Leah, "but if not, then so be it. Even Sunflower and I differ in some ways – she is Vegan for example, I am not. Whatever happens, it seems that Karma has decreed we come together at this time."

Emma was still finding herself fascinated by Leah's deep, soft, almost musical voice. With their experiences at the Foundation, she was sure these women would both be valuable members of the new community. Sunflower, she discovered, was a beekeeper as well as a gardener, while Leah was a herbalist and artist.

John and Dan returned soon after Emma and the others had finished the tea.

"Well that was fascinating," John exclaimed, "but I don't think I've ever seen as many rats in one area as I did walking round here. I think we should make tracks as soon as you ladies are ready."

Sunflower and Leah both had work equipment that they wanted to take but few other personal effects. Neither could drive, so all their possessions went into the trailer, while people crowded into the vehicle. They soon arrived back at Wester Cultain, to find Margaret and Tony waiting with the supplies they had collected and their van ready packed. After brief introductions all round, the small convoy set off for Knockside.

#

On arrival, Emma showed the new community members around and then offered them their choice of the rooms and cottages.

Margaret was the first to speak up. "Do you mind if Tony and I take the one-bedroom cottage, Emma? Tony can be a bit noisy at times."

Emma didn't really envisage Tony as the noisy type but readily agreed.

"Tony," Margaret shouted. "Get our things into the small cottage, then unload the supplies into the store room by the kitchen."

Tony waved back and trotted over to the Sherpa.

"You've got him well trained," laughed Emma.

Margaret smirked. "Oh he can be moody, but nothing I can't sort out." She leaned closer to Emma and whispered something, while glancing in Tony's direction.

Emma clamped her hand over her mouth to stifle a laugh and grinned as she watched Tony struggling into the cottage with a burden of bags. She didn't doubt for a moment Margaret's ability to 'sort out' her young consort.

She sent Morag and Dan off to find rooms, then asked Sunflower and Leah, "Have you found rooms you would like?"

Sunflower squeezed her arm. "We will only need the one room. It really does not matter which, as long as we are together."

"Then why not take the big one at the back?" Emma suggested. "It has the large windows in case you want to paint in there, Leah."

Sunflower stepped close to her. "Thank you, Emma, that is thoughtful of you." She stroked her fingertips down Emma's bruised cheek and tenderly lifted her chin. "And anytime you want to join us there, you know you will be more than welcome."

Emma swallowed and glanced at Leah, who lowered her eyes and bobbed her head in acquiescence. Leah's large brown pupils rose to bore into Emma's blue eyes, sending an unexpected shudder of excitement through Emma's groin.

The invitation was clear and Emma felt her face flush. She had never acknowledged such feelings before, yet could not deny the attraction of these women. The combination of Sunflower's strength and sensitivity with Leah's beauty and raw sensuality was a potent mix. After her recent experiences, Emma was not ready for any encounter of that intimacy. Nevertheless, these were women who would understand her feelings about her rape and who offered comfort and release without threat. If she completed the course of antibiotics and did not develop any infections, well, she was sure that the invitation would remain open. Who knew what might happen among this disparate group thrown together by catastrophe?

She felt a familiar warm fluttering tension deep within her. Reluctantly she tore her eyes away from Leah's gaze to softly answer Sunflower. "Thank you … I'll remember … Give me a little time."

Sunflower stroked Emma's cheek once more. "Any time," Sunflower promised, then leant forward and softly kissed Emma on the lips.

After unloading the trailer, John walked up the track to Knockside. He had taken into his workshop the weapons he felt would usefully add to those they already had. They were now stacked neatly alongside the ammunition, reloading supplies and other equipment. The remainder he piled at the back of his garage and covered with a tarpaulin. He arrived at the house barely in time to see the exchange between Emma and Sunflower, though he was too far away to hear their conversation. Stunned by what he saw, he quietly returned to his cottage.

Settling

The following day dawned cold, windy and wet. Sleet rattled the windows and the sky was dark with heavy clouds. Emma left everyone to themselves. They needed time to settle in but it was, she admitted to herself, also something of an experiment. She wanted to see what these people would do in their new environment.

She had risen early, showered then dressed in slacks and a warm jersey. After going quietly downstairs, she lit the Rayburn. When it heated sufficiently, she made herself some breakfast. Then she got a fire going in the huge fireplace that warmed the family room.

She sat cross-legged in front of the fire eating while she examined the large cosy room with its wooden floor, assorted rugs and reminders of a time now past. They could probably throw out the television and DVD recorder, though if they restored electricity to the farm there might be films and documentaries on disk that they would want to watch, she supposed.

The previous owners' ornaments were still there. Margaret and Emma had packed away many of the personal belongings but, she decided, too many ghosts of the past remained. They would have a good clear out and rearrangement to make the place feel theirs, a communal project that would help them to bond. Something else must be arranged too; they needed a meeting, a discussion, perhaps this evening after the main meal.

As Emma was sitting drinking her coffee and thinking over what she wanted to achieve at the meeting, she heard the back door open and quickly close. Footsteps clacked on the wooden floorboards and Leah appeared in the doorway.

"I thought I was the first one up," Emma said in greeting.

Leah sighed contentedly. "I've been out, enjoying the forces of nature."

"In that lot?"

Leah tossed back her head and laughed. "I love it! I love the wildness of it. It makes me feel so … alive."

"Coffee is enough to do that for me, first thing in the morning. Would you like some?"

"Mmmm, tea please. I'll just hang up my coat and get out of these boots."

She returned a few minutes later, as Emma was pouring the tea. Leah pressed up close behind her, then squeezed and rubbed her shoulders.

"That does smell good, thank you," Leah told her.

She backed away as Emma turned, but only enough to avoid the tea being spilled. They stared into one another's eyes for a few moments and then Leah took the cup from her and stepped back to lean against the big kitchen table. Leah closed her eyes, raised the cup to her nose and inhaled deeply then took a careful sip of the tea.

After a moment her long, curled lashes rose and slowly her gaze slid up Emma's body, until they again locked eyes. "Quite delicious," Leah murmured. "I look forward to savouring every inch of it."

Emma moved to return to the sitting room and her own coffee, knowing that she was blushing. "You mean every drop," she corrected, over her shoulder.

Leah's lips twitched. "That too."

A few seconds later, Emma heard Leah's footsteps ascending the stairs.

Dan was up next, hungry as always. Emma asked him if he could cook

"Me?" he asked in amazement. "No, nobody ever showed me how."

"Well that's about to change," she told him. "We'll have no passengers onboard this ship. Come on, you can start with scrambled eggs, I know you like those."

"Yeahhhhh!" cheered Dan, rushing off to the kitchen ahead of her.

Margaret and Tony joined them in the house mid morning, then Leah and Sunflower came down shortly afterwards.

Emma eventually went to wake Morag at about eleven. She gently shook the girl's shoulder. "Come on, lazy bones, it's gone eleven o'clock," Emma told her.

Morag squinted at her from over the edge of the duvet. "Sorry, Emma, I had a bad night, didn't sleep much."

Emma frowned. "What was wrong?"

Morag looked down. "Bad dreams."

Emma picked up Morag's hand and held it in her own. "I know, me too, but you're safe here now and things are going to get better."

Morag's eyes were pleading. "Are they, Emma? We really are safe now, aren't we?"

Emma put a confidence she wasn't entirely sure of into her voice as she answered. "Course we are. It's going to be hard work for all of us I think, not so much at first but as time goes on. But we're together now and we might find more people to join us, we still have lots of room … and John is with us."

Morag's face brightened. "Is he here?"

Emma had to stifle a laugh. "I haven't seen him yet this morning but I'm sure he's around. Now why don't you have a bath and get yourself dressed. It will be lunchtime before long."

Morag knelt up quickly and hugged her. "Thanks, Emma, you're a pal."

Soon after Emma returned to the kitchen, Margaret came to see her.

"So, what do you want us to do today, Emma?"

Emma had already thought about this. "I think everyone should take today to do their own thing, to settle in and explore Knockside and relax a little. I was going to suggest that we have a sort of meeting this evening. We do need to decide what our priorities are going to be and who is going to do what. If people want to do something practical today perhaps they could think about that as they wander around, make some notes even, if they want to." She hesitated. "Or am I thinking too much in ways that were right for before? Perhaps that sort of thing isn't appropriate now."

Margaret considered the suggestion briefly before she replied. "Well, many things have changed, but I don't see how we can unlearn everything we have done before, or why we should for that matter. We created conventions and cultures that restricted most of us in the ways we acted, sometimes for the better, to protect people from those who would hurt them, but sometimes simply through ignorance or lack of tolerance. Laws don't mean anything now so we have to protect ourselves, but I also believe many of us will be more confident than we were of throwing off old conventions that simply restricted our freedom to express ourselves openly, when doing so hurts no-one else. We might even develop whole new, more tolerant cultures. But some of the things we learnt about group working were useful. People developed ways of organising things within groups that actually made them run more smoothly and productively, most of the time." She laughed. "As long as we don't find any management consultants who survived we'll probably get along fine. If we do, I claim first chance to shoot them."

Emma nodded as she thought of the things she had heard and experienced since the deaths, her own actions, and reactions to the words and actions of others. She had always thought of herself as open-minded, but after everything that had happened and everything they now faced, people's differences of most kinds seemed even more irrelevant. Even among these few at Knockside there was a wide spread of what might previously have been considered unconventional living arrangements. Yet they had to work together, and that meant they had to know and understand one another, and maybe even to agree some rules.

She blinked and dragged her attention back to the matter in hand. "OK," she agreed. "We'll have a meeting. It doesn't have to be formal, but at least we might get to know one another better and work out where we go from here."

Emma asked Dan, to find John and see if he would come to the meeting but the boy returned saying John wasn't there. It was late afternoon when John drove into the yard and began unloading jerry cans from his trailer, into one of the barns. Tony spotted him through the window, so Emma went out through the blustery rain to meet him. She pushed the hood of her jacket back as she reached the shelter of the barn.

"Hello, stranger," she greeted him.

He smiled back at her, a little uncertainly. "Hi, Emma."

She frowned. "Is anything wrong, John?"

He shook his head. "I've been back to Kinloss. These are all cans of diesel. I've got two small diesel generators in the back of the Shogun. They won't provide enough power to give you electricity for the whole of the house but I thought they'd be useful for emergency lighting or power tools."

Emma nodded; still not convinced he wasn't merely changing the subject. Apart from a brief glance, he hadn't even looked in her direction.

John continued. "There's lots more fuel at Kinloss and Lossiemouth, petrol as well, but since your Land Rover and the Shogun both use diesel I brought diesel generators too. One type of fuel should simplify things. That way only the Sherpa needs petrol and maybe you can find something to replace that, if you want to. Otherwise somebody will eventually put the wrong fuel in something, guaranteed."

Emma was worried now and not about fuel. A couple of days ago, John had started talking about 'we' in relation to their little group. Now that the others had joined them, he had reverted to referring to them as 'you', as if excluding himself.

"John," she started, "we're going to have a meeting this evening after dinner, to discuss what we need to do and how we're going to do it. Will you join us, please?" She hesitated. "We really need you there."

John straightened from his task and faced her for the first time. "Well, if you're sure you want me there."

She stepped towards him and held his shoulders. "Of course we want you there … I want you there. You know more about this area and the country than any of us, and besides … I don't really know these others yet, you're already a friend."

She watched him searching her eyes, trying to confirm that they said the same as her words, and she wondered what had brought on this change in him. Finally he nodded and, to her relief, he actually smiled properly.

"What time?" he asked.

"Come about six o'clock and have dinner with us. We'll have a drink afterwards and when everyone is settled we'll start."

He nodded again. "I'll be there," then returned to unloading the cans.

After dinner the group settled in the big room. The fire was blazing and people found chairs or cushions to make themselves comfortable. Emma waited for a lull in the conversation before she began.

"I don't want to make this too formal but I think we'll get more done if we have some sort of structure. Can I suggest that we start by each person telling us whatever they want to share about themselves, their life and particularly about what special skills they have that will help us here at the farm?"

A general murmur of agreement and nodding of heads greeted her suggestion.

"Then we can each introduce any concerns or ideas we have and we can all discuss those. By the end I hope we'll have a plan of action, a list of things we need to do, in order of priority. Margaret has agreed to take notes of what we decide."

Emma looked around the group. Some people were smiling, some brows were furrowed in thought, but no one dissented.

"All right then, since it was my idea, I'll start," Emma volunteered.

She told them that she was born in Inverness and brought up in the same area. She had studied sociology at the university in Glasgow and then tried a variety of jobs before settling with a charity that helped refugees. She was an advanced First Aider and could drive but perhaps her most useful knowledge in their current situation came from her work with the refugees, from seeing the methods of doing things, such as farming, cooking and water gathering with basic tools that people in the west might consider improvised but which were the basics of life in their own countries for many of those she supported.

Morag was sitting on a cushion to Emma's left and went next. John, Dan and Emma had heard her story before but she related it again for the others.

"I can sew and cook and I'm good with computers but I'm not sure that's very useful to us anymore," she concluded, rather dejectedly.

Margaret who was sitting next to Morag spoke up.

"Don't worry, hen, we are all going to have to learn lots of new things and it will be all hands to the pumps. You'll find that you are better than any of us at something new we have to do."

Morag smiled up at her gratefully.

Margaret then briefly related her history. "I was a teacher, maths and then accountancy. I was born and raised in Lancashire but moved to Edinburgh and then Elgin five years ago, after my divorce." She grinned. "He was a prat, never did appreciate me. I have a flair for organisation and logistics. I enjoyed sailing, riding and cooking, including making my own bread. I'm not sure yet where my skills will fit in but I'm sure I can set my hand to most things," she concluded, giving Tony's shoulder an affectionate squeeze.

He was sitting on a cushion at the side of Margaret's chair. "I'm originally from Wick, but had to move to Inverness and then to Rothes for my job. I work – worked - in the stills," he said. "After everyone died I thought I would too, so I spent most of my time getting drunk. I was wandering about in Elgin – I'm still not sure how I got there – not really knowing what I was doing or going to do, when I met Margaret. She was the first person I'd seen alive since the deaths and she took me in." He glanced up at his partner, shyly. "I'm don't know what would have happened to me if she hadn't; she brought me to my senses."

He sipped his water before continuing. "I'm fit, used to play football for the local team, and I was pretty good at metalwork and woodwork at school. I guess with the metalwork and what I learnt at work I could make a still, for basic spirits for burning or cleaning or with better processing for drinking, but apart from that ..."

Margaret placed her hand over his ear and pulled his head against her leg, but not so tightly he couldn't hear, then stage-whispered, "He has other skills and uses but I'll save that for a ladies only meeting!"

Emma, Leah and Sunny chuckled, John closed his eyes and shook his head, and Tony blushed but grinned!

Sunflower was also sitting on the floor on a cushion but leaning back against the sofa next to Leah.

"Well I'm a Devonshire lass," Sunny said. "My parents had a market garden with a side line in honey production, so I grew up raising plants and caring for bees. I met my first and only boyfriend, big mistake, at college but it was not long before we joined a group of New Age travellers. We toured with them for a few years before we arrived at the Foundation. I stayed when the rest of them moved on."

Leah sipped her red wine then told them what she wished to of her story.

"I was born in Nigeria and orphaned when disease wiped out most of my village. My uncle, who lived in the next province, adopted me. My new family moved to Libya while I was in my teens. My uncle was an engineer in the oil industry. When I was of age I went to London to study for a degree in art and design. While I was there I drew the illustrations for a botany student who was doing his thesis on medicinal plants and their use in the Middle Ages.

"Through that I found an interest in herbalism. I learned about Findhorn from one of the other students. I had been there for only a few months after I finished my degree. I met Sunny the day after I arrived; she was leading a self-awareness expanding session. We have been together since that afternoon," she explained, then leant over to tenderly kiss Sunflower's cheek.

Dan was next, his story didn't take long but he finished with confidence. "I can't do much now but Emma is teaching me to cook and John is going to teach me to shoot and I'm ever so strong, really." He flexed his arm muscles to prove it and they all laughed.

John was sitting in the armchair on the opposite side of the fire from Emma and was last to speak. As was his way, he was brief, giving the bare bones and claiming far less experience and knowledge than Emma knew he really had.

As he finished Emma smiled warmly at him. "And if you believe that's all he can do, you'll believe anything," she warned the group, raising another laugh.

John actually blushed and grunted but as he raised his glass to his lips and sipped his whisky, his eyes met hers and Emma could see they were twinkling with pleasure.

"Okay," she announced, "lets take a short break so that anyone who wants one can get another drink, then we'll talk about our plans."

She levered herself out of the armchair and went to the kitchen to pour herself another whisky. John followed her.

"How do you think it's going?" she asked him, tipping Glenmorangie into his glass.

"They don't seem a bad lot. They have some useful skills, even if they don't all recognise them yet." Then he frowned.

"What's wrong?" Emma asked.

"I don't know," he confessed. "Somehow I think that there's more to Leah than she's telling us. Och, maybe it's my imagination or her way. We're all still new to one another – forget it."

Emma nodded then linked her arm through his. "We better get back," she suggested.

John allowed Emma to guide him towards the big room. He felt guilty and confused about his feelings, especially so soon after burying his wife and family but the warmth of Emma's arm through his gave him a surge of pleasure that he couldn't deny.

When everyone was back in place and settled Emma spoke again.

"Now we know something about each others' background and any special skills, perhaps we can move on to what we think we should do next. Let's go the other way around this time, starting with you, John, if you don't mind."

John took a sip of his whisky and a deep breath. "All right, there are a few things I think we ought to do. Firstly, if we want any more foodstuffs that are sold in packets or bags, like flour or sugar for example, we ought to get them together and into rat-proof containers as soon as possible. Secondly, I think we should gather a good stock of all sorts of goods we think we might want and store them here; at some stage it might be difficult to get into towns because of disease or weather or because we have competition from some other group, and in uncontrolled environments they'll go off a lot quicker."

John saw people were listening to him with interest and offering no arguments so far, so he continued.

"Thirdly, I think we need to consider our security. Everyone has had frightening encounters of one sort or another and as I was coming back from Lossiemouth today, four lads on motorbikes crossed the road in front of me. They didn't see me but I got a good look at them. They were all wearing leathers and they each had at least one gun across their back or on the bike."

Tony joined the conversation at that point. "I'm not arguing with you about our taking precautions, John, but I used to have a bike and everyone here carries a gun when we're out - not all bikers are thugs you know."

John nodded at him briefly. "I know, Tony, but that was a different time. From a practical standpoint a motorbike doesn't make sense in this environment. The roads aren't so blocked that you can't get around the abandoned vehicles in a car or van and there's damn all other traffic to have to get through. Big motorbikes aren't much better on fuel than a four-wheel drive these days and there's no shortage of fuel yet anyway, plus you can't carry much gear or supplies on a bike. About the only reason for going with a bike at the moment, is for the image or the thrill and those lads didn't give me the impression they wanted to foster an image of responsible, law-abiding motorcyclists."

Sunflower raised her hand. "But why would they bother us? So many things are available for the taking. They can scavenge from stores as easily as we can."

"Yes," said Emma, "but there's one thing here that they can't get in the stores."

"What?" asked Sunflower.

Morag interrupted, her face a mask of shocked realisation and her slender body trembling. "Us! You mean us, don't you, Emma?"

Emma nodded gravely. "Yes, any of the women, and not all the thugs out there would confine themselves to us." She glanced meaningfully at Dan.

Morag curled up and was silent.

The conversation rotated around the possible threat for some time, until Emma eventually held up her hand.

"All right, we all agree that we could face attackers and we all agree that we need to do something about it. What we don't agree on is what we should do. Sunflower thinks we should hide our presence or take only passive measures. John hasn't said much but I'd guess he's in favour of barbed wire, mines and machineguns, right, John?"

"For a start," he agreed.

"Well, John is the only one of us with any military experience; I think we should leave it to him to work out a defence plan that we can discuss in detail," continued Emma. "Any objections?" No one spoke. "Then will you do that for us, John?"

"Aye," he said. "I will."

Emma sighed in relief and returned to the discussion. "Right, on to other concerns – who's next?"

As the discussion moved around the room, each person brought up their own suggestions. John's idea of building up their stocks was agreed and the need to have a reserve store, somewhere at a distance but well hidden and protected from vermin, was raised and also agreed. Margaret was elected to organise and maintain an inventory of supplies on hand and needed.

They talked about acquiring a larger generator to supply electricity, particularly for lighting and refrigeration, the two things they missed most, but no-one was sure how to wire it into the system if they did find one and they were doing fine at the moment so it was pushed down the priority list.

The potential problem of attacks by dogs was considered and relegated to a sub section of John's defence plan. They decided to round up sufficient dairy cows for their needs; Sunflower volunteered to do the milking and to make butter and cheese. Leah and Emma would organise an infirmary in one of the spare rooms and equip it with a mix of traditional and herbal medicines.

In addition to the other supplies they all agreed that a reference library was essential; they would need to learn so many new things. Left unprotected, in unheated buildings, books would deteriorate and be damaged by vermin. And so the discussion went on.

It was late by the time they agreed to call a halt but Emma was pleased. There had been disagreements but they had formed a plan. People were starting to fall into roles that suited their talents and abilities. Over all, they shared an air of optimism and the beginnings of a sense of community.

Only Morag gave her cause for concern. After the initial discussion of a threat from the bikers Morag had contributed little and seemed to have withdrawn into herself. Dan had fallen asleep some time ago. Morag said nothing when Margaret roused her and Dan and sent them off to bed. As Emma banked the fire and prepared to blow out the last of the candles John came in from the kitchen.

His brow was furrowed with thought but it cleared as he saw her.

"Emma, I've decided to move up here to Knockside, if you can find room for me."

Emma sighed in delight and her face lit up. "Oh, John, of course we can." She hugged him hard and then stepped back. "What made you decide?"

"I've been thinking about it all day but the discussion tonight did it. It makes more sense for us all to be within the farm complex from the point of defending ourselves if needed and it's a waste of resources heating and lighting two places. My cottage and shop being right next to the road, it isn't even the best place for an alternative store; we'll have to think about that."

"When will you move?" she asked.

He thought for a moment. "Tomorrow. I'll start bringing things up in the morning."

"I'll help," she volunteered.

Whether from the excitement of progress or lingering bad dreams, Emma slept fitfully. For a while in the early hours she lay awake, listening, not sure whether she had really heard movement and a muffled cry or if it had been in her nightmare. Her fingers tightened around the handle of the kitchen knife under her pillow but she heard nothing else and eventually she drifted back to sleep.

#

The next morning, Emma was making coffee when she heard a shout from the yard. Sunflower burst in, tears streaming down her face, her words hardly intelligible through her sobs.

Emma held her tightly. "Sunny! Here now, whatever's wrong?"

Sunflower swallowed hard then pushed herself away. "Get the others, you've got to come now," she pleaded. "But not Dan," she added, "he mustn't see."

Emma fetched Leah but Morag wasn't in her room. Leaving Leah to comfort Sunflower, she then quickly called Margaret and Tony from their cottage. After they had all gathered in the kitchen, Sunflower led them out across the yard to the barn.

Morag's frail young body hung still and lifeless, her nightdress flapping around her legs, her face swollen and her tongue protruding. A rope from the rafters was tied around her neck. Emma stared in disbelief, unable to move, hardly able to comprehend what she was seeing. Sunflower buried her head against Leah, who also stared up at the body.

Margaret was the first to recover. "Get a knife, Tony, let's get her down," she commanded, even her normally firm voice trembling a little.

After they had laid Morag on the floor of the barn and removed the rope, Emma reached out to touch Tony's arm. "Will you fetch John, please, Tony?"

He nodded then ran off across the yard and down the track. A few minutes later John's Shogun ground to halt in the yard and he and Tony jumped out. Emma pulled herself as close to John as she could. He wrapped his arms around her and hugged her tightly, his right hand cradling her head against his shoulder, as he stared sorrowfully at the body laid out on the cold ground.

They all stood mute for some minutes, hardly aware of the bitter wind or the rain spattering against their backs, until Margaret again broke the silence.

"Tony, fetch a blanket and cover her up. The rest of you, let's get inside, we're doing no good here."

She bustled them all back to the house and into the family room. John built up the fire while Margaret put the big kettle on the Rayburn to heat. Tony came in while she was still in the kitchen.

"Tony, love, get some glasses and pour everyone a drink, will you? I think we need it, even at this time of the morning. I'll make tea and coffee."

Tony nodded silently. He found a tray, poured brandy into six glasses and then added mugs for the hot drinks.

"Good lad," she said, fondly.

Tony carried the tray into a room of people deep within their own thoughts. Each accepted the glass and a mug without comment, or with only a brief thanks. Each held together close with another, yet each was alone within their own memories, their own guilt at not recognising Morag's despair and the inevitable questions: Why had she done it? Was there anything they could they have done to prevent it?

Later that morning the rain fell continuously on the group gathered around a grave in a corner of a field, close to the outside of the farm compound. Sunflower said a few words of hope that Morag would be at peace and with love. If anyone prayed they did it silently, to their own deity. They all helped to fill the grave and then cover it with stones, taken from a pile that farmers had dug from the ground over the years. John hammered in the pointed end of a board into which he had carved Morag's name, age and date of death. Then the newly gathered, yet already diminished group drifted back through the wet to the farmhouse.

They had gathered again in the family room, which had become their meeting place. John spoke first.

"Well, none of us had known her long but Morag will be missed. I don't know about you, but I think she did what she did because she couldn't face the fear of being attacked again. Personally I prefer to deal with that by doing something practical to prevent it. While I was at Lossiemouth I spotted a stock of barbed wire and pickets by a truck. Tomorrow I'm going to fetch it and start making this place more secure. Who'll come and give me a hand?"

Everyone volunteered but it was decided that John should take Tony, Emma and Sunflower. Margaret and Leah would stay behind to start creating an inventory of the stores and equipment they already had and would need, together with a list of subjects on which they should find books for their library.

#

The following morning, Dan was stationed in an upstairs bedroom overlooking the track to the farm. They gave him a pair of binoculars and the title of lookout-in-chief, with the task of warning Margaret and Leah if anyone approached the farm.

He adopted his sternest expression and pledged that not even a mouse would get by without him knowing. He had accepted Morag's death with surprising calm; they could only guess if it was because he had seen so many deaths including his own mother and sister whilst he had known Morag for only a few days.

"After we have gone past, we'll take up the cattle grids by the gates at both the first fence and down at the end of the track. It'll prevent anyone driving straight in, give you some time," John told Margaret and Leah.

Emma loaded her pack into the back of the Land Rover, as she did for every trip.

John watched her, curiously. "Are you thinking of walking back then?" he asked.

Emma laughed. "I know we probably won't need it but you never know. In fact I think from now on I'll leave it strapped into the back of the Rover. The things in there could be useful any time."

"Okay," he agreed, "it's a good idea. What we used to call a bug-out bag - packed and ready in case you have to take off at short notice. It's handy if you're stuck away from base unexpectedly too. I'll make one up for the Shogun as well."

They set off in the Land Rover with John's trailer hitched to the back. Lifting the cattle grids was no easy task but with four of them they managed it and dropped them in long grass beside the track.

At the entrance to the airbase at RAF Lossiemouth they were stopped by the barrier across the main gate.

"Someone's been here," reported John. "I left the barrier up when I came away last time."

He climbed out of the Land Rover taking his rifle with him. "Get out of the vehicle but stay close and keep those guns ready. I'm going to do a quick recce."

Emma and Tony were both armed, but Sunflower still refused to handle a gun. Slowly John approached the barrier and the guardroom beyond but no challenge came. He searched through the guardroom and the police offices behind it without finding anyone but the now decaying corpses. He checked the key cases but as he had expected, most of the keys were missing; presumably taken by servicemen who had died at their workplaces.

John walked back to the barrier and lifted the metal beam.

"Bring it through," he called to Emma, waving her on with a roll of paper he held. "Everything seems okay here."

The other three climbed back into the Land Rover and Emma drove through the gate. John dropped the barrier behind them, slid into the passenger seat and Emma drove off, following his directions to where he had seen the truck and wire. When they arrived they found that they were in luck.

Whether people had been unloading or loading the lorry, the job was half done. Thick armoured gloves for handling the wire were by the powered tailgate, which acted as a lift. John started the truck to power the tail lift and they soon had the entire pile of wire and six-foot-long metal pickets on board. John inspected the load: coils of razor wire were stacked by reels of straight barbed wire, baling wire, pickets, gloves, wire stretchers, wire cutters, and two tubular picket hammers; everything they would need was there.

He climbed into the cab and Tony took the passenger seat. Then John called down to Emma, who was standing by the Land Rover.

"Follow me, Emma. I picked up a map of this place in the guardroom and there's something I want to check on at the other side of the airfield."

Emma called back okay and they set off around the perimeter road. It took them about ten minutes to arrive at a series of low, grass-covered, earthen mounds surrounded by a high double fence. John pulled up by a building next to the gates of the compound and jumped down from the truck. Emma got out of the Land Rover and joined him.

"What is this place?" she asked, intrigued.

"It's what they called the bomb dump," he said. "It's where they stored all the ammunition and explosives."

She gawped at him in surprise. "I was joking, when I talked about mines," she said.

He grinned back at her. "Aye, but I wasn't."

Emma drove with great care on the way back to Knockside. In the entrance building John had found both a site diagram and the keys of the mounded ammunition stores, together with the bodies of several airmen who must have worked there. She didn't know what John had taken from the stores and loaded into the trailer and she wasn't sure she wanted to know but towing it made her nervous.

They replaced the cattle grids so that they could drive in and then took them up again once they had passed. Margaret, Leah and Dan were waiting for them as they arrived back in the yard. Margaret waved as they all got out of the vehicles.

"Our lookout-in-chief warned us you were coming," she reported.

John ruffled Dan's hair. "Well done, I knew we'd left Margaret and Leah in safe hands."

Dan beamed.

For over a week they worked hard on their defences, retiring each night tired and sore in muscles that most of them had seldom put to such extended use. Having the right tools helped but was still a major task, at which John kept them unwaveringly. They could not complain. He worked twice as hard as any of them and kept on working after he sent them limping home exhausted. Sometimes he did not return to the house until after they had gone to bed. At the end of the week Emma called a meeting.

"Well, John, how are we doing?" Emma asked.

John's face was drawn and the skin around his eyes dark but he answered enthusiastically. "Very well indeed. We've closed all the gaps between the house, cottages and other buildings with wire. With the second load we brought from Lossie, we have triple-coil razor wire supported by straight barbed wire and tied into pickets, all around at twenty-five yards from the buildings and a straight wire fence five yards outside that to keep the animals off and inside it where necessary to remind us to keep away.

"That's important, because I've booby-trapped the razor coils. All the fences between here and the road are wire, not stone or hedge, so we can see out for at least a hundred yards. The grass in the fields might grow long enough to cause a problem later in the year but, for now, it's fine. The one route up from the road that was hidden was that gully and we have a mass of tangle wire, broken glass and a few other surprises mixed in with the brambles in there that should dissuade anyone from coming that way."

He sipped his tea before he continued. "Now we've got the pulleys in place, we can winch the cattle grids up and down and chain then padlock them when they are raised, so keeping them up is less of an inconvenience. We have a good selection of weaponry from pistols and shotguns to military rifles and machine guns; all I've got to do now is teach you how to use them. You all know that the wire marks the range at which you can effectively use the shotguns you have at the moment and we've agreed the places everyone would take and what to do if we're attacked.

"We've set up those battery-powered intercoms to let us talk to one another from the defensive positions, so we can move people to where they are needed. The only way into the buildings now, except for a well-trained and determined enemy, is up the track and through the gate. If a section or more of professional soldiers attacked us we wouldn't hold them but we can fend off a bunch of thugs without any problem and the dogs won't get in.

"By the end of tomorrow I'll have some alarm systems rigged up and then I think we can drop the sentry rota; I know it's tiring everybody with there being so few of us."

The whole group sighed in relief.

Emma smiled brightly despite her tiredness. "All right then, we've all worked damned hard but I think it's drawn us together and I think that we will all relax a bit more now knowing we are safer. Tomorrow we'll spend the day clearing up and doing some of the other tasks we put back. John can set up the alarm systems, then the following day is Sunday and I think we all need a day of rest. What do you say?"

They responded with a resounding cheer and several calls of, "Where's the whisky?"

Emma sat back. She had pushed herself harder than anyone except John that week but the sense of achievement and group spirit in the room right then was worth it. She glanced across at John intending to thank him but he was already asleep in his chair.

#

John must have gone to bed at some time because when Emma went down the following morning the chair was empty. He followed her into the kitchen as the kettle was boiling.

"Good morning," she greeted. "You must have smelled the tea."

"Morning, Emma, how are you feeling?"

She made a not entirely fake grimace. "Stiff all over, but it's worth it."

She poured water over his teabag and her coffee. "Coming through to the big room?" she asked.

He took the tea from her. "Thanks, yes let's do that."

John stirred the fire then added another log. "I'll split some more wood later, the stack's getting low."

"You don't have to do everything yourself you know," she told him, "you do more than enough. Let one of the others have a go."

He sipped his tea, before he spoke. "We need more people."

Emma mulled that over for a while. "There have to be more out there. If my estimate of one in ten thousand was right, that should mean about six hundred people are left alive in Scotland, another five thousand or so south of the border. Now we're secure and starting to get organised we really have something to offer any good people we do find."

"I wouldn't say we're totally secure," John observed. "There's still more to do but I think we're a lot better off than we were."

He took another sip of tea. "Sunny's ideas weren't all wrong, you know. We positioned the wire where it needed to go but wherever possible it isn't obvious from the road and our other preparations are as discreet as practicable. That isn't only because it's good security. I don't think we can, or would want to, spend our lives hiding but there's no point in making ourselves a target either. We don't want to get into any gun battles if we can avoid it."

"She appreciated it when you recognised her suggestions." Emma told him.

He nodded. "She can be a bit spacey for me at times but she's bright and she worked as hard as anyone on that fence. She might never touch a gun but she's a worker and she's never so much as murmured at doing her stint on watch. They've all done well and that's a fact."

"What else do you think we ought to do?" she asked, moving slightly to ease her muscles, almost in dread of what he might suggest.

John thought about it for a moment. "Not a lot actually, as far as physical work goes. The wire is a decent distance out, but I'll put some chicken wire frames over the windows that face outwards. They won't cut out any light but they would stop anyone lobbing bottles of petrol, or even grenades, in through the windows. Chicken wire never looks that out of place around a farm, even if it is over windows.

"Given time I'll take people through using the rifles and machine guns but the shotguns and buckshot will serve well enough for now. We should take some fire precautions too, for day-to-day safety as much as in case of attack. We're putting a lot of effort into Knockside; it would be a disaster to get burned out by accident."

Emma slowly rubbed her lips, thinking, then raised her eyes again. "Do you think we should prepare somewhere else, just in case? We've already discussed an alternate store."

John shook his head slightly. "Not to this extent. There's no point if we aren't living there. We might arrive only to find someone else had moved in." He swallowed the remains of his tea. "But we can clean somewhere out, put a good stock of tinned food and other surpluses there, well hidden so it won't be scavenged, generally make it liveable. Plenty of places, other than Knockside, would meet our needs. If it isn't obvious and we make it a bit difficult to get to and uninviting from the outside, maybe drop a tree or some power lines across the road or track, stage crashed vehicles blocking the road towards it – near where there's an alternative road to take – dump animal carcases around it, that sort of thing, people might take an easier option."

"You have got a devious mind," she said.

He grunted. "I saw a lot of this sort of thing when I was in the army. We did peace keeping ops in a couple of places that had minor wars or internal trouble. It didn't always work when people were facing armies of course but I saw examples where it made all the difference, where people had survived while all their neighbours had been killed by rioters or rebels or looters."

"How long were you in the army?" she asked, curious to know more about his experiences.

"Five years in the regulars. I was REME, an armourer. I might have stayed but my wife, Ruth, didn't like the barracks life and it was an active time so I was away a lot. Then I had a few years in the TA in the infantry. She was happier with that, even though I was away some weekends and for a couple of weeks a year it was just training. After I did one spell of 6 months on active duty overseas though, she put her foot down and said she didn't want that sort of worry again, so I packed it in."

The others all joined them over the next half hour. Emma was coming to realise that the previous week of hard work had not only brought them together as a community but had also created a routine, as well as taking their minds away from Morag's suicide. They usually washed or bathed before coming down, then made breakfast, or whoever was already cooking when others came in would often offer to cook for them too, then after eating they would set off to work. Today the work would be different but it seemed as if the routine had been established.

But none of the achievements could free her mind of a lingering worry that nagged at her. Despite the pills she had taken, her period should have started a week ago. She shuddered and felt bile rise in her throat. The idea of being pregnant to Jace or Al was too disgusting even to think about. She had checked the medical dictionary and was sure she was taking the right antibiotics to kill any STD. Disease or pregnant by one of her rapists; she wasn't sure which would be worse or what she would do in either case. Next time she went into town she would find some pregnancy test kits. All she could do about infection was watch for symptoms, take the pills and pray.

#

Over the course of the next few weeks the group achieved a great deal of what they planned. Roles and routines were becoming a part of their lives. The work was often harder than they had been used to, they squabbled as all people living together will, but they also started to have fun, to laugh together and even joke at one another's expense without causing offence.

Their stocks and library became extensive and they found and set up their back-up location. They camouflaged and protected it as John suggested. They found a few dairy cows that survived but they were dry. They penned pigs, brought some beef cattle and sheep into the fields nearby. They heard and even saw dogs and the bikers occasionally at a distance. There seemed to be six bikers now, including one woman, but if the bikers saw them, they didn't approach.

The weather was starting to improve and although still cool, this afternoon was beautiful, so Emma and Leah were taking a walk to see what medicinal plants they might find in the area.

Emma was feeling more relaxed at last. After having missed a month altogether, her period had finally returned and she had experienced no signs or symptoms of infection. According to the medical books she should have known by now if she had any of the common problems. There were other diseases she might not know about for years. They were things she could do nothing about and she had driven them to the back of her mind, but that didn't stop them haunting her dreams.

She had barely fended off Leah's teasing invitation to examine the plants at close range, lying down, when they heard a shout. They looked up, startled, to see a man coming over the hill in front of them. He was waving.

Contact

He was tall, well over six feet, Emma thought. His beard and long hair were black, his accent was distinctly east European and as far as she could see he was not armed. He approached with a beaming smile and open arms.

"Hello, ladies, such beautiful ladies," he called.

Emma thrust out her left hand in the universally understood gesture but kept her right hand behind her.

"Stop!" she ordered.

The man stopped, his smile wavering, his eyes showing confusion.

"Are you well?" Emma demanded.

His frown disappeared instantly, "Ahhhhhh, I understand. Da, I am well. I was sick just a little bit." He held up his right hand with the forefinger and thumb about an inch apart. "Are you well also?"

Emma dropped her hand. "Yes, we are well. My name is Emma and this is Leah."

"My name is Sergei. I hope you are not going to shoot at me too."

Emma let her right hand drift forward to her side, revealing the shortened shotgun he had obviously already noticed. Leah was regarding the stranger with interest but she kept her hands in her jacket pockets, in one of which, Emma knew, she had a pistol John had brought from Lossiemouth or Kinloss.

"That would be too much of a waste," said Leah, causing Emma to glance at her open-mouthed.

Leah returned her glance with a raised eyebrow and a small smile.

Emma cleared her throat, then asked, "Are you alone, Sergei?"

"Da, my shipmates, they all died," he responded, shaking his head sadly.

They led him back to the farm, where four clearly excited people greeted them. John stood back more cautiously, though he greeted Sergei civilly. Leah led Sergei into the house while John dropped back with Emma.

"Where did you find this one?" he asked.

"He came walking over the hill. I think he might be a Russian sailor."

John raised his eyebrows in surprise and they followed the others inside.

Leah and Sunflower had taken Sergei into the big room, where he dropped his backpack by the wall and removed his duffle jacket. He was wearing a brown leather belt over his jumper. John immediately saw the pistol holster attached to the left side of it but Sergei also removed both belt and holster then casually dropped them on top of his pack and jacket. They sat him in one of the armchairs by the fire and a few moments later Tony came in carrying a tray of drinks, closely followed by Margaret.

"I know it's early, but I thought we might stop work for the day, in view of our visitor," Margaret said, looking to Emma for agreement.

"Of course," agreed Emma, "this is an occasion."

With a drink in his hand and clearly pleased to be surrounded by friendly and interested company, Sergei relaxed.

Sunflower got in first, with the question on all their minds. "So where have you come from, Sergei?"

Sergei took an appreciative swallow of the malt whisky. "Ah, so much better than vodka," he pronounced.

He reached forward and ruffled Dan's hair. The boy was sitting cross-legged by the fire, enthralled by this foreign visitor. Then Sergei started to tell them his story.

"I am chief radio officer of the fishing support vessel, Helenska. I was first to hear the news of the terrible deaths. All my shipmates, they talked about it but we did not know what to do. Then a few days later the officer-of-the-watch spotted distress flares and soon after we found a lifeboat with four people on it, three women and one man. Many of the crew did not want to let them onboard but they said they were not sick and the captain he said it was the law of the sea, we must rescue those in distress." He stopped to take another huge swallow of whisky.

"Soon after they came onboard they started to get sick. The crew panicked and they put them back on a life raft and set them adrift without telling the captain but then we started to get sick too. The captain had me radio the fleet and we set course for Ullapool but we had one engine down, always we had engine problems, and it was over a week away. All the other ships stopped answering my calls and everyone onboard Helenska died before we got there. I do not know what happened to the other ships, they did not take anyone on board – perhaps they went home." He shrugged. "There was heavy fog in the Minch and I missed the buoys and ran aground off Skye. We were taking on water, so I took a lifeboat to row ashore. Then I walked."

Sergei swallowed the last of the whisky and held up his glass. "May I have another, please, it is very good."

Tony fetched the bottle and poured another round.

"Have you seen anyone since you started walking?" asked Emma.

"Da, many times. The first was an old man, in Kyle of Lochalsh, but he was crazy in the head. He kept calling me Yuri and asking if I had landed in my spaceship. When I told him my name was not Yuri he got very angry and pointed at me with a shotgun and sent me away. He did me a big favour I think. Next I came to a farm, near where the road from Kyle joins the road to Inverness. I saw the smoke from the chimney but when I went towards the house they shot at me. I do not think they meant to hit me but I went away anyway."

He took a moment to order his thoughts. "Then there were the people in the gas masks. I saw them near Inverness. They shot at me too, when I came close, and shouted at me to go away. I think maybe they were crazy also. I thought maybe everyone in the world was dead or had gone crazy, so I took a boat and I sailed on Loch Ness for a while. I caught fish and took supplies from the small villages; it was good but I did not see any people. In one village many dogs attacked me. I scared them off with my pistol but they chased me from where I had left the boat. Then I walked on the small roads over the hills and came to a little village, ahhhh, like the vegetable, Tomato."

"Tomatin," Emma corrected him.

"Da," Sergei agreed, "that is it. It was very weird there, no people, no bodies, no smell, nothing. Like they all just …. Poof!" he said, flicking open the fingers of both hands.

Everyone was sitting fascinated with his story, so Sergei took another drink and continued.

"Then I thought to go to Aberdeen. I have been to Aberdeen many times, good whisky, good beer, many ladies."

He aimed his smile round all the women, obviously starting to feel the effects of the malt.

"I thought I would find people there for sure. First though I met the men by Grand town-on-Spey."

Emma almost corrected him again but then let it pass.

"An older man was there," Sergei continued, "he was called Alan, and a younger one, who was Martin. At first they went to hide in their cottage when they saw me, but I called out and they stopped. They were friendly; they did not shoot at me. The old one lived there, the younger one said he had come from Dundee and it was very bad there. He had been in the hills but was trying to find his friend. Then he met Alan and was there a few days."

Emma raised an eyebrow at John. He nodded back in understanding.

"I'll take a drive down there tomorrow," he offered.

"Da, I will show you if you wish it. They were friendly people; they did not shoot at me. I stayed one night and then I want to get to Aberdeen, so I walk again," Sergei told them.

Emma winced; wondering if not shooting at someone was to become the new definition of being friendly. "Anyone else, Sergei?" she prompted.

His face grew serious. "The Hells Angels," he sneered. "I was walking on the road and they tried to run me down. I jumped out of the way and they went past but then they started to come back. There was nowhere I could run to, so I took out my pistol and shot at them. I think maybe I hit one. He fell off his motorcycle and the rest turned and drove off. They left him there. I was glad they went, because I had no bullets left, but my shipmates would never have left me." He scowled at the memory. "I was very lucky I think. I am not good shot. So I ran for a while, then I started walking across the fields and hills and only very small tracks, instead of on the roads and I think maybe I was a little bit lost. Then I saw the smoke from your house and I saw Leah and Emma. Now I am here."

Emma explained that she had come from Aberdeen and that they had searched but didn't know of anyone alive there now. She glanced at John but his face showed nothing. "So what will you do now?" she asked Sergei.

"I do not know. I cannot go home. If there is nobody in Aberdeen … I do not know."

Margaret stood up. "Well what I'm going to do now is make dinner, before you all fall over drunk," she announced. "Tony, kitchen!"

They offered Sergei a bed for the night, while he decided what he wanted to do. John showed him to one of the B&B rooms with an en-suite bathroom. He was, after all, a guest. Sergei thanked him and said that he would like a bath and to change before the meal. John returned to the big room.

"So," John asked Emma, Sunflower, Leah and Dan, "what do you think of our guest?"

"I think he's mega," announced Dan, conferring his seal of approval.

The adults all chuckled.

"Emma?" John asked.

"He seems okay. It even sounds as if he might have done away with one of the bikers."

"Leah, what's your opinion of him?"

She peered up from below lowered lids. "I think he is very interesting," she purred, gazing deep into Sunflower's eyes.

Sunflower smiled back gently while she stroked Leah's arm. "He has a good aura. I don't believe he will stay but I am sure we will see him again."

It was soon after four in the morning when Emma padded quietly back from the kitchen towards the stairs. She had awoken thirsty and in her hand was the glass of water she had refilled. She turned at the sound of a door softly closing, somewhere down the long corridor by the stairs. Leah was leaving Sergei's room. Moonlight highlighted every curve of the tall, beautiful woman's luscious and completely naked body.

Leah approached Emma quickly but silently, her hair flowing behind her like a dark veil, the balls of her bare feet skimming the carpet, her breasts jogging and glowing in the faint light seeping in through the hall window. The cold night air had brought Leah's thimble-large nipples erect, Emma noticed. Without speaking, Leah bent, kissed Emma softly on the lips and then slowly ascended the stairs.

The perfect curves of Leah's smooth bottom swayed deliberately as she climbed. She looked back as she began to mount the second flight, her lips gave the briefest twitch of satisfaction at seeing Emma still watching her and then she disappeared up the remaining stairs. Emma took a deep, trembling breath and closed her eyes briefly to catch the memory before she returned to her own room.

#

The following morning John, Sergei and Emma set off for Grantown-on-Spey. The windscreen wipers swished endlessly back and forward, fending off the newly returned wintry rain.

At one point as they rounded a bend Sergei shouted out, "Here! This was where the Hells Angels were."

John pulled the Land Rover to a halt. The tarmac was scarred and a pool of oil marked where the bike had lain. They hunted around for a few minutes and discovered it abandoned in a ditch at the side of the road but they found no sign of a body.

"Well, either they came back for him or the bike wouldn't work and he walked," surmised Emma.

She may have been right on either count but whatever had happened, they found the body of the biker lying at the side of the road about a mile further along. They left him where they found him and drove on.

Sergei told them that the cottage was near the other side of Grantown and they debated whether to go through the town or take the by-pass alongside the Spey and then back in. In the end they decided that Alan would likely know if any other people were around, so they took the by-pass. Avoiding towns, if they didn't have a good reason to visit, was becoming a habit, Emma realised.

The cottage they were seeking was one of an attractive row of four. The front gardens were all set slightly back from the road and even at this time of year their carefully-tended nature was obvious. Creeping ivy, intertwined with honeysuckle, covered the fronts of all the cottages. Most of the gardens were decorative, but one had been cultivated for vegetables and fruit.

As John drew up at the side of the road, the front door of number three was slowly pushed to, leaving only a tiny opening behind which they could see a face peering at them from the shadows.

They all climbed out of the Land Rover and Sergei opened the low gate calling out, "Martin, Alan, it is me, Sergei."

The door opened wider and a short, thin but sprightly man with a shock of white hair and prominent hooked nose came out to greet them.

"Hello, Sergei," he greeted, smiling broadly. "I see you have brought some friends."

"John, Emma, this is Alan, my friend who did not shoot at me," Sergei announced.

The old man snorted. "If I'd known you were going to drink all my whisky, and I'd had a gun, I might have done."

Sergei roared with laughter.

"Come on in," Alan invited. "I've just put the kettle on."

As they entered the hall, Alan called back over his shoulder. "Mind the batteries."

A row of twelve-volt batteries lined the hallway all along one side. Wires ran from one to the other and were tacked along the wall.

Alan led them into the small sitting room then invited them to sit down. "Tea or coffee?" he asked and having taken their preferences went off.

Emma stood up to follow him. "Can I help?"

"Thank you, my dear, that is kind of you."

The kettle was boiling on a butane-powered, double-burner camping stove. The wires that ran into the kitchen were connected to strip lights screwed to the wall and to a row of small tubes. A cool box whirred happily, plugged into one of the tubes by a connection intended for a car cigarette lighter socket. Alan bent down to a small refrigerator and as he opened the door, the light came on.

Emma gasped. "You have a working refrigerator?"

Alan picked a carton of milk from the fridge door and straightened up. "Yes, this is long-life milk but at least it tastes better cool."

"Does all this work from the car batteries?" she asked.

He chuckled at her amazement. "Well, they are actually called leisure batteries. They are made to provide steady power for caravans or boats, rather than bursts of power for starting cars. Both types are twelve volt but these last longer before recharging and can be recharged many more times. I was a caravaner, had a whole series of them over forty years and tinkered about renovating old ones. When the electricity went off, I first thought of moving into a van but then decided to convert this place into static version. The lights, refrigerator, cool box, and CD player all run on twelve volts. The cooker and heaters run on gas. I raided the caravan site and shop down the road. The refrigerator would run on mains electric or camping gas too."

"John must see this – do you mind?" she pleaded.

Alan laughed. "No, of course not, my dear."

John came through at her call, followed by Sergei.

"Have you seen what Alan's done?" Emma asked John, still awed by the neatly stapled wiring and multiple devices.

John nodded enthusiastically. "I certainly have. I was admiring the CD player and lights in the sitting room. But how do you charge the batteries, Alan?"

Alan was clearly pleased by his visitors' approval of his efforts and replied proudly. "I keep a little Honda generator out back. It goes for hours on a tank of petrol. It doesn't have a high-energy output but as well as charging the batteries it will run my power tools and a bench saw that I use for logs. I have solar panels for battery charging too but so far we have never had enough sun to use them for more than one battery at a time, and that takes at least a couple of days, even using both sixty watt solar arrays."

"Quite a set up," admired John.

Sergei interrupted their discussion. "Alan, where is Martin?"

"He's fetching water, that is our one problem now. The water stopped running yesterday and we are drawing from the tanks in the other houses."

John frowned. "Are you on the mains?"

Alan nodded. "I'm afraid so. Once the water in the other houses is gone we are going to have to move. We could get water from the river but I was down there yesterday and the banks are lined with dead fish. I think there must be pollution seeping in from somewhere."

"Which brings us to the real reason we're here," said Emma. "Let's wait until Martin gets back, then there's something we want to discuss with you both."

Martin turned out to be a fit young man, with short-cropped red hair and a strong Glaswegian accent. He had been a builder by trade and was working in Dundee when the deaths began. His hobby was backpacking and when things started to get bad in the city, he simply picked up his pack and walked out, heading for the hills.

He told them, "I followed the road to Kirriemuir then up the glen to Clova and over the hill from there. I stayed by Dubh Loch for a couple of days while I was feeling really rough. Then I went down into Braemar to find some scran and some meths for my Trangia stove. I'd been using an open fire but it was getting difficult to find dry wood. I went over Cairn Gorm, was going to stay the night at Rothiemurchus Lodge but it was full of dead.

"I had a look at Aviemore but a lot of other people must have had the same idea – bodies everywhere, the place stank. So I grabbed as much stuff as I could carry and went back up the hill and bivvied. I was planning to go right up north but I had a climbing pal in Grantown and thought I'd see if he'd made it. I met Mr Isaacs on my way. I tried Glen's house, he was right fit so I thought he might be okay but he was dead when I got there. Same as everybody else, I guess; at least I didn't see anybody alive."

Emma gave them the details of the community they were setting up and invited them to visit, to see for themselves if they might want to stay. Alan accepted gratefully. Martin said he'd check it out but he didn't fancy himself as a farmer. Mr Isaacs had been good to him, put him up and all, but he'd always intended to move on eventually. Emma was disappointed. Martin was a strong young man who would be an asset. Maybe Leah could persuade him, she thought, wickedly.

They helped Alan to pack his old but serviceable Mercedes estate then headed back towards Knockside. Alan wanted to call at the site to hitch up his caravan but they persuaded him to leave it for the time being. On the way back Emma sat in the front with John, while Sergei and Martin sat in the back talking. Alan followed behind in the Mercedes. They arrived home to find Tony and Margaret standing at the side of the track, rifles in their hands, watching over the field where the sheep were being kept.

John pulled up beside them. "Something wrong?" he asked, though the relief on their faces at seeing them back made the question irrelevant.

"Dogs!" Margaret said. "There were a dozen or more of them, all shapes and sizes. They must have slaughtered half the flock."

John could see Margaret wasn't exaggerating. "Well," he said, slowly, "It isn't a disaster for us, there are plenty of sheep about, but I suppose this was inevitable eventually and we can't let it keep happening. We're going to have to do something about those dogs. Did you get a shot at them?"

"They were too far away really and running about like crazy but we fired a couple of times and it scared them off," Tony told him.

"What can we do?" asked Emma. "We can't guard the sheep twenty-four hours a day."

John's face was grim. "Poison. The dogs will be back now they think they've found easy pickings, a couple of shots that didn't hurt them won't keep them away for long. We move the remaining sheep to another field and poison the carcases of those they've killed. I've baited foxes and corvids that way when I was a gamekeeper protecting poults. It isn't nice but it's effective. I'll go into town. I know what to get."

They left Tony watching over the sheep and drove the rest of the way into the farm.

#

Emma introduced the newcomers to everyone and then showed them around the farm. Martin was clearly taken with Sunflower and Leah but remained noncommittal about the idea of staying. Alan immediately accepted the invitation to join them, so Margaret took him off to find a room.

As John was preparing to leave, Sergei approached him. "John, do you have a radio, not for music but for communications?"

John shook his head. "We scanned the various wave bands, including short wave, but didn't hear anything. I thought about short-range radio, like CB, for while we're around or away from the farm but I haven't done anything about it yet. Why do you ask?"

Sergei's eyes scanned the farm buildings around them before he answered. "I have thought about what I am going to do and I do not think I am going to stay here, at least not for now. I am radio operator and engineer. There is your group here and I think there must be others, yes?"

"I suppose so, Sergei, what do you have in mind?"

"I think," Sergei said, "that I will try to set up a radio network. I want to explore this country all over and I think if I can help good people like you to talk to others, this will be a good thing."

John agreed. "Of course, that would be a very good thing."

"Do you know where we can get radios?" asked Sergei. "High frequency, short wave will be best."

John considered for a moment before replying. "Well, there were radio fans, they called them radio hams here, and shops that sold the equipment they used. The military would have radios of course, the police too I think, and ships, fishing boats, the coastguard and lifeboat. Probably the easiest place to find them would be at army bases. We've been getting stuff from the Air Force bases because those were the biggest around here but I'm not sure about their radios." He thought for a while, then continued. "I know there's a Territorial Army base in Elgin; I was a member for a while. We can try there."

"This is good," said Sergei. "If possible I will need a set I can take around with me and one for you here. If I can take more, good, if not, we find on the way."

"Who is we?" asked John.

"Ah, I talk to Martin on the way back, John, he wants to come with me."

John broke the news to Emma.

"I'm disappointed but not surprised," Emma told him. "Not as disappointed and surprised as I think Leah's going to be though."

John raised his eyebrows in question

"I'll tell you later. We're all going down to move the sheep in few minutes," she said. Sergei was standing by the Land Rover with Martin and called over to say he was ready but John called to them to come to the house first.

John took them to the room to which he had transferred the guns and ammunition.

"You said you were out of ammunition for your pistol, Sergei. We don't have anything that will fit your Makarov but you can have one of these Brownings instead if you like."

He offered Sergei a nine-millimetre pistol together with a webbing holster and belt, spare magazines and a couple of boxes of the Radway Green full-metal-jacketed military ammunition.

Sergei was delighted. "Ah, John, my friend, you make me very happy. I do not like to be out there with the dogs, on legs or motorbikes, without something to shoot with, you know?"

He seized John by the shoulders and kissed him on both cheeks and again on the right. John cleared his throat and cocked his head at Martin

"What about you, Martin?"

"I've done some clay shooting but I've never used a pistol. Can you spare me a shotgun?" Martin asked.

John picked up the Remington 870 he had taken from Al's shopping trolley in Aberdeen. "How about this?" he offered.

Martin accepted it gratefully, trying out the pump and swinging it up to point through the window. "Aye, that will do for me."

John gave him a box of buckshot cartridges, "For anything really serious" and two boxes of number-six-shot cartridges. "In case you want to take a rabbit or something."

"Right," said John. "Now if we meet anything nasty in Elgin you're ready and you have something to take with you on your travels. Let's get off."

With a wave to Emma and the others they drove off through the gates. John stopped by Tony who was still watching the sheep. "Seen anything?" John asked.

"No, but I heard 'em a little while ago, sounded like they'd found something else to chase."

John nodded. "They'll be back – they won't ignore this much easy meat. Don't shoot unless you have to. The others will be down to move the live sheep in a few minutes. See you later."

Tony put up his hand to stop them.

"John, do me a favour, see if you can find me some cigs," he pleaded. "I'm desperate for a smoke and Margaret made me chuck my last ones away. But don't tell her if you get me some, for God's sake."

John chuckled as he put the Land Rover into gear and they bumped off down the track.

They stopped in Keith to visit the vet's surgery. John came out with a large box, which he put into the back of the Land Rover. "For the dogs," he said, in answer to Martin's questioning look.

As he drove away he called back to Martin. "You were in the building trade, Martin, can you drive a digger?"

"Well I had a go once but I'm no expert."

"As long as you can lift the shovel a bit and make the thing go forward and back, that will do," John assured him.

They saw no one on the approach to Elgin but John was nagged by a feeling of something out of place. It bothered him for a while, until he eventually stopped the vehicle and stepped out. He peered back along the deserted road and then spun around, scanning forward towards the town.

"What is wrong, John?" asked Sergei, from the passenger seat.

John shook his head. "I don't know. Something is different,"

"But of course, my friend: no cars, no people, everything is different now."

John shook his head again, impatiently. "Not that, something is different from the last time I was down this road, something is missing."

He climbed back into the driver's seat, puzzled. It was probably nothing important but he was annoyed with himself for not being able to figure out what it was. They drove on, with him still wondering.

John eventually pulled onto a side road leading to an industrial estate at the edge of town, then turned into a compound surrounded by a chain link fence.

Martin laughed. "So this is why you were asking."

The compound was full of bright yellow trucks, bulldozers, diggers and rollers.

"But what is it for?" asked Sergei.

"I doubt that the gates to the TA compound are going to be lying open and they're steel, eight feet high, topped with spikes," John told them. "The place is surrounded by a brick wall, which is topped with razor wire and the office block windows on the ground level are covered with bars. We're going to need something serious to get into the vehicle yard. Take your pick, Martin."

John led the way out of the compound. Martin followed precariously in the digger he had chosen as nearest in operation to the one he had driven before.

John and Sergei watched in amazement as the mechanical monster lurched from side to side, destroying several cars and demolishing the front of a corner shop before they reached the Territorial Army buildings.

John climbed out of the Land Rover and approached the digger, staying cautiously clear of it on his way. "You sure you were in building, not demolitions?" he asked.

"Got here, didn't I?" Martin smirked.

John pointed to the red brick wall of the compound. "Let's see if you can wreck that as well as you did that shop."

Martin hauled enthusiastically at levers in the cab and the digger slewed around to point at the wall. He pulled another lever and the bucket of the digger smashed to the ground, shaking the huge vehicle and causing John and Sergei to rapidly back away. A bit more soberly, he worked at the controls, raising the bucket so that he could barely see over it and tipping it to point slightly downwards. He glanced at John, nodded and with a mighty revving of the engine surged forwards into the wall.

With a deafening crash, the bricks exploded inward towards the concrete yard beyond. Martin revved again, reversed and made ready for a second assault. But from the corner of his eye he spotted John, waving his arms frantically, crossing and parting his hands over his head to signal him to stop. Martin let the engine slow to an idle, allowing John to approach and open the door of the cab.

"That will do," John said breathlessly, "we only need to get in, not knock the whole place down. We can come out through the gates."

Martin grimaced in disappointment but he switched off the engine and jumped down from the cab.

The yard was covered with shattered brickwork for several yards inside the gaping hole that Martin had created. With Sergei and Martin following closely behind, John stepped carefully over the wreckage, ducking under the loose-hanging razor wire that now dangled like a strange Christmas streamer over the gap.

"What we want, for a start, is the unit commander's vehicle," John told Sergei. "That should have an HF radio as well as VHF radios fitted."

They found the green and black camouflaged Land Rover parked outside the main office block, identified not only by its profusion of radio antennae but by the square plate on the bumper, marked OC in white.

Sergei climbed into the back, squeezed past the map table and command centre installed there and soon called to them. "Yes, this is good. It is not the same as I have used before but I can work this."

He climbed out of the vehicle again, bending to clamber under the doorframe. "Can we get some tools? It will not take me long to get this out."

John tilted his head in thought. "Why take it out? Why not take the Land Rover with it fitted? You can stop anywhere, erect the antenna mast and be able to transmit within a few minutes. You'll need a vehicle anyway if you intend to cover the sort of distance you're talking about."

Sergei's enthusiasm was immediately apparent. "Yes, Yes, this is very good."

"There will be a trailer to go with the vehicle. It'll have extra radio equipment and probably admin kit, a tent, cooker, fuel cans and a generator too," John told them. He was right and it didn't take long for them to find it.

John showed Martin and Sergei over the vehicle, explaining about the dual fuel tanks and transfer switch, the strange multi-positional rotary light switch and various other controls.

Sergei shook his head regretfully. "Now I wish I had learned to drive."

Martin clapped him on the shoulder. "Don't worry, Sergei, I'll teach you and you won't even have to take a test."

They cut away the redundant camouflage nets and Hessian window covers but Sergei insisted that the map table in the back would be useful, both for navigating and for aligning directional antennae. John accepted the suggestion readily. He had worked with radios in the army but admitted he had never used the HF.

They entered the main building through an unlocked door. It was eerily silent, cold and echoing. The sound of their footsteps rebounded and multiplied, recalling the days when over a hundred men might have trod these corridors. The highly polished floors still gleamed in the light that filtered through the armoured glass windows.

They found the radio store on the ground floor, identified by neat black lettering on a polished wooden door plaque, but it was locked. Memories of his time with this unit flooded back to John, saddening him. Quietly, he led them along yet more hallways and up the stairs towards the orderly room where, he knew, the keys were kept. They found only one body in the building. It was the Company Sergeant Major, stretched out on a camp bed in his office next to the Orderly room. John had known him and out of respect drew up over the man's already decaying face the olive green blanket that covered his lower body. They quickly left the office and shut the door behind them. John took several deep breaths and swallowed hard before his stomach settled.

They retrieved the keys for both the store and the Land Rover from the carefully labelled boards in the orderly room. After a second's thought John also took the keys for the armoury and stores. He didn't intend collecting any more weapons or other supplies at the moment, but having the keys might make it more likely they would still be there if they needed anything in future. Back in the radio store Sergei found one additional HF radio, which they took, along with various tools, spare parts and cables Sergei identified as useful. These they loaded into the trailer, which they had hitched to the back of the Land Rover.

After a moment of thought John returned to the building and emerged carrying a large box. "Respirators, gas masks you'd call them, and rubber gloves. They might be useful for going into the towns," John explained, then laughed. "Oh and some cigarettes for Tony. I found half a carton on the bench in the store. He'll have to make them last, if Margaret doesn't find them."

John unbolted the huge steel gates and held them open for Martin to drive through. He was about to push the gates closed again, when he remembered the hole now breaching the side wall. He left them swinging as he headed for the Land Rover and home.

It was as they were driving out of Elgin that John realised what was missing. The bus and many of the lorries and cars which had been abandoned or parked beside the road were now gone. The sides of the roads from Lhanbryde to Elgin were all almost clear. Relieved at solving the mystery of what had changed but aware that it raised a new one of why they had gone and where, John's scalp tingled and the hairs of his neck rose. He shook his head and pressed the accelerator a little harder, suddenly anxious to be home.

#

It was now late afternoon and they were only a few minutes away when they heard the first, unmistakable, sounds of gunfire. John stopped the Land Rover and ran back to where Martin had pulled up behind him.

"Is it the dogs?" asked Sergei.

"Not unless they've started using guns," John answered, "that's a battle. When we get there, park in front of my place and we'll go up in one vehicle, and let's get a move on!"

When they started up the track, they found two wooden pallets had been dropped into the sump to replace the chained-up cattle grid. John guessed they wouldn't bear the weight of the Land Rover and they couldn't waste time winching down the grid, so they left the vehicle blocking the track and headed up the hill at a run. Slowing immediately before the bend, which would give them a clear view up to the farm gates, John motioned the other two to keep back then fell to his belly and crawled forward.

The cause of the gunfire was immediately apparent. Five heavy motorbikes blocked the track outside the fence before the farmyard gates. The bikers had made it that far but were unable to go any further because of the second cattle grid trough and the blistering hail of buckshot that was coming at them from the farm buildings.

One biker lay sprawled across the bikes; another two were taking cover behind them and firing towards the farm. As John sized up the situation, an explosion blasted out from somewhere to the left. It was immediately followed by a nerve-shattering, high-pitched scream that quickly died to a low, moaning whine. John guessed that someone had tried to cross the razor wire barrier and set off one of the booby traps.

A moment later a third man appeared running back towards the group at the bikes. John rose, aimed and fired in one smooth movement. Simultaneously, a volley of shotgun fire blazed from the farm defenders' positions. The man cried out once as he staggered and then toppled forward, dropping his rifle as he fell.

Realising that they were now caught between firing from both in front and behind, one of the two men hiding among the bikes shouted out, "All right, all right, that's enough. We surrender!"

Cautiously the two attackers began to stand up, holding their guns at arm's length. The firing from the farm immediately stopped. John had been taking aim even as the man called out and as he rose, John fired. The leather-clad biker was flung backwards and landed across the other man sprawled over the petrol tanks.

Martin cried out in shock. "John, no, they're surrendering!"

The final biker flung away his shotgun in terror and pleaded desperately. "No, no, it's over, I'm done!"

To the horror of both Sergei and Martin, John coldly worked the bolt of his rifle and then shot the final man dead. As the two watched, unable to move or speak, John calmly worked the bolt once more, bent over to pick up his ejected cartridge cases and then walked up the track towards the bodies strewn over the motorcycles.

The defenders slowly started to leave the buildings and gather by the farm gates. They watched John approaching, bewilderment, surprise and in a couple of cases anger etched on their faces. Sunflower was in tears. Her tiny fists were tightly balled and she was shaking as Leah held her close against her side.

John scowled down at the bodies. Pushing his foot under the corpse, he rolled over the final man he had shot. The lifeless eyes still stared out in a mixture of fear and surprise. "Is everyone all right?" he asked

Sunflower could contain herself no longer. "You murdered them!" she screamed. "They were surrendering and you murdered them!"

John rounded on her angrily. "Surrendering for what?" he demanded. "This isn't a bloody war. The Geneva Convention doesn't apply here. What were we supposed to do if we accepted their surrender – lock them up? Let them go? What?"

Alan joined the conversation. "I was a lawyer before I retired. They deserved a trial at least, John."

John closed his eyes and took a deep breath, fighting to control the adrenalin-fuelled aggression that was only now starting to drain from his system, to be rapidly replaced by a trembling ache.

"Alan, you were a lawyer, so would you defend or prosecute? Who would be the judge, the jury, the opposing council? You were all intended victims of their attack. You know what they came here for. You all saw it, fought it. Would there be any doubt about the outcome of a trial?" He waited but no-one answered.

"And then what?" he challenged. "When they were found guilty, then what? There could only be three choices: let them go, to pick up more guns and bikes and attack other people, until they had a big enough gang to come back to try to take their revenge …"

"We could have locked them up," screamed Sunflower.

"Where? For how long? Until they died or until they escaped, perhaps murdering some of us as they went?"

Sunflower's brow wrinkled and her mouth worked but she didn't answer.

John continued. "And the only other choice would have been to execute them. Well we couldn't let them go and we couldn't lock them up and the only difference between what I did and an execution is that my way was quick and without all the trauma for us and them in between."

Martin had walked up the track behind John and was standing, listening, equally nonplussed as the others.

Sergei joined them. He had been checking on the source of the screaming that had followed the explosion. He was carrying a military rifle. "It was the woman," he said. "She is dead. She had this." He held up the rifle for a moment.

Emma stared down at the body of the man John had rolled over. The last one he had shot. When she spoke, her voice was as devoid of expression as her face. "He was the one who was going to rape me in Forres, the day I met you, John."

John felt a wave of gratitude for her subtle support washing over him. Silently he searched the faces of rest of the group. They too, he knew, had been feeling the adrenalin surge, the fear and the excitement of battle and the elation of victory. His shooting of the two men brought a sudden, ugly end to that. The rapid reversal would have their emotions reeling in confusion. It had been their first taste of war and now they were starting to enter the post-combat drop. The guilt, the relief, the glory of still being alive, would be followed by a sudden, intense tiredness. He had to get them moving while they still could.

"Martin, will you bring the Land Rover up please?" he requested. "Sergei, will you give him a hand to get rid of the bodies? It doesn't matter where you dump them. Make it far enough away that we aren't bothered by the smell."

He knew it sounded harsh but he was deliberately trying to maintain their anger at the attackers, to dehumanise the dead enemy, to spare the feelings of his own side.

"Emma, drop the cattle grid please, the rest of you give me a hand with these bikes. We might keep a couple, drain the tanks of the others then we'll dump them."

Without question they started to do as he had directed. All except for Sunflower, who with a last sneer of disgust stalked back to the house.

When the bikes were safely into the farmyard he set the group yet more tasks: repairing the wire where it had been damaged by the explosion; siphoning fuel from the petrol tanks on the bikes; boarding up windows broken by the attackers' shots.

The community had done well, he knew. The alarm system worked. They had followed the defence plan and kept the bikers at bay, even killing one of them before he, Sergei and Martin returned. But they had also been incredibly lucky. The bikers were well armed but the defenders' only injuries were some cuts from flying glass. If the attackers had been better organised, had studied the defences before they attacked, had used better tactics, the result might have been different.

It was full dark when he brought an end to the work by asking Margaret to make hot drinks, with something strong in them. The remaining survivors filed back to the big room, quiet now, exhausted by the burst of emotions and activity.

John didn't join them. He went instead to the workshop armoury room where he had located his workbench and set to cleaning his rifle. He heard Emma enter but didn't look up from his work.

She gently laid her hand on his shoulder and spoke softly. "You were right, John. We wouldn't have known what to do, or it would have come to the same in the end."

"What I did wasn't right, Emma, but it was what had to be done under these conditions."

Emma heard the defiance in his voice but his face pleaded for understanding, for support, and for forgiveness and to her shock, she saw that his eyes were wet. She stepped forward, opened her arms and hugged him close to her. He made no sound but her body shook with the shudders of his fight to force back his emotions.

#

Sunflower sat crying in her room. "I cannot stay here. I cannot live with this."

She was cross-legged on her bed, with her back pressed against Leah's breasts. Leah's arms were tight around her and their heads were together, Leah's mouth close by Sunflower's ear.

"Tell me again, Sunny, tell me why all this is happening," Leah whispered to her.

"It is the will of the Universe," responded Sunflower, after a while.

"But why?" Leah persisted.

"Do you remember the poem, 'On a Sundial'? 'Loss and Possession, death and life are one, There falls no shadow, where there shines no sun.' From Belloc."

"And what does it mean?" Leah whispered.

Sunflower sniffed back her tears then swallowed. "Well, I think it means that everything is a circle, that there can be no good without evil or evil without good, no death without life, no darkness without light. That two sides exist to everything but both are part of the whole. When there is darkness, a great shadow, it must be cast by the sun, something good."

"Go on," Leah prompted.

"Man was destroying the Earth, polluting the water and the land and the air, changing the environment, killing more and more species of plants and animals every day. I believe it had to stop, for the natural balance to be restored. If it hadn't been the plague we would have starved from over-population, or when the oil ran out and there was no fuel to run tractors, or trucks and ships to transport food, or terrorists blowing things up and governments blowing up even more people in response, or something. So few of us live on the planet now, it will be centuries before that can ever happen again. Mother Earth has time to recover. Perhaps by then we will have learnt and will not make the same mistakes. The recovery of the Mother is the sun, the shadow is the deaths."

"And how is the death of those men with the motorbikes a part of it?"

Sunflower considered for a moment. "Their death is part of the darkness but it had to be, so that our light could shine, so that we could live. If they had not died, we would all have become part of the darkness."

Leah hugged her closer, whispering almost to herself. "You are the sun, your chosen name was meant to be. I am the needle, casting the shadow, one face to the sun, the other to the darkness."

Sunflower tried to twist around but Leah held her tight. "What do you mean, you are the needle?"

Leah pulled back a little and shook her head to clear it. She hesitated a moment before she replied. "Only that I fired a gun in the defence too, Sunny. I face the darkness and I am glad to have your light to comfort me."

Sunny relaxed and pressed Leah's arms against her body.

But Leah's thoughts were a world away, in another place and another time. In the confusion of the firing, no one else would know that it was her shot that killed the first biker coming up the track. Nor that it had been made with deadly accuracy.

While Emma comforted John, and Leah gradually prompted Sunflower to talk herself out of her anguish, the others talked quietly and slowly relaxed as the warmth of the fire and the whisky soothed their nerves.

They had fought together. They had seen men die and none of those who had fired knew whether it was their shot that had killed. They would never be the same again but as a group they would never be closer. Young Dan sat with them, now more than ever in awe of this new community of which he was a part and especially of John. He sat and listened as they talked. Never had he known such excitement.

That night Leah left Sunflower asleep, exhausted by emotion and their intense lovemaking. Moving silently through the house she made her way to the room Sergei and Martin were sharing, to take advantage of their burning needs and slake her own unfulfilled desires.

Meanwhile, in the small, detached cottage, Margaret and Tony pursued their own private passion until, aroused beyond further waiting, she rolled him over, grasped his hands in hers and thrust herself down onto his waiting manhood.

They were all discovering that exposure to deadly danger and seeing at first hand the mortality of others, can be a powerful aphrodisiac. Instinct inspired a desperate drive to perpetuate the genes, even when sense might have denied them.

Emma was as urgently aware of her own desires as any of them, and of John's need for support. But though she had never felt closer to him than on that night, still she could not drive away the demons that kept her from him. Trembling in silent frustration, she curled up, clamped a pillow tightly within her arms and between her thighs and sobbed until sleep eventually overcame her.

John had been in battle before, and taken lives in the process. He had suffered the dreams and memories over many years afterwards but thought they might finally have been past. He was grateful to have talked to Emma before she went to bed, but now he was glad to be alone. He poured another glass of whisky and hoped it would eventually bring sleep without any thought at all.

#

The following day, all except Alan, Dan and John slept late. When they did rise it was with a renewed confidence and relaxation and a buoyant team spirit that cheered Emma. Their attitudes to John also differed. Sergei, Martin and Margaret were friendly but cautious. Tony was almost overly friendly. Emma was tender. Leah was her usual respectful but distant self but Alan had adopted a rather superior attitude towards him.

Sunflower surprised him most, by coming to him, hugging him and kissing him on the cheek but her soft smile was marred by a pitying edge. Dan followed him around like a puppy, seldom saying anything but always there.

If in response he seemed quiet, they weren't to know that it was as much due to a hangover as any thoughts about their attitude to him.

Their task that day was to set up a working radio station. Under Sergei's direction they strung a wire between the roofs of two of the buildings. Sergei carefully aligned it using a compass then clipped on an insulator near one end. He measured along the wire a precise distance and then attached another insulator. To the centre of the length between the two insulators he fitted a connector for a long length of co-axial cable, the other end of which he connected to a tuner/amplifier, which in turn he connected to the radio.

He set up the radio in the meeting room, connected it to a pair of batteries and then switched on. The set hummed satisfyingly as the dials lit up. He tuned the radio to a frequency he had selected then showed them the few controls they would have to use.

Once Sergei was happy that the group knew what they were doing, he and Martin drove off in the army Land Rover. Everyone else gathered around the radio. About twenty minutes later they heard the agreed call.

"Hello Knockside, Hello Knockside, this is Mobile One, over."

Everyone cheered until Dan, who had been given the place of honour in the chair, with the headset over his ears and the microphone clutched in his small hand, twisted around and wearing his most serious face told them, "Hushhh, I'm trying to hear."

The others quietened with suppressed giggles and grins. As they listened intently, Dan carefully read from the piece of paper in front of him. "Mobile One, this is Knockside, hearing you loud and clear, over."

The reply came back instantly. "Mobile One, loud and clear also. Returning to base. Out."

Everyone cheered again and this time Dan joined in with them.

After Sergei and Martin returned, they quickly packed some supplies and their personal gear. They said a round of goodbyes and with a final reminder for someone to listen for their call at seven each evening, soon after the group's usual mealtime, they set out. They had decided to go through Inverness and then head north up the east coast. Then they would turn west and eventually south again down the west coast. They would work their way down to Glasgow, through Dumfries and Galloway, around the borders and then back through Edinburgh and Fife, taking any diversions along the way that contacts or instinct prompted to them.

It was agreed that Sergei and Martin would give directions to anybody who they thought might be suitable for the community and who was interested in joining.

Sergei had drawn some diagrams consisting of a centre circle with lines radiating from it, each ending in another circle. The centre circle was labelled M1, standing for Mobile One. Only one of the outer circles was labelled so far. That circle held the legend KS, which stood for Knockside.

John thought that the number of radiating lines was somewhat optimistic but then, why not? Margaret pinned the diagram to the wall above the radio table, together with a map to record the team's progress and set a lined A4 notepad and pen by the radio to record messages. They would not have long to wait to use them.

Directions

The first call came from Sergei the following evening, as arranged. Having travelled the roads through and around Forres and Nairn, finding no survivors, they had pushed on into Inverness. Eventually they crossed the Kessock Bridge, to camp on the Black Isle.

The group gathered round as Sergei's voice crackled from the speaker. "We found the people in the gas masks at a big fort, it was called Fort George. They were all dead, even though some of them were still wearing the masks. We too wore our gas masks in Inverness, they helped with the smell and we are being careful. Things were bad there, many flies, many rats. Over."

It was John's stint on the radio today and he answered, "You're right to be careful. I think we better start doing the same from now on. Over."

The call lasted a while longer but contained no real news. After Sergei signed off, Emma decided that, in view of everything that had happened, they should have a meeting. She began by checking on their current status.

"It sounds as if, now that the weather is warming up a bit, things are going to get even worse in the towns. How are our stocks, Margaret?"

"We're okay," Margaret told her. "We have good supplies of almost everything. There's enough to last us a while. I think about the only thing most of us are missing is fresh vegetables and fruit but we're getting plenty of fresh meat and we're all taking extra vitamins, so we'll be fine."

Emma nodded in agreement. "In that case I think we should stay away from the towns unless we desperately need something.

I don't see any point in taking unnecessary risks. There's nothing we can do about the bodies except leave them to decay over time. If there's a particular type of store or other building, like a library or museum, that we think we may need to visit more than once, we should find one that is clean or clear it out as soon as possible. Does anyone think differently?"

Most people shook their heads but then Alan spoke up. "It will probably mean we will lose the remainder of any food in soft containers. By the time we get back into a town it will probably all have gone off, or been spoiled by vermin."

Sunflower was undecided. "I agree that we should stay out of the towns altogether, if possible. We should be working towards being more self-sufficient anyway, but then I also think we should do a last search of the garden centres and farm suppliers for seed; we should be planting some crops by now."

"Sunny's right," John added, "but I'd like to make a trip to the BP depot outside Aberdeen, to see if we can find a couple of tankers of diesel. We're going to use a lot more for the tractor than we can take from petrol station tanks, even using that pump Alan rigged up."

The meeting devolved into a general babble of conversations crossing one another, until Emma stopped it by rapping her glass on the table.

"All right, it seems as if most people still have things they think we need to gather, so let's spend the next week concentrating on doing that. We should get it over with as quickly as possible, before the weather warms up. We must be as careful as we can now and then stay totally away from the towns unless it's an emergency. I think Sunny is right in something else she said too, we should be working towards being more self-sufficient and I don't only mean by having stocks of everything we can find. We should be planning what to do when the stocks run out."

"Surely that's a long way off yet," argued Tony. "We don't seem to have any competition around here and there's more stuff left than we could use in our lifetimes."

Sunny joined the fray again. "But we are just clinging onto the past, Tony. And anyway, it won't all last that long. Alan was right – rats, mice, insects, cats, dogs, even birds will get at anything in packets or bags. What vegetable seeds we could have perhaps planted if they were not eaten or spoiled will lose their vitality anyway, particularly any hybrids. Tins will rust and a lot of the food in jars will go off, much faster now that the buildings they are in will get too hot in summer and freeze in winter."

"Even petrol, diesel and other oil products break down in storage," John agreed. "I don't know exactly how long they'll last, but I think it's a couple of years at most for diesel and only a few months for petrol, unless they have been specially treated to prevent deterioration, like the canned stocks on the military bases are. Even so, at sometime in the future we'll try to use fuel, only to find it's decayed past the point where we can run vehicles or generators. That's why I want to use the tractors and trucks for as much as we can while we still can."

The group fell quiet, each immersed in their own thoughts. In many ways they had been living much as they had done before, except for finding alternatives for things powered by electricity. Since Alan's arrival even that had been restored to some extent, by use of generators and batteries. Now they were starting to realise that they were on borrowed time. Things were inevitably going to change, no matter how many supplies they tried to gather and store.

"It's going to get a lot harder, isn't it?" Margaret thought aloud.

Emma nodded. "I think so, an awful lot harder and we better start preparing for it now, so that we're ready."

An edge of desperation marked their scavenging over the following week but they also found their targets changing. In addition to food, medicines, batteries, fuel and seed, they began gathering hand tools and noting the location of museums or antique shops, where they might find older technology.

Books on self-sufficiency, gardening, animal husbandry and the use of tools became prime additions to their library. They each collected a bicycle. One day, to everyone's amazement, Tony drove slowly into the farm with Margaret following on horseback. More horses and riding gear and a small cart were added in the following week. Slowly but surely their ways of thinking and working began to take new directions.

#

Sean Applegarth was also reassessing his plans.

After escaping from Edinburgh, he headed north and west. Changing vehicles several times to overcome blocked roads and shortage of fuel, he used Service safe houses to rest overnight and take advantage of the supplies they contained.

Challenged aggressively by two men while he was looking for a new vehicle after running out of fuel, he simply drew his pistol and shot them. He believed that if they wanted to take on another survivor for no good reason and to wave knives at him in the process, what was left of the world was better off without them, and he gave them no further thought.

His destination was a personal safe house he owned in Kerrysdale, on the west coast near Gairloch. Like most operatives he possessed two such retreats that he had taken great pains to ensure were unknown even to the Service. This location was two former storerooms he bought, furnished and equipped over a shop selling local craft and tourist items. The other was in

Devon, useless to him for the moment but in an area he thought he might prefer after his mission was completed.

Cornwall was his birthplace and he had family there before The Death, but at the same time as he bought the Kerrysdale hideout he openly bought a cabin on a leisure facility on the Black Isle, north of Inverness, using his own name and bank account, and afterwards visited it for several holidays. He then also took up stalking and fishing, including sea fishing so that he learned to handle a boat in addition to being shown productive places to fish. That gave him a reason to visit various parts of the north of Scotland and inner isles on a regular basis, so that he could get to know the area well, while taking the opportunity to secretly visit the safe house to check and maintain its security and contents.

The rooms were bought with money he had liberated from a target during a mission overseas. He paid it into a bank account in a false name after being transferred through a number of offshore accounts. He chose the rooms because the building was routinely occupied but didn't contain anything that even a desperate crook might be tempted to break in for. The shop downstairs included a washroom and toilet attached, so it hadn't taken much to have the plumbing extended into the smaller upstairs room. The rest of the furnishings were sparse, but enough for his basic requirements. All of the interesting items he kept there were hidden in compartments under the floorboards or behind the false wall he installed.

On his way he considered whether the secrecy of the location was now of any relevance, but it also featured the advantages of isolation that he could extend by blocking a couple of local roads, while he waited for the pandemic to run its course.

He had initially encountered increasing numbers of living people, albeit more sparsely spread, as he travelled away from the major population centres, and quite a few seemed to survive for several weeks after he arrived at his safe house. After letting himself in, he opened up his hidden stores and set up his communications gear. There were only 2 messages waiting for him and neither was helpful. The second was basically a sign-off by the last remaining operator at HQ, wishing him luck.

But although he continued to monitor all channels, he eventually stopped finding any radio transmissions from commercial stations, military or other sources, and gradually the occasions when he saw other survivors dwindled.

He continued to live at the retreat, using his store of rations and water supplemented by things he took from obviously unoccupied holiday homes, houses at which there was no response to his knock, and boats in the harbour. After seeing no one, nor any passing vehicles or boats for over a week, he began to make nighttime reconnaissance trips through the area looking for lights or smoke but found nothing. Then he extended his search into careful daylight forays, but again with no contact. Finally he concluded that there could be no other survivors in his local area.

Satisfied that he was secure, he took some time to indulge himself. He moved into a plush house, drank fine wines and spirits, entertained himself with good books and music or movie DVDs played on a laptop computer powered by a car battery and inverter. When the battery went flat, he simply took one from another car to replace it. Now he helped himself to tinned and other preserved foods from local shops, the pub and houses, fresh vegetables from gardens, caught fish and shot one deer, and cooked them all on the Rayburn stove in the house he was using. Then he worked it off in the private gym the house also featured, took long runs or walks around the local roads and hills, and swam in the lochs, pushing himself hard to maintain his fitness.

This morning he decided it was time to resume his mission. There had been sufficient time for any die-off to be complete. If his target was still alive then there were less people for her to hide among. And last night his short wave scanner locked onto a very interesting transmission. Somebody, it seemed, was setting up radios to enable groups of survivors to talk with one another. From everything he had learned, the terrorist would almost certainly insinuate herself into a community, if only to eventually destroy it. He knew she was initially hiding in the northeast. She could have moved on, and there could be more groups than the one he heard of on the radio, but it was a start.

Now all he had to do was find out where this place called Knockside was located.

#

The news from Sergei and Martin was disappointing, until they reached the small village of Coldbackie on the north coast. "Hello Kilo Sierra, Hello Kilo Sierra, this is Mobile One. Over," came Martin's voice from the speakers.

"Hello, Martin," responded Leah. "How are you? Over."

"Is everyone there? Over," Martin asked, ignoring the question.

"Margaret and Tony are with the horses but everyone else is here. Over."

"Give them a call then," Martin requested. "I have someone here who wants to speak to you all. Over."

Dan ran off but soon returned with the two missing community members.

"Okay, we are all here now. Put Sergei on. What is so important? Over."

But the voice that came from the speakers was not Sergei's; it was feminine and with the unique lilt of the Highlands. "Hallo there, this is Mharie here. How are you all?" A pronounced delay was followed by a hurried, "Over."

Everyone at Knockside stared, transfixed, at the speakers. Half of them stood with their mouths open. Leah eventually recovered enough to speak. "Hello, Mharie, this is Leah. We are well. Are you? Over."

"Oh yes, dear, we're braw. Calum and Dougal and Isabel are here too." The gap was shorter this time. "Over."

"Ask her if they've been sick," whispered Emma and Leah relayed the question.

"Och aye, I was fair poorly and Dougal too. Isabel only a wee bitty but I think Calum must be pickled; he never had a thing. Over."

During the next half hour they discovered that Calum had come to the mainland from Sanday in the Orkneys where, so far as he had been able to discover, he had been the only one left alive. The other three were all from along the north coast. Dougal came from Thurso, Isabel from Wick, Mharie was still in her own home, where the others had joined her. They had seen no one else until Martin and Sergei drove up. They seemed to be living well; Dougal had shot a stag, Calum and Isabel were bringing in good catches of fish, lobster and shellfish, large stocks of peat for the fire and stove were available and, like Knockside, they had their own water source.

"Well, if it gets too cold for you there, we would welcome you here," Emma told them, while Leah held the microphone for her.

"Bless you, dear, but we are used to being on our own up here. We didn't see that many people even before God called them all. But you never know, we might come down for a visit one day and Sergei has fitted up a radio for us, from the coast guard station. We'll be able to have wee blether once he's gone."

With that Mharie handed back to Martin and, after a short chat, they closed down the radio for the night.

The radio call was the cause of much discussion that evening. Margaret carefully added the initials CB to one of the circles on the network diagram, then recorded the call sign, Charlie Bravo, location and names of the group in the notebook and pushed a coloured drawing pin into the map, by Coldbackie.

The excited Knocksiders discussed the possibility of fishing along the Moray Firth, which was only ten miles away and of seaweed as an alternative to the dandelion, nettles and sorrel they had begun adding to their diet. They even talked of boiling seawater to replenish their stocks of salt before they ran out. They had ploughed and begun planting but now they realised that other possibilities existed too. They could add variety to their diet if they had the time and, if they suffered a crop failure or other emergency, they could try alternatives they hadn't previously considered.

Much later, as John was heading up to bed, Emma stopped him in the hallway. "It's going to work, isn't it, John?"

He smiled at her hopeful face. "Aye, I think so. I would still be glad to see more people here before the fuel goes bad but I think we're going to be all right."

She kissed him lightly on the cheek. "Good night then, sleep well."

As she watched John climb the stairs, Emma felt better than she had at any time since before the deaths. Actually, she confessed to herself, since well before the deaths. She trembled and squeezed her thighs tightly together, as she leaned against the banister. She had long ago given up any hope of seeing Robert again. The situations she and John had survived together had brought them extremely close. Damn it, she wanted him. She wanted to be with him but even as she wondered whether to follow him upstairs, the now familiar and hated panic started to shake her. Cramp sent a spasm of pain searing through her insides. She clung to the banister, shutting her eyes to fight off the demons, cursing her weakness and damning Jace and Al to hell for what they had done to her.

The time was approaching mid afternoon, several days later and everyone at Knockside was about their various tasks, when the insistent ringing of their alarm system startled them from their activities.

John had taken the vehicle-activated customer-alarm cable from a garage forecourt and rigged it to a car battery and to a bell outside the house. The cable ran under a covering of mud across the track, before the first cattle grid. It was wired along the fence line, all the way up to the house.

Most of the group no longer carried a gun when they were near the house and they all now dashed for the buildings as the bell rang out. John had his rifle by him, as always, and walked to stand behind the cover of the wall by the farm gate. Emma had been in the house and joined him a minute later, after switching off the bell. The shortened shotgun was in her hands, a bag of cartridges slung over her shoulder.

While John and Emma watched the track, heads bobbed into view above the hedge. Two people were slowly making their way up the hill. When the visitors rounded the bend, John and Emma could see they were a young woman and a teenaged boy. The couple waved when they spotted John and Emma.

When they reached the level of the barbed wire, John called to them. "Stop there, please."

The couple stopped and stood still, waiting. Neither of them was carrying a weapon as far as Emma could tell, though the woman had a small backpack slung over one shoulder.

Emma stepped from behind the wall. "Are you well?" she shouted.

"Yes, we both had the disease but we are both well now," the woman said.

Emma took a pace towards them. "What can we do for you?"

"It's more what we can do for you – I'm a vet ... and a doctor as well, these days."

Emma saw John's face relax before he too stepped from behind the wall. Together they walked down the track towards the newcomers.

"Hello, I'm Fhionna and this is my assistant, James," the woman informed them. "We have a Range Rover at the bottom of the track but we couldn't bring it in because you have the cattle grid tied up."

"Just a security precaution," said John, "we can get your Rover later. Come on in."

Emma led the way into the kitchen and offered Fhionna and James tea or coffee.

"Coffee for both of us, please," Fhionna said. "James takes his black, I'll have milk if you have it."

"Where have you come from?" asked John, "and how did you know we were here?"

Fhionna smiled. "We met a couple of friends of yours first thing this morning, Sergei and Martin. They were on their way down the west coast as we were heading north. Like them we were searching for other survivors, though for our different reasons. We've taken on a sort of roving brief, wandering around finding people. There are some groups like yours, some individuals. I'm doubling as a doctor when needed. I'd never worked on humans before but I haven't heard of a surviving doctor, so I'm the best they're going to get. I don't think anyone will report me, do you? Are you all well?"

Tony had gone to the gate to keep watch, in case anyone else came up the track. The others were now crowding into the kitchen, eager to meet the newcomers.

"Have you met many others?" asked Margaret eagerly. "I'm Margaret by the way." She held out her hand to Fhionna who shook it.

"I'm sorry," said Emma, "let me introduce you," and proceeded to do that for everyone in the room.

"We've met a few, but widely scattered," Fhionna told them. "The biggest community so far was about twenty to thirty strong. They're down by Galashiels but they'd gathered from all over central and eastern borders region. Then twelve have sort of come together near Oban, though they live spread out rather than as a group. They seem to get by in various ways, hunting, fishing, and scavenging. Mostly it's ones and twos, some small groups. How many of you are there?"

"Eight now," Emma told her, "though we'd welcome a few more."

"Well, the four at Invermoriston might be glad to see you. They're struggling a bit. They're the nearest to you as far as we know," James told them.

"I think Sergei might have met them some time ago but he said they shot at him," John said, doubtfully.

Fhionna shook her head and took a sip of coffee before replying. "Most people were rather paranoid in the beginning. I'm sure you'd get a different reaction now. They were certainly friendly enough to us. Approach openly and leave your guns in the vehicle and they'll be fine."

"Who are they?" John asked.

"Three men and a woman," she told him. "They're a mixed bunch: a lorry driver, a journalist, a fisherman – the woman and her husband had a shop before he died."

"Are they all well?" asked Emma.

Fhionna gave a small shrug. "The fisherman had fallen and dislocated his shoulder. The others had tried to help but couldn't put it back. His arm was in a sling but he was in a lot of pain. I soon fixed that by setting the shoulder. The woman had a cold but that's all it was, though it was making the others very nervous."

Alan had recently arrived and now joined the conversation. "Have you had any trouble on your travels, Fhionna?"

"Surprisingly little. Early on, four people – two men and two women - stopped us on the road. They ordered us out of the Range Rover at gunpoint and then made us back away. Then they ransacked the vehicle, took all the food, the spare fuel and James' shotgun. Luckily they left my bag when I told them I was a vet and that if they used any of the drugs they would kill themselves. They stole the First Aid kit though."

Emma's face showed her bewilderment. "But why didn't they scavenge from shops, like the rest of us?"

"I asked the same question. The man who was the leader seemed to be absolutely paranoid about any contact with people or anywhere there might be bodies. He said they were keeping away from everyone. They were heading into the hills to stay isolated, 'until it all comes under control,' to use his words."

"How many people do you think are left alive?" Leah asked.

"What do you think, James?" Fhionna asked her assistant.

"We've probably met a hundred in all but there might be more in the cities. We've stayed clear of cities or big towns. Some small towns you can't avoid but we detoured around Glasgow, Edinburgh, Perth and Dundee, and Inverness. It's getting so you catch the smell even at a distance. The further north you come, the fewer people you see."

"How are people coping?" asked Emma.

Again Fhionna wrinkled her brow in thought. "I'm no psychiatrist but it seems to vary a lot. Almost everyone has a fear of disease of course, but many seem okay mentally apart from that. I think everyone went through the usual reactions to disaster: shock, denial, fear, anger, depression, resignation and then eventually, for most who really are surviving, determination. Some worked through the whole list, some seemed to get stuck at one point or another. We've met some who've become virtual hermits. The people by Galashiels have centred on religion, led by a Mormon chap. Then you have the drunks – we've seen more than a few of those, and although we haven't come up against any, we have heard of groups or gangs who have gone wild, become predatory."

Margaret's face was set and her voice hard as she spoke. "We had an encounter with some of them, on motorbikes."

Fhionna stopped to take a drink of coffee. "I wondered about the barbed wire and the cattle grids." She took a moment to think before continuing. "Some people can't bear to be alone; they've become dependent, while others have found a new strength. There have been suicides, survivor-related guilt or simply unable to cope probably. Not many who would have been classed as clinically insane are surviving. Some people are using the situation to do all the things they would have liked to do before but were inhibited by laws or opportunity. Then there are those who seem to be in denial, trying to hold on to as much as possible of what they knew before. All in all, it's a wonder everyone isn't totally mad. Those doing best are people who have some sort of purpose outside of pure survival."

Emma gave a short, ironic laugh. "Survival has been enough for us, it's been hard work and we think it's going to get harder. We're starting to gather hand tools and learn new skills for when the tins and fuel run out or go bad."

"But that is a purpose, Emma. You're planning and learning for the future. For a lot it's mere day-to-day survival, and basic at that in many cases. They haven't the skills, the understanding or the will to do more than that. Are you still going into towns?"

"Not any more. We have most of what we need and we're concentrating on planting some vegetable crops and tending the animals."

Fhionna nodded approvingly. "That's good; it's already risky. We went to see a small group that a man living on his own had told us about. When we arrived, three of them were dead and the other very ill. She died soon afterwards and I still don't know what it was that killed them. One of the women had broken her leg and the others had taken her into a local health centre, to do what they could to fix it. They must have picked up the infection while they were there. James and I quarantined our selves for two weeks afterwards but didn't show any signs or symptoms. We had taken every precaution though."

Fhionna sipped at her coffee again and then continued. "If you do have to go into buildings or areas where there might be infection, wear gloves and tightly closed protective clothing, be careful of what you touch and stay away from the rats or any other animals. It isn't the animals themselves you have to be worried about so much as their fleas and the other insects, with the diseases they will now be carrying. Make sure that before you open them, you wash in disinfectant solution any food tins that were on shelves, in case the rats have urinated on them or insects have crawled over them. And pay strict attention to hygiene, hand washing especially."

Panic touched Margaret's voice as she responded. "We haven't been washing the tins and I handle the stock all the time."

Fhionna was practical. "Nothing you can do about that now," she said, "and you all seem healthy enough. From now on wear rubber gloves to handle things until they've been washed. If you have tins still in boxes or polythene wrap, you could give the outsides a wipe over with a cloth soaked in disinfectant and still wash the tins before opening them. Do you have disinfectant?"

Margaret seemed to have calmed from her first panic but the nervousness was obvious in her voice as she said, "Yes, lots of it, we collected a good stock of all sorts of cleaning materials."

"Then clean your stocks, just to be sure. They're probably fine but there's no point in taking risks you don't need to. Have you any medical facilities or supplies here?"

"Leah and I set up an infirmary and gathered what we think is quite a good stock," Emma told her.

Fhionna nodded. "Good. I'll check it for you if you like. As I said, some things we can't identify let alone treat, but a lot you can deal with yourselves. Ninety percent of cases doctors saw before The Death could have been treated at home by the patient and most would have cleared up in time without any treatment at all."

After they had finished talking, Emma and John took the vet and her assistant around the farm and animals. Fhionna identified mastitis in one of the milk cows and a sprained ligament as the cause of the limp one of the horses had developed. She treated them both but she was generally happy with their health.

"You should get those cows in with the bull," Fhionna told them. "You'll be wanting milk and to renew your stock. You're lucky even those three survived without being milked for so long. They must have been going dry before the owners died."

"We haven't had anything from them since we got them," Emma told her. "The milk in your coffee was reconstituted milk powder. We thought we were getting it wrong because none of us had milked before, or because we weren't feeding them properly."

Fhionna shook her head. "They'll do well enough on grass. So will the horses but they'll need some oats as well, if you're going to ride or work them much. You'll have to think about fodder to keep them over next winter too. One of the cows is bulling now, it's probably too late for the other and the third could come ready any time in the next three weeks. They usually come ready every twenty-one days when they aren't carrying but it only lasts about eighteen hours. Keep them in the field with the bull; he'll know when he's wanted. You do have a bull?"

"I know where there is one. We'll get him over," John said.

Fhionna gazed out over the fields. "What are you planting?"

"Potatoes and peas as the main crops. Cabbages and oats were already planted. We've got patches of other things including some salad vegetables and herbs in a smaller plot we surrounded with rabbit wire to use as a garden," Emma told her. "We also collected good stocks of seed for neeps, mainly for the animals. That will go in next. Then there will be sprouts and other greens for over the winter."

"What about next year?" asked Fhionna.

"We plan to let some of the crops go to seed. I know some things are hybrids and we probably won't get such good quality or yield but less of the stored seed will germinate each year anyway, so we have to do something."

Fhionna laughed. "I'm a vet not a farmer; you know more about that side of things than I do. I wasn't even a keen gardener."

"If we can get enough good seed, we're going to use a four crop rotation," explained John. "That's partly why we've chosen to plant what we have or are going to, leaving one field fallow for a couple of years. There's plenty of suitable land so it doesn't have to be strictly four fields in rotation and we're only going to be planting enough for double our yearly needs and maybe some to trade … if we ever find anyone to trade with."

"It's going to be hard work. Why double?" asked Fhionna.

"I wish it could be more. There's an old rhyme, I can't remember it exactly but I think it goes something like, 'One to wither and one to grow, one for the mouse and one for the crow'. You have to plan for some losses from what you put in. And yes, when, not if, we have to go back to using horses for the ploughing, the work will be a lot harder," he answered.

Fhionna gazed at the tractor and its huge multi-bladed disk harrow. "They won't pull that."

"We've already located some horse-drawn equipment at an agricultural museum. They used to do demonstrations so it's in good working order," he explained. "We saw several ploughs, harrows and hoes, carts and a good selection of hand tools stored there. We haven't collected any of them yet, been too busy, but they're under cover and we'll get anything we need in time to service it before it's used. That's where Arnie and Sophia, the Cobs, came from. I know they had a pair of Suffolks there as well but we couldn't see them anywhere."

"Will you start to use it straight away?" James asked.

John's brow furrowed. "We thought about it. Sunny thinks we should move to using only renewable resources immediately but the rest of us aren't ready for that yet. We've decided that we'll use whatever we can of the things we know while we have them and gradually learn the old ways. We must be grateful that we have all this stuff available, to give us the breathing space to do that."

"You're doing remarkably well," Fhionna complimented.

John glanced at Emma then back to Fhionna. "We've had our share of problems," he said. "Let's go and fetch your Range Rover then you can come to the house for a drink and tell us your stories."

As they walked back across the concrete yard, Emma took John's hand and squeezed it. It was, he knew, a gesture of hope, of companionship. Nevertheless, her small fingers felt good in his big but gentle grasp.

After dinner they all settled comfortably around the fire for Fhionna and James to tell their tales.

Fhionna started. "I was living Dumfries. I was a junior partner in a country practice there. I was headed for Ayr to check on my brother and his family when I found James. He was wandering alongside the road desperately searching for anyone else alive. He had intended to study electronics, now he's learning to be a vet." She smiled at her young assistant.

"After we met, we went on to Ayr but my brother and the family weren't there. The car was gone but the dog was still in the house, so they must have intended to go back. James broke open the door for me but Bruno ran off. He never did like me after I neutered him."

John coughed and the others laughed.

Fhionna grinned back and resumed. "We went back to my place for a few days while we thought about what we wanted to do. I decided that if my clients couldn't come to me, then I must go to them. James decided he wanted to stay with me, to learn a profession that would be useful in the circumstances we have now. So we packed up the Range Rover and set out on the grand tour, to see who we could find."

Emma interrupted. "And you found about a hundred? I thought there might be more, maybe six hundred."

"Well, we've only seen about one hundred but this is a big country for two people to search. We haven't been into the cities so there might be people there and the rest may well have gone to remote places. It will take months for us to cover every area and even then we'll inevitably miss people."

"At least two lots of you are on the lookout for people now," John reminded her. "You should co-ordinate with Sergei and Martin. They're doing much the same as you, but for a different reason."

"Speaking of which," said Margaret, "we haven't had the radio call tonight."

"The set is on and ready," confirmed Alan. "I checked the frequency and the battery but it all seems okay."

Sunflower's face showed her concern. "I hope they're all right."

John tried to reassure them. "They're probably in a spot where they can't get a signal. All sorts of things can cause that. Sergei said those bombs made a mess of the ionosphere HF uses to bounce the signal. If they don't get through tonight they will tomorrow."

The arrival of friendly visitors was cause for excitement and celebration, so the chat went on for a while before evolving into party. As the others drank and talked, Emma called to James.

"James, will you help me mark a map with the locations of all the groups and individuals you and Fhionna have met, please?"

James trotted over to her, enthusiastically. "'Course I will, Emma, much as I can remember anyway. And from now on anyone we meet, who Fhionna thinks wouldn't be a threat to you, we'll tell about Knockside."

Emma spread a map on the table and with much conferring they gradually marked it with a highlighter.

Fhionna came over to join them and added a couple of extra locations that James had forgotten.

Emma leaned over and kissed James quickly on the cheek. "Thanks, James."

The boy blushed bright red and hurried away mumbling about finding the toilet.

"Careful," advised Fhionna.

"Why?" teased Emma, "because he might get the sort of crush on me he has on you?"

Fhionna threw back her head, laughed then gave her a playful prod in the ribs. “Let’s try giving Sergei a call,” she suggested.

Flames

The bullet burst through the windscreen with a crash like a tray full of glasses dropped by a careless waiter. Sergei ducked instinctively and Martin swerved the Land Rover wildly from side to side, accelerating hard at the same time. Another shot whined off the back of the Land Rover. Martin threw the vehicle into a skid that almost tipped them over.

Air hissed through the filter of Martin's gas mask as he inhaled greedily.

"Slow your breathing down, Martin, or your eye pieces will mist up," Sergei warned. "You can't drive if you can't see."

"I ken, I ken!" Martin snapped, his accent thickening both because he was home and with tension, "but you try driving in this damn thing when somebody is shooting at you. We should nae have come into Glesca."

"It is the biggest city, Martin. It was necessary, I think."

"Aye, with the biggest nutters too. Why did they shoot as us? We hadn't done anything."

Sergei thought for a moment. "I still say we should paint this car a different colour; maybe they do not like soldiers. In some places in Russia many people did not like soldiers. Here they shoot at us. It has been the same since I came ashore; all the time people shoot at me. I think maybe we should fly white flag from aerial, yes?"

"Aye, well, ye might be right, ye ken, we could at least put a Saltire on the roof and sides."

Sergei frowned at his partner, mystified. "A what?"

Martin laughed. "A Saltire, the Scottish flag, cross of St Andrew. Sorry, Sergei."

"But would not a Union Jack be better?" asked Sergei.

Martin roared with laughter. "Not unless you want them using machine guns and anti-tank rockets instead of rifles it wouldn't."

Then their laughter stilled. Martin had driven into George Square, in the centre of the city. At the west end of the square a dais had been erected. It was draped with cloth and the religious ornaments of various faiths. The bodies of representatives of differing religions, defined now only by their clothing, lay around them. Layering the red asphalt of the square were thousands of bodies of those come seeking salvation. They were alive and heaving now only with the predation of rats that outnumbered them.

Martin pressed down hard on the accelerator, anxious to pass the stench that penetrated even the charcoal filters on their masks. Squeals and squelches rose around them as the Land Rover bumped across a river of rats that swirled backwards and forwards from the drains and alleyways. They left the square at speed, heading east, a few seconds too soon to see the fire engine enter the square from the south.

The first truck was followed by a second, which navigated to the opposite side of the square. After they halted, the motorised high-pressure nozzles above their cabs swivelled back and forth, directing a torrent of liquid over the heaving mass, reaching to the centre and overlapping as they went, soaking the bodies with hundreds of precious gallons. Then the bright red trucks left as swiftly as they had arrived, one still trailing a stream of their cargo.

Rats emerged, sniffing, disquieted by the disturbance and the rain of stinking fluid. But too late. Along the tail of evaporating petrol left by the fire engine ran a ribbon of searing flame. With a roar the square exploded in a thunder of igniting fuel and the shriek of a hundred thousand rats in their death throes.

Martin slammed on the brakes and both he and Sergei swivelled in their seats as the inferno erupted behind them.

"What the..." Martin would have finished his inquiry with 'hell' but it was far too appropriate.

"Go!" yelled Sergei. "We go NOW, Martin!"

"Yez no wrong, pal!" Martin gasped, as he accelerated through the gears at a rate that would have made Jackie Stewart proud.

Glasgow was Martin's hometown but the mass of abandoned cars and wreckage meant no straight route was possible. Without the four-wheel drive, high ground clearance and heavy-duty tyres of the Land Rover, they would not have got out at all.

Switching lanes and weaving around the streets, Martin eventually found himself driving east again. After a few minutes he pulled the vehicle to a halt. In front of them lay a huge mound of rubble that would have blocked the road to any ordinary vehicle.

Engaging low ratio gear, Martin pushed the Land Rover up the jumbled mass of brick, dirt and concrete. At the top he stopped, unable to believe the scene spread out around him. To the right and left, for as far as he could see, no building still stood along the one and a half mile stretch between the river and the motorway. A seemingly endless swathe of rubble was all that remained, for a distance of maybe fifty yards either side of what had been a chain of roads.

Down at last from the man-made hill but still mesmerised by the devastation, Martin nearly collided with the bus that blocked the road. What he couldn't miss, a moment after he stopped, was the insistent tapping of a shotgun muzzle on his side window. Martin slid the window open.

"You all right, pal? You're not sick?" the man with the gun demanded.

Martin shook his head. "You?" he asked in return.

"There's no sickness here, not that Effie and Joshua can't deal with, anyway," he assured them. "You army then?"

Martin removed his mask and sniffed carefully. The stench of rotting flesh was much less here. "No, pal, just took a loan o' one of their Landies."

"Where you come from then?"

Martin gave him a quick summary of their journey and purpose.

The man raised his head from the Land Rover window and called to an unseen colleague. "Hey, Andy, let these in. The Big Man will to want talk to these two."

Another man climbed into the cab of the bus and it pulled back, but only far enough to let them by. They were then stopped by yet another bus across the road. As the first bus drove forward again, restoring the roadblock, a boy of about fourteen appeared as if from nowhere and clambered onto their bonnet.

He shouted through the empty frame where one side of the windscreen had been. "You go where I tell you, an' no where else, right?"

Martin nodded.

Sergei also removed his mask. "The smell is not so bad here, Martin."

"I think someone's been doing some clearing," Martin responded, and then put the Land Rover into gear, while the second bus reversed to let them pass.

Within a few minutes they were directed into a huge retail park. On a communication tower above it hung a great sign proclaiming it to be The Forge. From a walkway above the sign, a man with a rifle briefly checked them through binoculars, then returned to scanning the surrounding area.

Martin followed the boy's directions until he was directed to stop in front of what had been a furniture store. A tall man, spare now but with the look of having been heavily built, came out to meet them. He stood straight, watchful, with an obvious air of authority that was reinforced by the highly polished belt and holster around his waist. This, Martin guessed, was 'The Big Man.'

They eased themselves out of the Land Rover and after a moment's hesitation Martin left the shotgun in the rack. Led by the boy, they walked across the tarmac car park to meet the tall man.

"These here are the ones come in over the hill, Mr Hendrie, sir," the boy introduced.

Unexpectedly, the man smiled. "Thank you, Robbie, away you go."

The boy grinned back and ran off.

Hendrie's face lost all but a fraction of good humour as he moved his attention to Martin and Sergei. "You are travellers I hear, wanting to establish communications. You better come in."

His about-face to re-enter the furniture shop was parade ground smart and his long pace fast enough that they had to hurry to catch up. The furniture had mostly been cleared or neatly stacked, presenting no barrier to their passage to the office at the back.

Hendrie seated himself in a luxurious office chair behind a large desk and pointed them to two straight-backed chairs in front of it. The source of his information about them became obvious when he unhooked a small radio transceiver from his belt and precisely aligned it alongside the blotter on the desk.

"So then," he began, "tell me your story."

The Big Man sat quietly, his hands neatly folded on the desk, his eyes flicking between them as they provided the details of their journey and encounters with other survivors. Occasionally, Hendrie asked quick, direct questions and noted their answers on a lined pad in front of him. Eventually Martin came to the explosion in George Square.

"That was my men's doing," Hendrie informed them. "We have been waiting for a day with a strong wind blowing to the west to take the fire away from here. You saw the firebreak on the way in but it will be better if the fire does not come this way at all. Glasgow needs clearing out. We have started in this area but a lot more must be done yet. After the fire from George Square has burnt out, and as soon as conditions are right, we will burn outwards from our firebreak to there. It isn't a perfect solution but it is some form of control."

"But aren't there any people living in that area?" protested Martin. "And what about all the stuff in the shops?"

Hendrie huffed, impatiently. "We moved a great deal of the useful equipment and supplies to The Forge and posted notice of what was intended, all around the city, over a week ago. There will inevitably be some loss of potential salvage but anybody with any sense will have moved out by now. The clearance is vital. The damned vermin are multiplying every day."

"There was someone still near the square," Sergei said. "They shot at us."

Hendrie's face twitched in a spasm of disinterest. "If they are shooting at people without cause, then they will be no loss."

He stood up. "Now, I like your idea of establishing contact with other survivors, especially this vet-come-doctor of yours. We have a nurse and a pharmacist here but no doctor. Work out the details with my second-in-command. She will find you somewhere to stay and let you know the set-up here. I think you will find her directing operations at the supermarket across the square. Name's Jeannie. In the meantime I need to talk to my men about the progress of the fire. Good day."

Clearly they had been dismissed, so Martin and Sergei left the office and strolled across the car park in the direction of the supermarket.

"What do you think, Martin? He was a soldier I think, no?"

Martin shook his head. "Chief Inspector William Hendrie, late of Strathclyde Police. I've seen his picture in the papers and on television often enough. Black and White Hendrie they used to call him. Not one the villains liked to tangle with. Straight as a die. They say he broke a man's jaw for offering him a bribe. There weren't many like him, I'll tell you."

In the supermarket they asked for directions to Jeannie and were pointed to a slim woman with a shock of white hair. She was in the process of carrying a case of tinned peas from a pile of goods in the centre of the floor to a neat stack at one side.

"Excuse me," interrupted Martin, "are you Jeannie?"

The woman hoisted the case onto the top of the stack and turned to them with a brilliant smile. She had the wickedest gleam in her eye Sergei thought he had ever seen. "I am, and you must be the radio men. Welcome to Glasgow."

"News travels fast here," Martin said, in surprise.

She laughed. "It does and visitors from outside the area are always news. Come into my den and have a cup of tea."

Jeannie led them up a metal staircase, to a small booth overlooking the warehouse floor behind the shopping area. On a desk against the wall a space had been cleared for a double-burner gas cooker with a small kettle on it. A container of water, packets of tea and coffee, a tin of milk and a bag of sugar, together with some mugs and spoons, were neatly arranged beside the cooker. She lit one ring of the stove and moved the kettle onto it.

"I always have the makings ready for visitors, or anyone who needs advice or a shoulder to cry on," she told them. "Now, how long do you expect to be staying?"

"For as long as it takes us to find and set up a radio link," Martin explained. "Maybe a couple of days, maybe more."

Jeannie thought for a few seconds. "Then we'll put you in the hardware store with the other transients. It's warm and dry in there and there's plenty of space."

"Transients?" asked Sergei

"We have a system here," Jeannie explained. "One hundred and fifty-seven men, women and children are permanent residents. Most of us live in the tenement blocks across the road. About another fifty people come for occasional shelter and food or medical attention. Anyone may trade either goods or labour in return for food and other items. Some come simply to be with a gathering of people for a while, but everyone who stays must contribute in some way. We lack little in the way of hard goods but fresh food or fuel is always welcome.

"If someone doesn't have goods for trade, they can work for what they need. For manual labour we give food and shelter while they are here plus one day's extra food, or other items of comparable value of the person's choice, for each day worked. Or, the visitor can register credit to the same value.

"If people, like you, have specialist skills, we will negotiate a contract that both sides find acceptable. We try to persuade those with special skills suited to a fixed location to stay here, to set up shop if you like. We have a tailor and a cobbler, two carpenters and some other trades."

Martin shook his head in amazement. "That's an impressive system, Jeannie, and not that different from the way things used to be."

"This is still a city," Jeannie reminded him. "It helps people to adjust if we can work as much as possible in the way they used to. We also run a sort of bank and trading scheme. I keep records of all work done or goods brought in and the credit to which people are entitled in return. They can then trade that credit for work or goods from other people at any time. So if two people want to trade, they agree a price in credits, come to me and I transfer the agreed sum from one account to the other. Sometimes people ask for a credit note, which they can use like money. We discourage that though, because our facilities aren't sophisticated enough to prevent forgery if someone had access to the right equipment."

Jeanie poured boiling water onto the teabags and left it to brew for a minute, and then passed the cups across, together with milk and sugar. "Of course many of the skills we need now are different from those we used to need. Before the plague I ran an agency for temps. There isn't much demand for secretaries now but my administration skills are still valued. Others can be employed on the demolitions and salvage or moving bodies for cremation and we have converted the parks into garden areas for growing food, so gardeners are needed. The residents all do guard duty in addition to other work - we don't entrust guarding to transients - and everyone receives a ration allowance plus credit according to the work they do. The old systems of motivation and reward still work, people haven't changed that much."

Sergei and Martin were enthralled, but eventually Sergei spoke. "You have much good here," he agreed, "but not everyone comes. Someone shot at us in the centre of the city as we came."

Jeannie's face grew sad. "We know of loners who couldn't cope or who prefer to be alone and at least three other groups in the city, apart from ours. A man who was well known as a gangster here leads one of them. His lot are the reason we need armed guards and the other cause of our creating the firebreak.

Open ground makes it easier to see anyone approaching. The other two groups are centred in areas where they lived I suppose, one to the south and one on the western edge of the city. We have reasonably friendly relations with the people to the south but we don't hear much from the others."

"You may hear less if the fire spreads far enough from George Square," observed Martin.

"I know," she admitted, "but that open mortuary had to be dealt with and the gangsters also live near the city centre. Besides, the river and the motorway provide natural firebreaks in places, so it is doubtful the fire would spread that far. If it does, they will have plenty of warning."

"Emptying and destroying the shops might make you even more of a target too," Sergei added.

"That's partly why we never take everything. We want to persuade people to join us but we don't want to make them so desperate they might attack us instead. Animals or people are much more aggressive if they are backed into a corner. It also takes too long to empty all the shelves in a shop; we don't have that much spare manpower. The fire will destroy a lot, of course, but usually we take the stock that is in boxes or containers and leave the things that are on the shelves for others, unless it is something we especially need. It's more efficient and it leaves people with options. Gathering the main stocks into a few locations where they can be protected from damage by weather or vermin is also absolutely necessary."

"Some friends of ours in the north had the same idea, although they're a much smaller group than yours," Martin told her. Then he remembered. "Sergei, we forgot the radio call."

Sergei checked his watch. "It is too late now, they will have disconnected. We will call them tomorrow."

"One thing puzzled me, Jeannie," Martin said. "How did you manage to clear that firebreak so quickly?"

"Explosives, controlled fires, a wrecking crane operator and careful selection of the route," Jeanie explained. "Poor building standards when some of it was put up helped too. How did you come into the city, by the way?"

"From the west," Sergei answered.

"And where are you going next?"

"We thought of heading towards Edinburgh, or down into Dumfries and Galloway," Martin told her.

"Well if you intend to use the motorway when you are heading out again, you will have to go east a way before you get onto it. We have it blocked on either side of the area we now hold."

Martin nodded. "Thanks, Jeannie, but for now we should get ourselves settled in."

Jeannie signed and handed over two ration vouchers. "It's about time to eat. If you would like to join us, come over to Pizza Hut."

Martin's jaw dropped. "Pizza Hut?"

Jeannie laughed. "We've converted it to our communal kitchen and dining area. No side orders or ice cream fountain and it might not even be pizza, but you will be fed."

The following day, Sergei and Martin awoke to the strong smell of smoke and the unmistakeable odour of burning flesh. The wind had changed direction during the night and was now blowing towards them. A black pall speared through by flashes of flame hung over the city.

It was decided that the safest way for them to travel in their search for radio equipment would be down river, by boat to the docks. So guided by two of The Forge residents who knew the area and escorted by four more, all heavily armed, they set off.

It was a productive trip, during which they collected a total of six short-wave radios and accessories. One they set up at The

Forge on their return and another they left for the group who had based themselves on the southern edge of the city, to be passed on at their next visit. That evening Sergei again made contact with Knockside.

#

Sunflower was on radio duty.

"Hello, Sergei, how are you? We were worried last night when you didn't make contact. Over."

"Hello, Sunny, we are well but we have quite a tale to tell you this evening. Are the others there? Over."

"Yes, we are all here and so is Fhionna, she would like to talk to you afterwards. Over."

"We will do that but first I have to tell you why we did not call last night …."

Sergei recounted the whole story while the group at Knockside gathered round the radio to hear him. When he was nearing the end of his account, the call was interrupted by the distinctive crackle of gunfire, interspersed with louder explosions. Sergei signed off hurriedly, leaving them all wondering what could be happening.

Sergei and Martin dashed from the building where the radio had been installed to find a confusion of running, shouting people. Gunfire came from the direction of the barricade by which they had entered the complex and then from the north, towards the motorway.

They felt useless and uncertain of what to do. Earlier Jeannie had apologetically informed them that all non-residents must hand in their guns. They would be returned when they left, she assured them, but it was a necessary security precaution to prevent infiltration by bandits who might then attack from inside the enclave. They spotted her crossing the car park and ran after her.

Martin caught up with her first. "Jeannie, what's happening, can we help?"

Jeannie shook her head. "The gangsters attacked the barricade on the road first but that was a diversion; they were really after the garden in Alexandra Park. They came off the motorway. It's stupid. They aren't trying to steal anything, simply to destroy it. It might be a revenge attack for our burning of the city centre. Talk to Effie at the dispensary, she might need stretcher-bearers."

And with that, she rushed off towards the furniture store where Hendrie had his office.

The gunfire rattled intermittently for almost half an hour but once the people of The Forge got organised, the gangsters were no match for their numbers and determined defence.

For the next hour Sergei and Martin helped fight fires and to carry the wounded from the barricade and garden area to the dispensary. There Effie, the pharmacist and Joshua, the nurse, assisted by two trained First Aiders, tended to them as best they could.

The total casualty list was four defenders dead, several minor injuries and five more seriously injured. At least two of the serious casualties would probably not recover. Three gangsters had been killed and two captured. The garden area had been badly damaged by petrol bombs and weed killer that had been sprayed around liberally.

Sergei and Martin watched as the two captives were dragged into the square.

"What will you do with them, Jeannie?" Martin asked.

Her face set as she answered. "We will try them and if convicted, which seems likely, shoot them."

"How do you try them?"

"William presides as judge. No lawyers are allowed; he asks questions of witnesses. The defendants represent themselves. Then a jury of seven people who were not witnesses vote in a secret ballot. We use seven so there can be no tied vote. Then William pronounces sentence."

"What are the options?" asked Sergei.

"It depends on the crime. We've had thefts, rape, damage and fights. It can be banishment, a work sentence then banishment or a firing squad. There are no light sentences except for the very young."

Martin glanced at Sergei then back to Jeannie. "You've got more options than we've seen elsewhere."

Both the trial and the execution, which immediately followed it, were open for any of the residents to view. The trial was held in the furniture store and most of the residents not on essential duties attended. The convicted attackers were taken beyond the outer barrier, tied to lampposts and then shot. It was considered essential that people should see that justice was done, Jeannie told them. Both Martin and Sergei decided to forego the opportunity but they couldn't fail to hear the two volleys of gunfire that signalled the end of the attackers' lives.

After breakfast the following morning, Martin and Sergei packed up the Land Rover. For the work they had done on the radio and their help with the wounded, the Land Rover's shattered window had been replaced and they had been paid a week's worth of rations and a bottle of whisky. They left two of the days rations on account with Jeannie, principally to maintain a link with the Glasgow community. Jeannie walked across from the armoury to return their guns.

"Well, good luck. Stay in touch and if you want to return to trade, or to stay, you will be welcome."

"Oh, I'm sure we'll be back this way," Martin told her.

They drove out of The Forge heading east once more, and then for the nearest motorway access and, eventually, Edinburgh.

The Knockside group cheered that night, when Sergei and Martin established contact to say that they were safe and had moved on, but their story sparked another discussion.

Margaret was the first to speak. "You know, the situation in Glasgow got me thinking. At the moment they're storing up as we are, but on a much larger scale. They are actually bartering some of what they have for labour and skills but how long can that go on? What will they do when their stocks are gone? Cities were built on taxes as well as trade. Who are they going to tax?"

Tony agreed. "And it isn't only them – what about Sergei and Martin? Even when they've found everyone that wants a radio and set them up, how will we run the radios when the batteries go flat and we can't run a vehicle or generator to recharge them?"

Emma looked across at John and he nodded for her to speak for him.

"John and I have been discussing this. I know that all of us are looking to the future, learning to ride and take care of the horses and bikes. We're working on using the horse drawn plough and hand tools, but we have to be much more organised about it. We've been bumbling along so far. We must start thinking about every diminishing resource we have: food, fuel, ammunition, candles, everything. We have to calculate, as accurately as we can, what our usage will be and how long it will last. Then we have to take some time off that to allow for wastage or increased use or other unforeseen circumstances."

She stopped for breath. "Once we've made that calculation, we have to plan how we're going to replace our resources with something sustainable. We have to know what materials, skills and so on we are going to need and plan how we're going to achieve that in the time we have. If we don't, we're going to run short and be caught unprepared."

"Even if things last us for years, what about Dan and any other kids? They won't all last their lifetime. So, what do we do?" asked Tony.

"Well the calculations are my job," Margaret told him, "but I'm going to need help from all of you. From now on, every time you use something that we can't replace, I need you to make a note of it, even if it's mental one, but don't forget. I'll get the details from you at the end of the day and after a month or so I should be able to make reasonable estimates, allowing for seasonal differences." She sighed. "And I thought my accountancy days were over."

John now joined the conversation. "Once we know how long we have, I think it will give all of us an incentive to develop the necessary skills. We've all already got our specialities; in some cases it will be a case of one or two people developing those. We ought to have at least two people who can do any job, just in case. We haven't had any problems since the bikers, for example and you did all right with the shotguns, so I haven't pushed the weapon training but what if the Glasgow gangsters Sergei told us about were driven out by Hendrie's lot and came this way? I doubt they'd join a community and become farmers."

Emma took the floor again. "What I suggest we each do, is think seriously now about our own jobs and what we need to learn to continue them and also choose another skill we're interested in. Then we can work with whoever is doing that job, so that we can learn it too. That way we all have someone to help or take over if we are ill. Any skill Margaret decides we're going to need, that isn't already anybody's speciality, we'll take volunteers for."

Alan stood up. His face was red and his lips tight. "Don't you think we have enough to do? The work has already at least doubled since we collected all these animals. Now you suggest we take on even more work and train ourselves in the skills of medieval farmers as well. Where do you suggest we find the time for all this training?"

John's eyes narrowed as he faced the retired lawyer. "If we don't learn new skills there will come a time when we don't eat, or know how to treat illnesses with herbs, or have light in the evenings. You may not be around by then but Dan will and for a long time afterwards I hope."

Alan snorted. "You may well be right. I might not be here by then. Possibly none of us will be. It might be more productive if we all put our efforts to restoring society rather than opting out for some utopian rural idyll, or running around playing Rambo." And with that he stomped out.

"What the hell brought that on?" John asked the silent room. "Alan has never complained about the work before. Nobody asks him to do more than any of the rest of us do."

Leah sighed. "I was talking to Alan yesterday. He had a nice life before all this happened. He was retired, well-off financially. He and his wife toured in their caravan whenever they felt like it, often abroad. He's been working harder, physically, than he has ever done, even as a young man. He's missing the old life and now he's having pain in his chest. I've made mixture of hawthorn and valerian for him that should help but he's frightened. He is sixty-seven you know."

John's face softened. "I never realised. I knew he was retired but he always seemed so fit." He shook his head. "I'll find him and apologise."

"I'd leave it, John," suggested Emma. "He'll come back when he's ready. We'll have to make sure we don't put too much on him if we can, without being over-protective."

Alan didn't reappear that evening but he did join them for breakfast. The entire group took part in teaching Dan. Some taught practical things, some academic. Alan was taking the lad off for reading when Emma called to him.

"Alan, can you spare me a minute before you start?"

"Of course. What can I do for you, my dear?" he asked.

"It's about the idea of our becoming more self-sufficient and yet still recovering some of what we have lost."

Alan tilted his head inquisitively but didn't speak.

"You know how you put together all those batteries and circuits for us? Well I was wondering if we could take it a step further. Do you think you could research alternative power? To generate electricity properly, I mean. Not on the scale of that huge turbine they had at Findhorn but enough to give us light and maybe some refrigeration or other facilities."

Alan raised his eyebrows in interest. "That is ambitious. However, it would save all this messing about with candles and gas cartridges and prevent food being wasted in the summer. Yes, all right, my dear, I'll look into it," he said, "in my spare time."

Emma frowned as if in thought. "I think we should give it more priority than that. If you don't mind I'd like you to concentrate on this as your main project, apart from teaching Dan."

"But what about the other work?" Alan objected.

"We'll manage. Things are steady at the moment. John and I are going over to Invermoriston today, to see if we can recruit the four from there."

Alan reached out to touch her arm. "That's nice of you, my dear, but I'm all right really you know, despite my little outburst last evening."

Emma lowered her head shyly, as if embarrassed at being caught out. "All right, I'll admit I'm concerned but I really do think this is important. I'm sure it isn't going to be easy, either in the design or construction but I'm also sure it will be worthwhile."

Alan's eyes flicked from side to side as he visualised his task, then he bobbed his head in acceptance. "All right then, but I must still do my share of other work. I will not be carried."

"Agreed. As long as you take care, then as Dan would say," she put on a serious face and a deep voice, "that's a deal."

#

Emma had to admit to herself that it was a relief to be away from Knockside for a while. They were taking minor roads to widen their search for other survivors and avoid the towns. Heather and bracken-covered hills rolled away from them, interrupted only by stretches where the forests hugged close to the roadsides, stretching out their branches across the gap as if to join hands with their cousins on the other side. Burns gushed and gurgled beside them, disappearing only to emerge again from below the road in their onward rush to the rivers.

At one bend Emma braked sharply to avoid a family of roe deer lying in the road, enjoying the warmth of the tarmac after the deep cold shadows of the forestry plantations. The deer climbed to their feet and stood, their noses twitching, staring at the Land Rover as if irritated by the troublesome disturbance of their sunbathing. Then they sprang into the trees, to vanish as if they had never been there.

A few miles on, as the Land Rover crested a small rise, a plastic sack spilling out a bundle of rags beside the single-track road caught Emma's eye. Yet another body she supposed, but then it moved. A bedraggled form scampered to its feet and scrambled away. Emma stomped on the brakes. The wheels locked, causing the vehicle to slide, tyres grating against the tarmac until the Land Rover shuddered to a stop.

Emma leapt from the cab and called after the retreating man. "Wait, wait, it's all right, we won't hurt you."

The man who spun to face them was filthy, emaciated, his grey-white hair and beard a tangled mass. Yet, under the old fertiliser sack draping his shoulders as a cloak, the rags he wore had once been a double-breasted business suit. Barely discernable beneath it were the remains of a striped shirt and a tie. He scooped up a stone and hurled it at them, then another, before scampering away again.

"Get away, leave me alone, you're not there, I know you're not there. Leave me alone I tell you."

Emma desperately called after him. "Wait, we are here, we're real, we can help."

The man stumbled away up the hill, his hands waving them away behind him. "Demons, ghosts, get away from me, get away!"

Emma was about to pursue him when John caught her arm. "Leave him, Emma, the poor beggar's too far gone."

She spun to face him, her face a mask of anguish. "But he's alone! We can't leave him all on his own."

John shook his head. "There's nothing we can do for him. He doesn't need us, he needs a mental hospital."

Emma watched in tortured concern, while the man staggered over a rusty barbed wire fence and thrashed his way into the trees of a plantation.

John steered Emma into the passenger seat and took over driving. She sat quietly for a long while, her hands clenched in her lap, her head hanging down, her face pale.

"We should have helped him," she whispered, "nobody should be so alone."

John made no reply, simply reached over and gently squeezed her arm.

When they arrived at Invermoriston, they searched for over two hours for the house that James had described but they could see no smoke and no sign of life. They called at several farms and cottages in the area but all held only the stench of rotting flesh or nothing but vermin.

They found signs of recent occupation in only one. Even there it was a lack of things that made the difference. No smell, rats, thick dust, or bodies tainted the rooms.

"Where could they have gone?" Emma asked.

John shrugged. "Anywhere. James said they weren't having a good time of it, maybe they went to join one of the other groups."

Emma shook her head in dejection. "We have to find more people soon, John."

John laid his hand on her shoulder. "We will but we aren't doing so badly for now, with the eight of us."

"Eight, including a boy and an elderly man with a bad heart."

He gently put his finger and thumb under her chin and lifted it. "And you and me, Margaret and Tony, Sunny and Leah. God what a bunch."

Her face brightened a little. As she gazed up into his eyes her expression softened. His arms felt strong and safe, his eyes were warm and caring. For long seconds she searched his face, then her head slowly tilted back and her lips parted. She trembled, her breath coming in short shallow gasps, while her heart pounded.

John saw the invitation in her eyes and mouth. He wanted this, wanted her and his body instantly responded but his mind boiled with doubt. Was what he was seeing what she meant? Was it right anyway? Slowly he lowered his lips towards hers.

Emma watched his face drawing nearer. She felt herself stretching as if pulled upwards, as her mouth opened to meet his. Closer, closer, any second now their lips would meet and then … with a gasp she tore her face away from his, burying it against his shoulder, gripping his jacket hard in her clenched fists, pressing her whole body against him while it shook as if in the grip of a violent fever.

John raised his head and closed his eyes, squeezing his arms tight around her. His mouth was dry, his throat tight. His head swam with a cauldron of longing and disappointment, tempered by guilt and anguish for her hurt, but spiced with anger for those who had caused it. But, was there something more? Or was he fooling himself? Ten years age difference separated them, but did that matter any more? Had it ever mattered? He was still troubled by the memory Emma and Sunny's kiss, when the newcomers first arrived at Knockside, but she hadn't been teasing him a few moments ago, of that he was sure. Maybe, when the time was right, when she trusted him enough, they would find out.

Gradually the torment wrapped in his arms calmed and he felt her muscles relaxing. Emma's body sagged with the exhaustion of spent emotion.

Her eyes were red, her cheeks wet with tears, as she pulled her head back. "I'm …."

John let go of her with his right hand and quickly touched his fingertips to her lips. His own lips curled in a sorrowful half smile as he shook his head. She lowered her face back to his shoulder.

His voice was gruff. "We'd better be getting back. There's nothing here for us, that won't wait until another day."

His voice might have been hard, but Emma could see that his face belied it. She let go at last and moved towards the door. This would not happen again, she decided. Not until she was sure she wouldn't hurt him. Not until she could, finally, give him what she was now sure they both wanted. There had been no mistaking the desire for her in his eyes. Nor where his body had been pressed against her thigh.

#

The smoke had been visible for miles. With a fear born of near certainty, Emma's foot pressed down harder on the accelerator. The rising shriek of the Land Rover's engine matched the mounting scream of pleas in her mind.

When they passed Huntly and cleared the crest of the hill, her hopes evaporated. From there they could see the smoke and flames blasting skyward from Knockside. John's eyes narrowed and his lips whitened, while he scoured the scene for information.

After Emma had brought the vehicle to a shuddering halt at the first cattle grid, John leapt from his seat. Within seconds he had dropped the grid. Jumping onto the bonnet he waved Emma on up the hill. At the next cattle grid they both sprinted from the vehicle into the farmyard, to a scene from Dante's wildest imaginings.

Margaret bellowed instructions, while she and the others ran frantically with buckets of water to hurl over the burning barn, then back to the house again for more. John and Emma choked, their lungs seared by the heat reflecting from the buildings and concrete yard and the all-encompassing smoke.

Seeing Alan and Sunny emerge from the back door of the main farmhouse carrying buckets of water, John summoned his breath then yelled, "Forget the barn, we can't save it. Soak the house."

Alan cupped a hand to his ear. "What?"

"The house, the house, soak the house with water. Leave the barn."

Alan rapidly nodded his understanding and emptied his bucket over an already charring window frame. Sunny quickly did the same. John and Emma dashed in through the farmhouse door, to find more buckets. Sunny relayed the message to Tony.

As John and Emma struggled back into the yard to join the fight, fire exploded from the barn. Lifted by the blast, their feet left the ground and they were thrown hard against the farmhouse wall. John staggered upright but a whole series of explosions followed the first and his body screamed with pain as the blast smashed him against the stonework. His ringing ears didn't hear Emma's cry, or the shattering of the windows but instinctively he twisted to throw himself over her, while a hail of broken glass and burning fuel spattered down on them.

When the blast subsided, John rolled Emma over and over to douse the flames licking along her jacket. Only then did he tumble himself along the ground, fighting to extinguish the flames scorching through his own clothes. A blanket descended on his head and shoulders and his nose recoiled from the smell of burning wool. Choking, he pulled the stinking material tightly around him and battled to his feet.

Desperately, John whirled around. Emma still lay at the base of the house wall. Through the empty window frame, he could see Tony and Dan beating jackets down onto a smouldering carpet. Sunny and Leah fought side by side, flailing with hearthrugs at a smoking window as flames flickered up the paintwork. Margaret emerged to pour a bucket of water over Emma's steaming clothing. Alan was close behind her, with yet another bucket of water.

John turned towards the barn then ducked instinctively, when another explosion blasted the barely identifiable shell of a jerry can upwards a hundred feet.

He watched stunned as it fell back, with a thud, among the crops beyond the barn. Of the metal-framed barn itself little remained except four twisted girders that marked its corners. The shell of the Shogun still blazed and pools of flame billowed dense black smoke. But the blasts had scattered debris out towards the fields and the fuel spilled from heat-ruptured cans was, at last, starting to drain down the sloping concrete floor of the barn, away from the house.

For another hour, everyone drenched the house and swatted small patches of flame. Eventually, all fires on their home were out and, unable to do any more, they allowed their blackened, stinking forms to collapse against the wall, exhausted.

Gratefully they tilted their faces upwards to the welcome coolness of drops of rain, which smeared soot in streaks down their drained faces. Small fires still burned in what had been the barn but they posed no further threat.

Steam wafted from the house and other buildings. Raindrops hissed then fizzled into extinction on hot metal and ash. Debris lay everywhere. The house was singed and battered but still intact. The wooden workshop by the barn was gone. Barbed wire that had sealed the gaps between buildings, hung in tatters.

Emma stared through stinging, streaming eyes at the ruins in front of her. Their fuel was gone. The generators were gone too and many of the tools they had collected. Their bikes had disappeared, vaporised, she supposed. All that identified where the Shogun had stood was a metal chassis and the still smouldering masses of steel wires that had been tyres. She didn't have to see to know that every window that faced the yard was smashed. It seemed ludicrous to think it but still she knew they had been lucky. They should be grateful John had never brought the fuel tanker he had wanted.

The house and cottages still stood, as did the stone-built animal sheds with their corrugated iron roofs. The animals were all fenced in the fields and couldn't run far. Most of the crops would be unaffected. Their stores were safe. Everyone in the group was burned, cut, and bruised to varying degrees but they were all alive. They could rebuild, must rebuild.

Emma heaved herself unwillingly to her feet. Her head hurt and when she put her hand back to feel the lump, her fingers came away sticky with congealed blood. If it was drying it could wait, she decided.

"Come on, you lot, let's sort out the house then we can get ourselves cleaned up. We can't do any more out here."

Weary faces flopped towards her in protest but with moans of exhaustion, people pushed themselves upright to follow her.

They found boards and cardboard packing cases to shut out the weather from some of the windows and clear polythene from the gardening supplies to cover those where they needed more light. Their fire-fighting efforts had left the carpets near to the windows soaked and all the ceilings in the rooms on the farmyard side of the house were blackened but when they finished their temporary repairs, the house was habitable. The reek of smoke they could live with for now.

One advantage of the house having been a B&B was plenty of bathrooms. Tension started to fall away along with their ruined clothing, as they exchanged it for the ecstasy of a muscle-easing bath or streaming shower. Clean after several showers and a long soak in the bath, Emma dressed then knocked at John's door. They coated one another's burns and cuts with antiseptic and a sealing spray then gratefully headed for the kitchen.

Margaret was ahead of them. She sent them through to the big room, where she and Tony had already spread sheets over the smoky furniture. A tray of spirits, mixers and glasses stood on the table. Alongside it mugs of tea and coffee steamed invitingly.

Emma sighed in relief. "Margaret, you work miracles."

Margaret laughed. "No, I just work Tony to a frazzle."

Tony entered with plates of sandwiches. Sticking plasters decorated several parts of his face and head. "Someone talking about me?"

"About you, not to you," Margaret retorted. "Fetch some salt too, please, Tony."

Tony went off muttering, "Slave driver," under his breath.

Margaret reached out and gave his rump a playful slap as she called after him. "I heard that."

They could see his shoulders shaking as he chuckled silently.

Gradually all except Dan filtered in to join them.

"He's fast asleep, but at least he showered first," Sunny assured them.

When everyone was settled with something to eat, John asked the inevitable question. "Does anyone know how it started?"

"I saw it first, I think," volunteered Tony. "I was going out to check on the sheep. It was already blazing by then but it seemed to have started at the side where the generator was running. We'd been charging up some batteries."

John sighed. "That could have been it. Maybe the generator overheated or the exhaust ignited a bit of spilled fuel or the hydrogen from the batteries exploded. I don't suppose we'll ever know."

"Does it matter?" asked Emma. "However it started, and whatever we've lost, the important thing is that we're all still alive. Things can be replaced, people can't."

"You didn't find anyone at Invermoriston, then?" asked Alan. "I'd forgotten about that until now."

Emma shook her head then glanced at John. "Only one poor man who had completely lost his mind. He ran off when we called to him. We kept to the back roads but saw no sign of anyone but him, either there or anywhere along the way."

"Ah well, we will have to keep looking elsewhere," Alan said.

"Speaking of what we lost, do you have lists, Margaret?" John asked.

She nodded. "Pretty full inventories. The big things were the tractor and the Shogun, bicycles, fuel and generators of course and the tools both for the fields and in the workshop."

John frowned. "I know we said we'd stay away from the towns and other inhabited places, Emma, but this is an emergency. We need to replace some of those tools at least."

Emma sighed heavily. "You're right, of course. If it had only been the power tools and vehicles I would have said let's make do but we need hand tools and a reserve of fuel."

"The tools we can get at that big B&Q and the farm suppliers on the industrial estate this side of Elgin, where we went before. We only saw only a couple of bodies and the hardware stores don't attract vermin like food shops do. That way we don't have to go into the town at all. If we want fuel in cans we'll probably be best getting it from Lossiemouth. There's already some stored that way there and we don't have to go through the town to get to the airbase either."

"All right," Emma announced decisively, "but you take maximum precautions and a minimum of risks. We aren't doing this to then have you, or all of us, go down with some new disease."

John nodded in agreement.

"Tony, will you fetch some candles, please?" asked Margaret.

Sunny flinched. "I'd sooner we used the battery lamps, if nobody minds."

"So would I," added Alan.

"I think a few of us would prefer not to have open flames around at the moment," agreed Emma. "Okay, let's use lamps. Hopefully we'll all have settled down a bit before we run out of batteries. It's time we set up some of your twelve-volt lights in here too, Alan."

"Lamps then, please, Tony," Margaret said. "And I think we better add fire extinguishers to our list for tomorrow, John; big, industrial, water, foam and powder fire extinguishers, for both in here and the outbuildings."

John closed his eyes and gave a tired sigh. "We'll take the four-tonner that we brought the wire in. It's parked at the back of my place."

Neighbours

By the time they had finished loading up at the hardware superstore outside Elgin, fire extinguishers filled almost half of the space in the back of the RAF lorry. Much of the rest was packed with hand tools, glass and wood. The store had been pleasantly clear of bodies or vermin but even though the industrial estate was on the edge of town, the smell of putrefaction was strong on the cold morning air.

Tony helped John to push the tailgate of the truck upright and then, as Margaret joined them, asked him, "What now, John?"

"We'll leave the four-tonner here for now and go on to Lossiemouth in the Land Rover. We should find ourselves a trailer for the cans of fuel somewhere on the base. After the fire, all I found of my trailer was the wheel hubs."

Margaret was driving the Land Rover, so John took the passenger seat as navigator and Tony climbed into the rear. They would have to drive three miles back towards home before they turned onto the side road John intended to use to get to the RAF station.

As they rounded a bend on the side road, which was really no wider than a track at this point, Margaret braked fiercely. They were approaching a cross junction with an even smaller track. The road they needed to take, on the other side of the junction, was completely blocked by cars.

They had been jammed together side-by-side between the high banks and tall bushes bordering the lane and extended several cars back. Some were facing them, some sideways on, all seemed to have had their tyres punctured or wheels removed and many contained bodies. At the back of the roadblock John could see a familiar bus.

"Well now I know where the vehicles that were on the main road disappeared to," he exclaimed.

Tony leaned forward to see through the windscreen. "What do we do now?"

John thought for a moment. "We'll have to go round the Elgin by-pass, and then up the A941. It could be that someone is living further along this track and wanted to block the approach. After we've got the fuel we'll see if there's another way in, make contact with them. Back up, please, Margaret."

Margaret looked puzzled. "Couldn't we take the track to the left, John? It seems to go back towards the road."

John shook his head. "We could; but when a road block is the other side of a track junction, it's usually because someone wants you to take one of the side roads and in that situation I don't like doing what people seem to want me to do. An officer, leading a convoy I was in, took us down a road like that in Africa, because of the difficulty of reversing the whole convoy. We drove straight into an ambush."

"But surely that wouldn't happen here," protested Tony. "They would never know when anyone was coming."

"Maybe," agreed John. "It could be that they're simply giving people an easy route away from them. I prefer not to take the risk."

Margaret slipped the Land Rover into gear and twisted to look over her shoulder as she reversed along the route they had come. She slowed as they came to the gate to a field, and then backed into it to turn the Land Rover around. Within minutes they were on the main road and heading towards Elgin.

Although they would not go through the main part of the town, the road they were on was still lined on either side by offices, industrial estates and some houses. Before entering the built-up area they all put on gas masks. Even so the smell filtered through to them.

"Phew! This smell is definitely getting stronger," complained Margaret.

John agreed with her. "Aye, well, the weather is warming up and the bodies have been there a while now. I reckon it could be autumn next year before it starts to fade. Give it a couple of years and the smell may be gone out here, though not in the houses."

When they reached the roundabout on the by-pass, John directed Margaret onto their new approach road. They had left the town and rounded a bend when they came to yet another roadblock. The main road was two lanes wide at this point but the obstruction was equally impassable.

"So it wasn't only the lane," John mused. "I think whoever did this is trying to block off Lossie completely."

Margaret faced him so that he would hear her more clearly through the gas mask. "Is there any other way in, John?"

"Aye, a couple, but I think I know what we'll find."

Margaret turned the Land Rover around once more. As they drove back to the roundabout John noticed that two side roads from the town, that he could have taken, were also blocked. He hadn't been looking for it before but whoever had done this had been thorough.

They reached the town and headed out on the Inverness road. It wasn't long before John directed them onto yet another side road, now heading towards the coast. Every road and track leading from it towards the airfield and town of Lossiemouth had been carefully blocked.

"Okay, so now what?" mumbled Tony, through his mask.

Though they couldn't see it, John smiled. "This is a Land Rover, not a mini. We go cross-country. We can take the masks off now we're clear of the town," he said, removing his own respirator.

At the next field gate John told Margaret to stop and Tony jumped out to open the gate.

"Leave it open after we drive through," John called to him. "We might want to come out faster than we go in."

After they had cleared the gate, Tony clambered back onboard.

"High ratio four-wheel drive would be best for a ploughed field like this, Margaret," John advised.

She grimaced. "In that case I think we better change places. I can learn about off-road driving another time."

"Keep that Mossberg 500 ready, Tony." John instructed, referring to the eight-shot, pump-action shotgun that Tony had taken to replace the Beretta 686 skeet gun he was carrying when they first met. The Beretta was a fine shotgun but not nearly as useful for their purposes now as the Mossberg with its extra magazine capacity, shorter barrel and folding stock.

Tony pushed the back door of the Land Rover open slightly and held it that way with his foot. He held the pump action with the barrel resting across his knee, aiming out of the back. It wasn't obvious but it was ready for fast use, as John had taught him.

John drove across the field they had entered and then another, before finding a gate which let them out onto a track which led towards Lossiemouth. They had to detour around blockages in yet more places but they were making their way steadily towards the airfield and town.

"They've been thorough, but whoever put up these barriers is used to driving on roads not country," John commented. "Still, it would have been more than enough to put off anyone who didn't have a four-wheel drive or who didn't have a real reason to head this way."

They were now passing the ruins of Duffus castle and would soon be nearing the end of the airfield.

"We'll go in through the crash-gate," John told them. "Once we're on the airfield we shouldn't have any trouble, but be ready in case others are already there and don't like us on their patch."

The crash-gates were locked but using a pair of wire cutters John had put into the vehicle for this eventuality, Tony cut away part of the fence next to the gate post, squeezed through and then pushed the gates open from inside. As he climbed back into his seat, he picked up the Mossberg.

"From now on, whenever you get out, take the shotgun with you, Tony," John warned him. "You never know when you might need it."

John drove straight to the transport yard to collect a trailer. Then they headed for the fuel compound, where he had previously stocked up on cans of diesel. The transport pool had been open but a new padlock shone on the gates of the fuel compound. John took a hacksaw from the back of the Land Rover and began to cut through the hasp.

Margaret climbed from the cab and nudged Tony. "Keep your eyes open. If someone has bothered to lock these gates, they might not take kindly to us helping ourselves."

Glancing up, John saw that Tony was watching the roads approaching their position. Margaret was next to him. The twelve-bore Baikal side-by-side hammer gun, which she seemed to have adopted as her own, was in her hands. The gun suited her; strong, reliable, unpretentious but extremely capable. She had not yet drawn back the hammers but John knew that she kept both barrels loaded. In the house, the gun stood in the corner, by the head of the bed she shared with Tony.

The padlock fell away. John put the hacksaw back with the other tools he had stored in the Land Rover then called to

Margaret. "Will you keep watch please, Margaret? I'll back the trailer into the compound then Tony and I will load the fuel."

Margaret waved her agreement and John reversed towards the fuel cans. It didn't take long for the two of them to fill the trailer with green painted jerry cans, each of which had the black painted top that denoted Diesel fuel. They roped down a canvas cover over them, and then John drove out while Tony closed the gates.

They were about to drive away, when a military Land Rover came around a corner between the buildings thirty yards in front of them and braked sharply to a halt.

"Everybody out, fast!" commanded John.

He leapt from behind the wheel, his .308 Sako in his hand, while Tony and Margaret ran to the other side.

Tony dashed a few yards to the cover of a trailer-mounted fire extinguisher. Margaret stayed close to the Land Rover. As he thumbed off the safety catch of his rifle, John heard the double, "clack, clack" of each of the hammers of Margaret's Baikal being cocked.

Two men and a girl jumped from the RAF Land Rover. Each of them carried an L85A2 military rifle, fitted with a twenty-round magazine. The girl stayed by the back of the vehicle. The driver stood behind his open door. A man of around fifty emerged from behind the passenger door and limped to the front of the bonnet. His right leg trailed slightly but he seemed to ignore it, as if he was so used to the hindrance he no longer gave it any thought.

"Who are you and what are you doing here?" he called.

John sized up the situation quickly. Margaret and Tony would not fire without his lead, unless they saw an obvious danger. From his position, John could easily shoot the girl. Tony was furthest to the left and although he would most likely aim to shoot through the Land Rover window, any buckshot that hit the aluminium door would, at this range, go straight through to wound the other group's driver. Margaret's shotgun was pointed at the man who had challenged them, so he would be her target.

In the hands of soldiers, the L85A2s with their semi or full automatic firing capability, optical sights and large magazine capacity would have outgunned John's group, but the people in front of them did not hold their rifles like soldiers. Tony and Margaret's shotguns might even give them the advantage, if it came to shooting. John wanted to avoid that if possible.

"I'm John, this is Margaret and Tony," John told them, deliberately using first names in an attempt to personalise and so ease the situation. "We had a fire that destroyed our fuel reserve, so we came to get some more for the tractor."

"And you thought you'd help yourself to ours, did you?" snarled the man facing him.

"What do you mean 'yours'? This was an RAF station, the fuel here doesn't belong to you or anyone else now," John countered.

The man scowled. "It's ours by right of possession. You say you want it for your tractor; well we need it for our fishing boat. You have no rights to it either and we've claimed it. Now back off or we'll start shooting." He hefted his rifle but he still hadn't brought it up to point at any of them.

Again John scanned the opposition. The girl seemed nervous but her rifle was pointed at the ground. The driver had his rifle pointing roughly halfway between John and Margaret, though he kept glancing anxiously towards Tony.

John still wasn't yet ready to shoot. These people were doing no more than his group would in the same situation. They were only trying to protect their own survival. The fact that both sides were nervous could yet lead to disaster but Margaret and Tony had been blooded, these may not have been. He would keep trying.

"If you shoot, we'll shoot. We're all trying to survive. Getting into a gun battle isn't a good way to do that. People on both sides are going to die."

The girl was moving closer to the back of the Land Rover. The driver kept switching his attention frantically between John, Tony and Margaret, while chewing his bottom lip. Finally he spoke. "He's right, Terry. There's no need for this. There's plenty of fuel for us both, isn't there?"

The leader angrily turned towards his driver, lifting the muzzle of his rifle unconsciously as he twisted.

"Shut up, Hamish! I'll han…."

Before he could finish, Margaret cried out a warning and the Baikal in her hands roared. Four thirty-two calibre lead balls struck Terry in the chest, one severing an artery, another hit him in the right shoulder, yet another in the stomach and a seventh tore into his neck. He staggered backwards, as the Land Rover windscreen shattered under the impact of the buckshot that had missed him.

Terry's head snapped round to face them, his expression one of disbelief. His already dying body rocked as he gasped for breath and tried to maintain his balance. He fought to raise his rifle but it was too late. He collapsed forward, the L85A2 falling unfired from his hands.

John's Sako was up and aimed at the girl before she could move. For a moment she stood motionless, stunned, and then dropped her rifle. Her hands flung up to cover her face and she fell to her knees, wailing.

John's eyes now flashed to the driver but the young man was already dropping his rifle too, his hands rising in surrender. Hamish's face was ashen and his mouth open in terror, as he backed away from the vehicle door.

John snatched a look at Tony, desperately hoping that he would not fire.

Tony had the butt of the Mossberg pump action in his shoulder and the muzzle aimed unerringly at Hamish. His body was taut, leaning forward to combat the recoil when he fired. The knuckles of his right hand gleamed white as they gripped the pistol grip stock and the muscles of his left forearm stood out starkly as he grasped the fore end, ready to pump another round into the breech as soon as he had fired. His finger was on the trigger, already starting to squeeze as John yelled.

"Tony, don't shoot!"

Even as he steeled himself against the recoil, John's shout penetrated Tony's concentration. His finger flicked forward off the trigger. His eyes shot first towards John and then back to his target. Slowly, trembling with repressed adrenalin, he lowered the muzzle of the shotgun, his gaze fixed on the man he had been less than a second from killing.

Margaret continued to stare at the man she had shot. The Baikal was still at her waist, from where she had fired it. Without thinking, she opened the gun, picked out the fired cartridge and dropped it, reloaded with another then snapped the gun closed. Her brow creased in a puzzled frown. "I didn't mean to fire. I didn't want to shoot him. He was bringing his rifle up," she explained.

John nodded in understanding, and then walked forward to pick up the dead man's rifle.

He hung the L85 over his shoulder by its sling and then walked towards the kneeling girl. Her face was still buried in her hands, her body shaking with muffled sobs. John retrieved her rifle too then stooped over, took her by the elbow and gently pulled her up.

"It's all right, lassie, it's all over now," he reassured her.

Her hands crept away from her tear-stained face but stayed clasped, as if in prayer. She was an attractive girl in her late teens, with lustrous auburn hair and a model figure but her eyes were wide with terror as she asked, "You aren't going to shoot us?"

John shook his head. "It was a misunderstanding. Margaret thought he was bringing his rifle up to fire. Nobody's going to shoot you."

The girl closed her eyes and took a deep, shuddering breath. "I thought I was dead. I thought you were going to kill us all."

John guided her around the front of the Land Rover, pushing the driver's door closed as he led her to stand by Hamish. He picked up Hamish's L85 and placed it and the other two on the bonnet. Margaret had moved to stand beside him. "Are you okay, Margaret?" he asked.

She nodded and even gave a small smile. "Yes, I'm all right." Then she turned her attention to Hamish and the girl. "I'm sorry," she told them. "I really didn't intend to shoot him but he started to point his rifle at John."

The girl glanced nervously between Margaret and the body in front of the Land Rover. "We hadn't known him long. We only joined up last week," she said, and shrugged as if to close the matter.

"Who are you? What are you doing here? Are there any more of you?" asked John.

The girl took a deep breath and visibly calmed herself. "I'm Claudyne. I was at Gordonstoun School. After everybody died it got really stinky, so I moved into one of the farm cottages. Hamish saw the smoke from my chimney and came to investigate. I was on my own for a week. He was the first person I met after everyone died. We have six in the group," she glanced at Terry's body, "five now. The others came with Terry on his boat."

"Where are the rest?" asked Tony, who had joined them.

Hamish kept glancing at Tony, as if expecting that at any moment Tony would raise his shotgun and shoot him after all but his face was starting to recover some colour and he now answered Tony's question. "We've taken over some cottages down near the harbour. They'll be there or on the boat. We've been living off fish mainly, together with some scrounging and a bit of shooting. We were coming to get some diesel for the boat when we saw you."

"And how are the others going to take the news about Terry?" asked John.

Hamish shrugged. "Nobody liked him much but he was the one who got us organised, and he was the one who knew about the fishing."

"Sheenagh won't miss him, that's for sure," interjected Claudyne. "They were sort of together but he liked his own way and used the back of his hand to make sure he got it. It didn't stop him trying it on with me either."

Another thought came to John. "Was it his idea to block off all the roads?"

Claudyne shook her head as she admitted, "No, that was mine. Hamish and I had already started when the others arrived. A mob of bikers came through one day and almost caught me in Lossiemouth. After that we got a map and began moving cars and things to close off all the roads."

"Terry decided it was a good idea anyway," added Hamish. "He said anything we couldn't get in Lossiemouth we could get from somewhere along the coast and that it was safer travelling by sea than on land. He sort of took over the roadblock idea as if it was his. That was why he was so angry when he saw you. He didn't think anyone would get past the blocks."

"All right," said John, "let's tell you something about our set up and then you can take us to meet the rest of your group - if you will."

He explained what they were doing at Knockside, their brief history and told them they were ready to welcome new recruits. "Do you think any of your people would be interested in joining us?"

Hamish shrugged. "We can ask."

John nodded towards the body. "What about him?"

"We'll take care of him," Claudyne offered. "We'll take him out on the boat; he would have wanted to be buried at sea."

John and Tony helped Hamish to put Terry's remains in the back of the RAF Land Rover but John unloaded all the rifles then put them in the back of the Knockside vehicle. They followed Hamish and Claudyne out of the base and down towards the harbour.

Sheenagh met them at the door of the first cottage, trying to pat her untidy, mousy hair into some sort of order to cover the bruise on her right temple. She was as thin as a plaice seen sideways and could have been anywhere between thirty and fifty, John decided. But her eyes were piercing blue and she smiled when she saw them. "Well I'll never, new people!"

Two men came out of a cottage further along the row to join them. One had to stoop to get through the door. The other was of average height, heavy but wearing clothes that seemed a size too big for him now. Neither of them was armed, John noticed.

"Where's Terry?" the shorter one asked.

"He's in the back of the Land Rover," announced Hamish. "There's been an accident. Terry's dead."

John watched their faces carefully. They showed some surprise but neither shock nor great emotion.

"What happened?" asked the tall one.

Hamish nodded towards Margaret. "This lady thought he was about to shoot at them, so she got in first."

The heavy man grunted. "He probably deserved it."

Sheenagh shook her head and sighed. "Well what's done is done and no undoing it. Will you take him out in the boat later, please, Hamish? There's some chain in the shed."

Hamish nodded.

Her smile again flashed at John, Margaret and Tony. "Well, come in, come in. You're our first visitors. The kettle is on and you can tell us all about yourselves. Come on, all of you." And with that she ushered them through the door into the stone-built cottage.

A fire burned in the hearth. Aided by the low ceiling it produced a cosy atmosphere. The kettle steamed on a metal trivet that had been fitted in front of the fire. Old but comfortable furniture crowded the room. Somehow Sheenagh seemed as if she was a part of the house, even though she had only been there a week.

The tiny room could barely contain them all, but Claudyne and Hamish perched on the deep window sill and Morris, the tall man, tucked in his arms and legs like a Swiss army knife being closed as he sat on the floor.

"So who are you and where have you come from and are you going to stay?" Sheenagh pestered. "I'll warn you now – start talking or I'll never shut up." And her face glowed once more.

Again John recited their story, emphasising all they had achieved but admitting to their various problems, including the recent fire. At the end he put their proposition. "So we want more people. Emma is the organiser but we all have an equal say in things. If any of you decided to join us the same would be true for you. If you don't like the farm, or us, you can always leave again."

The Lossiemouth five were thoughtful and John decided not to interrupt their deliberations.

Sheenagh spoke up first. "You sound like good people, John, and I can only speak for myself, but I came from Fraserburgh. I've always lived by the sea; my people have always been fishers. I don't think I would want to leave it. The rest must choose for themselves."

Morris looked to Graeme, his counterpart, who nodded. "Sorry, John. We have a radio at the Coast Guard station and we'd like to keep in touch. You're our nearest neighbours as far as we know, but this place has all we need with the RAF camp there with its stores and fuel, that's why we moved here. We like the small group. We wouldn't want to move in with a lot more people."

Sheenagh smiled at them, gratefully, causing John to wonder whether her renewed availability might not be a part of their reason for deciding to stay.

Claudyne and Hamish were whispering to one another. Eventually Claudyne spoke for them both. "We're staying too. I love going out on the boat for the fish, lobsters and shellfish we catch. It's just too cool here. Sorry."

"We would like to trade though," added Hamish. "Sea food for fresh vegetables or oats or milk. Anything you have in surplus really."

John grimaced. "That will be a while yet. I won't pretend I'm not disappointed but you know where we are now if you need us. We'll give you a copy of the radio network and our frequency. Sergei will agree a call sign with you. It looks as though Saturday night is going to be a regular chat night with most people logging on to blether. Maybe we'll talk to you then. There's plenty of fuel in the compound so we'll keep what's in the trailer, if you don't mind, but from now on we'll take our fuel from Kinloss, leave Lossiemouth for you."

#

John, Margaret and Tony collected the four-tonner from Elgin and then returned to Knockside. The news of their nearby neighbours caused both great excitement and equal disappointment, because no newcomers had chosen to join them at the farm.

Nevertheless, Emma was encouraged and said so. "Even if they don't want to come here to stay, we're near enough that we can help one another if needed. It's good to know we have neighbours."

"And it will be good to trade," added Alan. "I do like a bit of fresh fish."

John put down his tea mug and stood up. "Aye, well, they gave us some fish to bring with us but before dinner we've got vehicles to unload and there's plenty to do. We better get to it."

The next few days at Knockside were spent cleaning up the aftermath of the fire and repairing the broken windows. The remains of the curtains were thrown out, as were the carpets in the affected rooms. They cleaned and scrubbed the walls and thoroughly aired the house to help remove the stench of smoke.

They dug a pit, well out in the field on the opposite side of the track from the farm, for their new fuel store. The bottom was fitted with a drainage pipe and filled with gravel and then pallets laid for the cans to stand on. The sides were shored with planks and the pit covered with a tarpaulin. They positioned blue, dry-powder fire extinguishers by the side of the track near the entrance to the field. In every room, every corridor, every corner of the farmyard, there now stood bright-red fire extinguishers.

New barbed wire was added to fill the gaps where the barn and workshop had stood. They had lost some of the cabbages in the field behind the barn, burnt or ruined by fuel and oily smoke or damaged by the explosion but it wasn't too bad. The main losses were the generators and the horse-drawn farming equipment, for neither of which they had yet found replacements. They now had to charge batteries by switching them around on the Land Rover.

Saturday night was becoming a busy time on the radio, though some people on the network were keeping an open channel to listen for calls at other times too. On that Saturday night they had been talking for about an hour. Margaret was exchanging cookery tips with one of the Oban group. They were discussing making bread without yeast.

"And how long did you have to let your starter stand before it was ready, Ailsa? Over."

"Well it depends how you like the taste, dearie; the longer you leave it the sourer it gets. Start with your starter quite fresh, until people get used to it and then experiment. Over."

The speakers crackled for a moment before an unfamiliar voice joined the conversation. "Well landsakes! Howdy, folks. Jack McCauley outside Menard, Texas here. Over."

Everyone stared at the speakers open-mouthed. Margaret was first to recover her composure.

"This is Margaret Hilton in Scotland. Did you say Texas? Over."

"I surely did. You folks are the first people I done spoken to in nearly three months. Over."

"And you are the first person we have heard from outside Scotland. How are things there, Jack? Over."

"Lady, this might not even BE Texas no more. I ain't seen a living soul since the plague got done. I was starting to think the good Lord had left me in my own private hell. Over."

"We think about six hundred people are left in Scotland, Jack. Texas is bigger than this whole country; maybe in time you'll find others. Over."

"Might be, ma'am, but there were a lot more alive till the second plague hit. That rightly took most of those who were left. Sounds like you-all's real crowded there compared to here. Over."

"A second plague?"

"Yes, ma'am. The first was like influenza but it hit your chest real hard, then when that seemed like it was over there was another, sort of like smallpox. People got a blazin' fever, came out in blisters and just up and died. Over."

Margaret shivered. Until now they had all assumed that everywhere had been affected in the same way.

"There were no reports of this second plague here, Jack. We hadn't heard of it before. Over."

"I'm not rightly surprised, ma'am. There wasn't much left in the way of newspapers or radio or TV here by then either. I only knowed about it on account of I saw it happening. Over."

"And how are you, Jack? How are you surviving? Over."

"Aw hell, ma'am, pardon my French, I never did care much for people no how. There's plenty of beefsteak on the range. Me and ol' Howly make do just fine. It surely is good to talk to y'all right now though. Over."

"Howly?"

Jack laughed. "Yes, ma'am, this flea-bitten ol' pooch don't talk much, lessen he scents a rabbit, but he listens real well. Anyways, I couldn't help but hear you all were talkin' sourdough. If'n you want a recipe for sourdough biscuits I reckon mine will beat the britches off any in Texas. Over."

Their first international contact left them both excited and terrified.

"What if the second plague exists here?" asked Tony. "It could be down in England and we've never heard about it."

Alan added his warning. "People from the borders could contract it. If Fhionna or Sergei and Martin go down there they could bring it back with them."

John was doubtful. "The second plague seems to have sprung up in the States after the first one started to die down. If they were right about it being spread by terrorists, it could have been a second strike. Maybe not so many people were vulnerable to the 'flu' over there."

Emma agreed. "There doesn't seem to have been any need for it here. The first disease wiped out most people anyway."

"But it could do," insisted Tony, "we don't know what all the people in Scotland died of."

Margaret reached out and slapped her partner's shoulder. "Calm down, Tony! Look, if both germs were loose up here we would have been exposed to them and none of us have been affected. Still, it does bring home that we should be careful of strangers, I suppose."

Tony hung his head, but did settle.

"I'll rig up an intercom down by the first cattle grid," John volunteered, "and we'll put up a sign asking people to use it before approaching."

"Yes, but what if they have already been infected but don't know it?" asked Sunflower.

Emma came back into the room carrying a book she had fetched from their library. "It says in Black's medical dictionary, that the incubation period for smallpox is three to seventeen days but that the person is only contagious once the blisters appear. As long as people haven't been in close contact with someone at that stage they should be okay."

Alan sighed. "That might be true if this was ordinary smallpox, but if this other disease was developed as a weapon it must be more deadly and more easily passed on. Who knows what its characteristics might be?"

Emma was becoming increasingly concerned about Alan. His attitude was becoming negative. Walking seemed to tire him. He was losing weight and had lost the energy he always displayed when they first met him. He now regularly slept during the day. Often she would see him absent-mindedly massaging his chest and left arm, as he was now. Leah's potions no longer seemed to help, so Emma had given him a supply of aspirin but he looked to be weakening daily.

"You're right, Alan," she agreed, "but what can we do – cut ourselves off entirely? That didn't seem to help those people at Fort George despite all their precautions."

"If a virus was developed as a weapon wouldn't it be designed to spread quickly?" Leah suggested. "In which case if we were sure a visitor hadn't been in contact with anyone who was ill for, say, a week or ten days, and they weren't showing any symptoms themselves, shouldn't they be all right?"

John interrupted before the discussion could go further. "We're guessing, and it isn't doing us any good. I suggest we ask Fhionna to talk to Jack and then make some recommendations. Damn it! I wish she had a radio in her Range Rover. Where was she going next – anyone know?"

"She's coming down here," answered Margaret. "She and James were at Coldbackie to treat a gash on Calum's leg. But she said it might be a couple of days. Dougal told them he'd spotted smoke while he was out stalking and they were going to scour the area he thought it might have come from."

John frowned in thought. "Then we'll have to get as much information from Jack as he can give us, for when she gets here. He said he would be back on tomorrow evening, or tomorrow afternoon as it is for him."

"And in the meantime," said Emma, "we'll put up that sign and intercom and, oh, I don't know, play it by ear if anyone we don't know shows up, I suppose." Tight-lipped, she snapped the book closed and paced out of the room.

John frowned again but this time in concern, then picked up his glass of Glenmorangie before following her.

He found her in the room they used as a study and library. She was sitting at the table staring at the medical book in front of her but it was closed. He nudged her arm and offered her his whisky.

"That wasn't like you, Emma, what's wrong?"

She shook her head, hesitated then took a sip of the single malt before handing it back to him. "Thanks. Oh, I don't know, John, it seems never ending; first the deaths, and then … Aberdeen, and then Morag, the bikers and all the work and not finding anyone who wants to join us and then the fire and Alan being unwell and now this new worry. We don't seem to get anywhere without something else coming along to make it worse.' Tears filled her eyes. She sniffed and shuddered. "Do you know, I even had second thoughts before taking your drink?"

He gave a brief grunt. "I'll go and take a sup from the bottle; it'll keep you off the whisky."

Emma laughed but smiled gratefully. He offered her his glass again. She took it, drained it, and then handed it back. He stared down into the empty tumbler in mock horror.

She stuck her tongue out at him. "Serves you right. Keep me off the whisky indeed. We better find a distillery before you drink us dry."

Then she stood up, put her hands on his shoulders, leaned forward and kissed him on the cheek. She pushed herself back and stepped away. "Thanks, John. I just needed to blow off steam."

He nodded. "I know. It isn't easy but we'll get there, you'll see."

#

Fhionna and James arrived not two but three days later, to find them in sombre mood. "If our visiting makes you this glum, we'll go again." Fhionna said, frowning.

Emma shook her head. "It isn't you, Fhi. Alan died yesterday."

"Oh, I am sorry. What happened?"

"It was his heart. He'd been getting weaker for some time. Leah found him when she went up to call him, after he missed breakfast yesterday. He must have died in the night. We buried him beside Morag."

"He wasn't a young man and he hadn't been used to this sort of workload," Fhionna observed. "I see you've had some other problems too. I had heard about the fire but I didn't realise how much damage there'd been."

Emma sighed. "That isn't the only thing. Come in and have some coffee and I'll bring you up to date." Then she faced Fhionna's young assistant. "And how are you, James?"

"I'm good thank you, Emma. Fhionna is teaching me lots."

Emma glanced at Fhionna. "I'll bet she is! Come on in."

James' neck was blushed bright red as she ushered him in ahead of them but Fhionna glared and playfully dug Emma in the ribs.

"Oh, by the way," Fhionna said, "you have some new neighbours, Wallace Urquhart and Rachel Cowan. They're at a place called Littlemill."

"I know it," said Emma. "Near Nairn."

"That's it. James and I have taken to mainly using the back roads, avoiding towns and widening the search. We saw their smoke."

After they were settled in the kitchen with a hot drink, Fhionna continued. "They're a nice couple. Wallace is in his mid thirties, used to be a fireman in Inverness; rather dishy actually. Rachel is twenty-two. She lived and worked by Littlemill; her father had a farm there. That's where they're living now."

"Any chance they would want to move here?" Emma asked, hopefully.

"You could visit and talk to them. We told them about you of course, but they actually seem to be doing rather well. Rachel is pregnant; she might like to have another woman around but she's a strong and confident lassie, she doesn't seem overly worried about having the baby. I'll be keeping an eye on her though."

"When is she due?"

"Oh, not for another six months yet. Wallace is the father. Now, tell us all your news."

Emma giggled. "She didn't hang about, did she?"

Fhionna gave her a knowing look. "You haven't seen Wallace."

Emma told them about the fire and the people John had met at Lossiemouth. Then she came to the radio call and their contact with Jack, in Texas. "So what do you think – are we at risk from another disease?"

Fhionna shook her head thoughtfully. "I doubt it very much, not of that sort anyway. I never heard of any second disease. There could be all sorts of things breeding in the towns of course, and not everyone is being careful enough from what I hear." She took a sip of coffee. "That lot in Glasgow have been trying to get me to visit but they haven't had anything so serious that Effie and Joshua couldn't cope. They sound healthy enough and they're continuing the burning program but I don't fancy going into a city if I don't have to."

"I don't blame you," agreed Emma. "So you don't think we have anything to worry about?"

Fhionna drank more coffee and thought about it for a while. "It makes sense to be cautious. Question visitors to find out when they last had contact with others and if they had any sign of illness. If you're in any way unsure, keep them at a distance. If you want to be hospitable but not let them in here you could always let them use John's cottage or his neighbours'."

"His neighbours' cottage is empty; he buried them after his own family. We'll see about preparing that. Thanks, Fhionna. Will you tell all the others this tonight? It'll reassure them more coming from you."

"'Course I will. We'd like to stay for a day or two anyway if you don't mind. We've been on the road pretty much constantly for ages now."

"Stay as long as you like. You two are always welcome. Come on, we'll get your stuff into rooms."

Late the following morning, Emma was accompanying Fhionna and James on their inspection of the animals, when they were startled by the howls of a dog pack, closely followed by a volley of shotgun blasts.

John ran from the farm, his Sako .308 in his hand. "Who's out there?" he demanded.

"Margaret and Tony went down to clear up your neighbours' cottage," Emma told him. "It must be them."

Another two shots boomed out.

"Get back to the farm and close the gate. I'll go to see what's going on," John called, as he started to run down the track.

"Be careful, John," Emma shouted after him.

She and the others hurried back to the farmyard and pulled the barbed wire wrapped gate closed behind them. As the gate bolt clanged into place, they heard another shotgun blast from the bottom of the hill, closely followed by a series of the sharper cracks of John's rifle firing, then nothing.

A few minutes later Sunflower ran from the farmhouse. "Emma! John is on the intercom. He says he needs a vehicle and Fhionna down there quickly. Tony has been hurt, Margaret too."

"Is there room in your Range Rover?" Emma asked.

Fhionna shook her head. "It's packed."

"Take the Land Rover then, the keys are in it. James, help me with the cattle grid, please."

Fhionna ran first to the Range Rover to grab her medical bag and then to Land Rover. Meanwhile Emma and James swung open the gate and ran down to the fence to lower the cattle grid. They had barely got it down as Fhionna arrived. She drove straight over and down the track.

Sunflower, Leah and Dan were all standing by the gate, while James and Emma waited anxiously by the cattle grid.

After what seemed like hours but was only five minutes, they heard the whine of the Land Rover as it forged up the hill.

Fhionna drove past at speed. Emma and James winched up the cattle grid once more before hurrying after her.

They arrived back at the house to find everyone in the kitchen. Margaret was sitting on a chair. Leah was swabbing blood from Margaret's right arm and Sunflower cleaned a rapidly-swelling series of bite marks on her right calf.

With her left hand Margaret was stroking Tony's hair. He was laid on the kitchen table. His face was ashen, his eyes were closed and he was shaking. John was cutting away Tony's trousers, to get at bites on his left thigh. Fhionna was pressing a blood soaked pad firmly against his neck.

"James, get my other bag from the Range Rover, please," Fhionna requested. "I'll need anti-tetanus and broad range antibiotics. They're in the red pouch. Sutures too. Emma, can you get me some more pads, please. Once I stop the haemorrhaging, this will need stitches."

As Emma rushed to get the pads, tears were running down Margaret's face. Her words were punctuated by sobs. "Brave boy. The dogs were all around us and he laid straight into them. One of them knocked away his shotgun so he was tearing them off me with his bare hands, and then a terrier got him by the neck. It was hanging there, swinging around while he strangled the Alsatian that was biting my leg but he wouldn't take care of himself until he had got that dog off me. Then he managed to get at his knife, stood in front of me, stabbed the terrier and started using it to batter the others away. He was so brave."

Fhionna glanced up briefly. "He'll be fine, Margaret, don't worry. Once I finish my needlework on him you'll be bossing him around in no time." Then she laid her hand on Tony's shoulder. "This is going to hurt, Tony; I don't have enough anaesthetic to use it for stitching. I have to save it for more serious surgery."

His eyes opened. He nodded and gripped Margaret's hand tighter.

Fhionna took pads from Emma and her bag from James then swabbed the lacerated wound.

Margaret gave a tearful cough, half laugh, half sob. "I'll give him what for, making me cry like this."

Tony twisted his head slightly towards her. "Sorry …"

Fhionna pushed him back down "Keep still or you'll bleed all over her and then you really will be sorry."

"There were so many of them," Margaret continued. "We came out of the cottage and they rushed us from down the road. We shot at them and tried to get back into the house but they were too quick. We got off a couple more shots then they were on us."

"You got some of them before they got you anyway," John confirmed.

"I know, but they were frantic, barking and biting like they were mad."

Emma started in alarm. "Mad? You don't mean …?"

"Rabies?" Fhionna asked, then she shook her head. "No, the government sent out a notice to all vets about a week before the deaths started to escalate. It was already bad on the continent by then and they ordered all animals in quarantine to be destroyed. Any animal that wasn't killed will have died in its cage. I don't know how far they got but they also started to put down all the dangerous animals and reptiles in the zoos. The non-dangerous species were to be released, to fend for themselves. The chances of rabies getting into the country now are less than they were before the deaths."

"But what about the Channel Tunnel?" asked John.

Fhionna's face wrinkled as if in confusion then it cleared. "Of course, you wouldn't know. I was talking to a vet friend in Dover after the extermination order came through. When the situation became serious on the continent, our government was still keeping it quiet that there had been many deaths here. A mass of people tried to come through from France and the government ordered the tunnel to be flooded. Apparently it was built into the design from the start, at the MOD's insistence, in case there was a threat of invasion."

"Flooded? With the people still in it?" queried Sunflower, aghast.

Fhionna nodded. "They tried to warn them but most of the mob took no notice, they kept coming. I heard over four hundred were in the tunnel when they let the water in. It probably only made a few days difference for them anyway."

"Then why are the dogs so vicious, if they aren't sick?" asked Emma.

"They've gone wild. There hasn't been enough time for natural selection to take its toll, so all sorts of dogs are hunting in packs and probably not doing it very well. They're hungry, frustrated, confused and desperate. They might even blame people because they're not being fed any longer," Fhionna told her.

"Most of them will die come the winter, if not before," John added. "Eventually the ones that survive will interbreed and we'll probably end up with a new species of wild dog, to replace the wolves that were once native to Scotland."

"What happened to the rest of the ones that attacked Margaret and Tony?" asked Leah.

"Margaret and Tony accounted for quite a few. I got three more; the remaining four or five ran off," John told her.

Fhionna nodded as she finished suturing the wound in Tony's neck. "There, stitching to make a quilt maker proud. You're lucky it missed the artery, young man. Now, I'll give both of you some jabs and a course of antibiotics to take for the next seven days. James and I will stay a few extra days, if that's all right, Emma, so that I can keep an eye on things, but I think you'll both be fine."

She checked the bandages that Sunflower and Leah had applied. "That's good. Let's get Tony to bed. I've given him a sedative. Margaret, you go with him, or rest in the sitting room with your legs up, please. Emma, how about another cup of coffee?"

Hunters

Sweat trickled down John's neck. Slowly he reached out his hand to Dan's back and gently but firmly pressed the boy down onto the ground.

He positioned his mouth close to Dan's ear and whispered, "If you stick your head up here the rabbits will see you. There's no cover in front of or behind you. They'll see your head bobbing up and it'll frighten them."

Dan gave a tiny nod of understanding.

John pointed to a spot a little way forward. "See ahead of us, those big thistles? If you look between those, the rabbits won't see you and you can watch what they're doing. If they're sitting up, looking around, they're nervous, so we'll keep still for a few minutes until they relax."

Dan's head bobbed up and down eagerly and he took a deep breath before he moved. Keeping his head low and his stomach on the ground he began to creep towards the thistles. He crawled using his elbows and knees; his little fists turned upwards, his air rifle across his forearms.

The rifle was a .177 BSA Meteor Mk6 Standard. John had shortened the stock to fit Dan's small frame. The ten foot-pounds of muzzle energy it produced were ample for practise and for hunting, out to the twenty-five yards he currently allowed Dan. The rifle was not fitted with optical sights either. John wanted the boy to learn to use the open sights effectively first. They were quite adequate for the range, particularly with Dan's young eyes and it avoided adding any extra to the less than six pounds weight of the rifle.

Dan reached the thistle patch and worked his camouflaged face close enough to see through them. The field in front of him sloped away from the grassy mound at the base of the fence, beside which they had been crawling. The well-drained hillside, rough grass and patches of gorse provided a near perfect environment for the rabbits, which were hopping around, chasing one another and eating, totally unaware of his presence.

As he watched, a large buck rabbit chased another in a circle then stopped again to feed. The rabbit it had been chasing ran closer to Dan then it too paused to nibble at the grass. Dan slowly turned his head towards John then nodded in the direction of the field of rabbits. The green netting tied bandana-style around his head scratched against the thistles as he did so. John crawled forwards; using the same technique he had taught Dan.

The rifle resting across his own arms was also a BSA but in this case the Meteor's big brother, a .177 Supersport Mk2 carbine. This rifle was fitted with a silencer and a Simmons 6-18 x 42 Whitetail scope sight, with a matt 'black granite' finish.

He reached Dan's side and peered between the plant stems. He estimated the rabbit at twenty-two yards. Only a hint of breeze stirred the air and the Meteor was sighted in for twenty-five yards. Dan could aim dead on. The rabbit was a buck, three quarters grown, young and healthy, probably one of a late litter from last year. John nodded his assent then edged sideways a few feet to give him room.

Dan rolled onto his side. With his right hand he grasped the small of the stock. Reaching forward with his left hand he gripped the Meteor's barrel immediately behind the fore sight and gave it a sharp tug, unlatching the barrel at the breech. Steadily he pulled the barrel towards him. The molybdenum grease-coated spring compressed silently, as the cocking lever fixed below the breech pushed back the piston. With a muted click, the notch in the piston locked into place with the corresponding sear on the trigger.

From the leather pouch John had made for him, Dan took a .177 Eley Wasp pellet. He inspected it carefully to make sure he could find no damage or deformation of the skirt, nor any dirt adhering to it. Satisfied, he pushed it into place in the breech then closed the barrel.

Rolling onto his front he pushed himself back from the thistles then brought the rifle into his shoulder. Using his toes he eased himself forwards slightly, so that the muzzle cleared a blade of grass but did not protrude beyond the thistles. Then Dan settled his body, spread his legs for balance and consciously relaxed, slowing his breathing as he had been taught. It wasn't easy. He was excited and desperate to make John proud of him. This was his first shot at a rabbit.

Mirroring Dan's actions, John prepared his own rifle. He would not fire unless the boy's shot wounded the rabbit. If Dan made a clean hit or a clean miss, he could discharge his own pellet safely into the ground afterwards. Letting go with his right hand, John pushed his holster, containing the pistol he was carrying in case of an encounter with dogs, round to the small of his back where it was more comfortable.

He could sense his pupil's nervous tension but the lad was doing well. Dan's rifle barrel was shaking slightly with his excitement but steadied now as he calmed himself. John breathed out and took aim, waiting.

The rabbit hopped a pace closer, faced to the side and sat up, its nose twitching Perhaps it sensed something, perhaps their movements had caught its eye or one of them had made a slight sound that its sensitive ears had detected. It tensed. From beside John came the sharp crack of the Meteor's discharge.

In the view of his scope the rabbit stiffened, stretching upwards, then slowly toppled onto its side. Its back legs kicked twice and then it was still. John looked towards Dan. The boy exhaled with a whoosh and grinned widely. John smiled back and nodded towards the rabbit. Dan leapt to his feet, climbed over the wire fence and ran towards his prize.

John stood, pivoted away from the field into which Dan had run, pointed his rifle at a patch of soft mud, released the safety catch and fired. The pellet embedded itself in the ground with a thud. He followed Dan over the fence into the field now empty of rabbits, except the one at which the boy was staring.

As John joined them and dropped his hand onto the lad's shoulder, he could see that it had been a good shot. A small disturbance of the fur on the rabbit's head was the only sign of where the pellet had hit but it was in line between the eye and the base of the ear.

"Well done, Dan. That was a good stalk and a good shot," he complimented.

Dan's expression was less certain now and John could guess exactly what he was thinking. He still vividly remembered his own first kill and the turmoil of emotions that accompanied it. He squatted beside the rabbit, picked it up and stroked its fur.

"You know, some people say that the only reason rabbits were put on the earth, was to provide food for other things. They make all their predators work for their meal but they taste really good, aren't very bright, and don't live long even if they don't become a meal for something."

He smiled gently at the boy's interested face. "Everything lives and everything dies. In every case one animal can't live unless something else dies. It's part of the process of life and it benefits both species. In our situation we're closer to Nature than we were before and I think both this rabbit and we are fulfilling our natural purpose. What do you think?"

Dan tilted his head quizzically. "Is this what you meant when you talked about respecting what you hunt?"

John nodded. "Yes. You treated this rabbit with respect. You wouldn't have hunted it if we weren't going to eat it or unless it was eating our crops. When you did hunt, you did it in a way that didn't frighten your quarry, or put it under stress and not until you had practised enough on targets to know you could kill it quickly and with the minimum of pain. If we were to throw this rabbit into the bushes now, it would be a waste and there would be no respect." He winked, and then said, "I think we should clean it and have it for dinner. What do you say?"

"Can I do it?" Dan asked.

John laughed. "Too right you can do it. You don't get all the fun part without doing the messy bit as well."

He first showed Dan how to lay the rabbit on its back and stroke his thumb down its belly to squeeze out the urine. Then he took out his old Opinel No8, twisted the metal collar to lock open the blade and handed Dan the knife.

"If we only wanted the meat, we'd skin the rabbit here and leave the pelt and guts for the foxes or crows but I'm curing the skins so we'll paunch it now and I'll show you how to skin it later."

Dan nodded his understanding, so John continued.

"First take a pinch of the skin on the belly and pull it towards you."

Dan did as he was told. "Like this?"

"That's it. Now push the point of the knife in just enough to make a small hole … Good lad. Now hold the knife in the palm of your hand with the edge up," he adjusted the knife's position for Dan, "so that your fingertips shield the point. That's so you don't puncture the insides. Push into the hole you've made and cut forwards towards the chest."

The sharp edge of the blade sliced easily through the skin and fur, revealing the rabbit's innards. Dan pulled back his head and wrinkled his face in disgust. "Awwww, phew, that stinks!"

John chuckled. "You'll get used to it. We haven't finished yet, now comes the messy part. Put down the knife. Now reach inside and pull out all the guts."

Dan's mouth dropped open. "Eh?"

"You can't get them out otherwise. Come on, your hands will wash."

Reluctantly, his face screwed up in revulsion, Dan complied.

"Good lad. Now push your finger inside and right out back between the legs."

Dan did as he was told causing a few droppings to pop out of the anus.

"Nearly done. At the front of where you pulled out the guts there's a membrane, a thin layer of skin. Push your fingers through that right to the front then pull out the heart and lungs."

Again Dan complied.

"Okay, that's it done. Not so bad, was it?"

Dan was not at all sure he agreed and he frowned. "Yuck!"

John showed him the liver and how to check for white spots, which might be a sign of infection, and where the kidneys had been left in the body cavity.

"You can eat the liver, if it's in good condition; you just have to pinch out the gall bladder … like this." He pinched the small tube at the top of the dark green, bile-filled sack between his nails, pulled it away from the liver then threw it out into the field

"If the bile from the gall bladder gets onto the meat it will spoil it, make it taste bitter, so be careful when you're doing that. If you're really hungry you can eat the heart and lungs too and we could use the rest of the guts for fish bait or hang them over the river until the maggots that drop off attract fish. Then we'd use maggots to fish there ourselves. We're still finding dead fish along the banks though, so we're leaving the fishing for now, maybe next year. The rabbit will do for today."

John hocked the rabbit, threaded one back leg between the bone and tendon of the other leg then handed it to Dan to carry.

"Right, let's get back and show them what a hunter you've become."

Side by side, with Dan swinging his kill and regularly lifting it to admire, the successful hunters headed home. One was quietly proud, the other beaming.

Emma met them as they strolled into the farmyard. "Hello. Home are the hunters, home from the hill…" she misquoted.

John winked at her. "Dan is the hunter, not me."

"I see that. Well done, Dan." She hesitated, and then asked, "John, have you got time to talk for a few minutes?"

"Let us skin this rabbit and get cleaned up, then I'll be with you. Ten minutes, okay?"

"Okay."

"How's Tony this morning?" John asked. "We were out before they were up, I think."

"He's fine." Emma assured him. "The infection that developed in his leg seems to be clearing up well. Doesn't seem like a week ago since the dogs attacked, does it?"

John shook his head.

Emma followed them into the end of the cattle shed, where John had set aside other furs for preservation. She watched as he showed Dan how to skin the rabbit. When he finished, John pinned the pelt to a board, ready for scraping and curing. He and Dan washed in the sink at the end of the shed and then Dan ran off to take the rabbit to Margaret in the kitchen.

"Okay, I'm all yours. What's up?" John asked Emma.

"There's nothing wrong, but your coming in here is what it's all about. I've been thinking that we ought to do some building while the weather is fine."

"Building what?"

"A new barn for when we cut the hay, a stable, a new workshop and anything else we might need."

Emma let her gaze roam around the dingy old shelter, with its mingled smells of horses, straw and rabbit. Knockside had been almost perfect for setting up their new community but the fire had cost them dearly.

John's eyes followed Emma's as they tracked around their surroundings. "You're right," he agreed, "and now is the time to do it. I wonder if we could persuade Martin to come up for a while to help out. We're going to need to build a forge too, eventually."

Emma blinked. "Why do we need a forge?"

"If we're going to work the horses, they'll need to be re-shod every couple of months or so. We brought some shoes from the museum but they were ruined in the fire."

"Do you know how to shoe a horse, or make the shoes for that matter?" Emma asked.

"No," John admitted. "So the sooner we build the forge and somebody starts to learn, before we need them, the better. Didn't Tony say he was good at metalwork?"

"At school yes, but I'm not sure he'll ever have made a horseshoe."

"Well, either we learn to do it ourselves or we find someone who can and who'll trade their skills for whatever we can provide. Either way, it's one of those skills that we're going to need again."

Emma looked doubtful. "But even if we did find someone with the skills and who would come, what could we trade? I doubt we'll have much food to spare."

"I've been thinking about that. I can cure skins and I've started experimenting with tanning leather, from the hides of the deer and cows we kill for meat. All my tools for leatherwork are still down in my workshop at the cottage. I can make all sorts of harness and other goods; it was how I made my living before the 'flu', after all." He took a breath. "Then we have the medical potions you and Leah are working up. If we can find some hives, Sunny can produce honey, and candles from the wax. Margaret and Tony have made a smoker and a dehydrator, so we might have spare jerky; damned good it is too. We could even hire Dan out as a rabbit catcher."

"You have been thinking about it, haven't you?"

"Well, I reckoned that, if communities did get together, it was going to come to trade eventually. It'd be a big community that would have all the skills they needed in-house. Sergei and Fhionna are already ahead of us. They're like the traders of the Middle Ages, travelling around selling their goods and services as they go. There might be others take up with that idea. And what about the people in Glasgow? They have the right idea but too many are living off what they can scrounge rather than what they produce. Still, given time, that might change."

"We should talk to all of the others on the radio network about this. Develop a list of the skills or products available in each group, so that everyone knows where they can trade and for what." Emma suggested.

"Good idea. We could call it Emma's Yellow Pages. It might save a lot of work too. If there's already someone who is a farrier and wants to trade for something we have, we won't need to build a forge or learn to make horseshoes, though we might do anyway, as insurance."

Emma's face grew sad. "Alan should have lived to see this. It could be the start of what he talked about."

"I don't know about that, but it might be the start of a real hope of survival, especially for Dan and the other youngsters."

Emma's mouth dropped open and her eyes widened. "Of course, Yellow Pages. Damn! I feel like an idiot."

"What?"

"Yellow Pages, John. We've been relying on our knowledge of the local area and what we've seen as we drove around but even though the phones don't work, the directories are still good as lists of where we could locate things. We might find bee keepers listed where we could get hives for Sunny, for a start."

John nodded enthusiastically. "It's certainly worth a look. Why didn't we think of this before?" he asked.

"With no phones working, it never occurred to me."

"Nor me, but with directories and maps we can locate things we need and choose the places that are going to be closest and safest to get them. The new listings are still going to be important though, old directories might help us to find things but for skills we need up-to-date information."

They were leaving the shed when Sunny came running into the yard waving her arms, and jumping up and down. "Lambs! One of the sheep has two lambs. Do come and see."

Margaret followed her into the yard, the Baikal side-by-side hammer gun over her arm and a Browning pistol, which she had requested from John after the dog attack, holstered at her waist. John coughed to suppress a laugh; all she needed was a set of buckskins and they would have to break into a chorus of Oklahoma.

Margaret called out, "And more are on the way."

Emma linked her arm through John's and together they strolled towards the track, to have a look at the new arrivals.

"I think the building is going to have to wait a while," he said. "The lambs will need guarding and we have to get the rest of the planting done this month, both in the garden and in the fields."

Emma agreed. "We need to move the cows on to the next field and move the sheep and horses onto the one the cows will have just left too. It won't be long before we have litters of piglets as well, thanks to the boar that got through the fence. I wonder if any of the group from Lossiemouth would come to give us a hand, in exchange for produce later."

"We could ask, but I think we might need them even more come harvest time and by then we'd have some of the garden crops or bigger lambs and pigs to pay them with there and then. We don't want to pester them too much."

"I suppose not," Emma sighed. "It looks as if we're going to have to plan on doing whatever we can, with the people who are here and no-one else most of the time. It shouldn't take us long to finish the planting though and I suppose we could let the sheep and pigs go free. You could hunt one when we wanted the meat."

"We could, but that would take more time than when they're close and they'd be more vulnerable to the dogs. Let's see how it goes," John suggested. "If it turns out that we can't cope with everything as farmers, then we might have to go back to being hunter-gatherers for some things."

Emma nudged him. "But you'd enjoy that, you know you would."

John smiled. "I don't deny it's easier on the back than planting and hoeing but we need to grow things to build a surplus for the winter. In some societies, in cold climates, they either kill off surplus stock and preserve the meat or let the beasts free to roam in winter and gather up again in the spring.

"Hill farmers do that with their sheep anyway. It saves having to grow crops to feed livestock over the bad months and in some ways it's good for the animals, because the weaker ones don't survive. It leads to stronger stock in the end. The disadvantage is having to hunt in harsh weather, if you haven't preserved enough."

For a while they stood in companionable silence, enjoying the moment while they watched the sheep and lambs. The sun warmed them. The sheep bleated peacefully in the field. From a tree nearby a woodpigeon cooed out it's mating call. John took a deep breath, unwilling to spoil the mood but knowing there was still much to do and decide.

"But to get back to what we were talking about before, we can all discuss a list of things we still need, or need to replace, and use the directory to find the best source. We should certainly try to locate some bees and look for those building materials, even if we don't fetch them yet."

Emma nodded in agreement. "I think we should see if there's a source for windmills too, not big ones, one of those that go on the roof or on boats to charge batteries. We can't keep running the Land Rover as a battery charger, it uses too much fuel and we haven't been out any distance for a fortnight."

They stopped their conversation again for a while, to lean on the field gate while they watched the two lambs staggering around, their noses battering up at their mother's belly as they suckled. But too soon the peace was shattered by the clamour of a dog pack over the other side of the hill.

John lifted his head. "I could put down some more poison. It sorted out that first pack that attacked the sheep."

Emma's brows knitted. "Have we still got any?"

"It's in my garage. I left it there to be well away from all the other stores."

"I suppose so then."

"I'll take a walk round after we've moved the animals, see if I can spot a recent kill to use. I'd sooner not attract them in this direction at all if we can help it."

Emma nodded. "I don't like using poison but it's better than losing the lambs. Only, be careful, John, please."

#

John plodded back towards Knockside. He had laid out poison on the opposite side of the hill from the farm. The dogs had killed a sheep and her lamb from a flock that roamed wild there but had run off at his approach. He shivered a little in the chill wind that replaced the morning's warmth and looked up at the gathering rain clouds darkening the evening gloom. He was walking along a ride in the wood, alert for either dogs or a shot at a deer, when he saw the horseman. The horse was pulled in to the side of the track and its rider had parted the branches of a tree, to hide him from view while letting him scan the area below him.

The man sat easily on the big brown mare. It was a fine looking horse John had to admit. A horse built for riding not for working. The man was the opposite. The rolled-up sleeves of his brown and green check shirt revealed thick, muscular forearms and the material above his elbows was taut over his biceps. Close-cut, dark hair showed from under the brim of the green canvas Tilley hat that shaded his eyes. His shoulders were broad and his belly flat as he sat up in the saddle surveying Knockside and the fields around it through a pair of binoculars.

Behind him, a neatly tied bedroll with a camouflage waterproof jacket over it was fastened across full saddlebags. The butt of the rifle protruding from the scabbard in front of his right leg looked to belong to an M16. A 12 bore Benelli M3 Super 90 shotgun was slung muzzle down across his back, over a sleeveless, green, fibre pile body warmer.

For a moment John puzzled over what was unusual, and then he realised that the sling allowed the gun to be worn so that it was not only muzzle down but also the right way up. It was an arrangement that would allow the Benelli to be swung forward for instant use. John had never used one but he knew the Benelli was of superior quality. Few had been available to civilians in the UK.

John had been stalking silently forwards and was now a few paces off the track, watching the man from beside a mature Sitka spruce, about ten paces behind him.

"Do you know if the people down there welcome strangers, or are they likely to shoot without asking your business?" the rider asked.

The man's voice shocked John for a moment. Firstly because John had been sure he hadn't been detected, secondly because it was a cultured, though not affected, Home Counties accent. He glanced around but saw no one else to whom the question could have been directed. He stayed where he was and took a deep breath before he answered. "They won't shoot you without good reason but they've dealt with trouble before."

The man had still not tried to turn around. "I guessed that. Someone who knew what they were doing put those defences together. You?"

"I had a hand in it," John admitted.

"You're damn good in the woods too. I never heard you, the horse did. Do you mind if we talk face-to-face?"

John tightened his grip on the stock of his rifle and pushed off the safety catch. "As long as you keep your hand away from that Benelli."

The man pulled back gently on the reins and squeezed in with his knee. The mare backed up a couple of paces and slowly turned around to its left. Even before it started to move John had sidled back and across to a different tree.

The rider's eyes settled on John's previous position then scanned rapidly for the three seconds it took him to detect John's new stance. He nodded slightly as if in silent confirmation to himself. "Damn good," he murmured under his breath.

John watched him ease his shoulders under the body warmer. He knew that the rider understood that had he reached for the shotgun as he guided the horse around, he would now be dead.

"It's going to be a bad night but it's been a warm ride today. Do you think I could get some water for the horse down there? I did have the bug by the way. I take it all your group did too."

"We've all had it," John confirmed. "But before I take you down there, would you mind telling me what you're doing here?"

"Following a … passion," he said. Then added, "Riding around the country, living off the land. It's a dream come true."

"Have you had contact with anyone else recently?"

"I haven't even spoken to anyone for nearly a month."

John nodded then stepped from behind the tree. "Ride on down, I won't be far behind you."

"Thank you. I wouldn't be bothering you but my horse could do with some oats as well as water and it doesn't look like a night for camping in the woods. I'll happily sleep in the barn and I'll pay you in work but that's about all I can offer."

John's face remained passive but he felt his suspicion ease, a little, at the offer of payment. "A hand with the work is always welcome but we can talk about that later. I'm John McLean. I'll introduce you to the others when we get down there."

The visitor nudged his horse forward and started down the hill at a walk. As he twisted in the saddle his jacket rose up, giving John a glimpse of the distinctive handle of a Gerber Mk2 fighting knife. John's eyes narrowed. This man might be living off the land but the weapons he carried belonged to a soldier, not a countryman.

Sunflower was in the kitchen helping Margaret prepare dinner. She peered out at the gathering storm and saw John and the horseman coming down the hill. "We are going to have one extra for dinner, Margaret." she announced.

Margaret looked up from the garlic she was chopping, one of the last in their stock she had noticed, and crossed the big country kitchen to join Sunny at the window. "Hmmmm, John Wayne by the looks of it."

Sunny smirked. "I better tell Leah, she won't want to miss this."

Margaret frowned. "Doesn't it ever bother you, Sunny?"

"What, Leah's interest in other people?" She smiled gently. "No, of course not. I do not own Leah, I am simply grateful for what we have together."

Margaret shook her head in disbelief. "If it was a woman riding in and Tony showed an interest, I'd tie his balls up so tight he'd not want to think about her, let alone try anything."

Sunny giggled. "Yes but Tony would probably enjoy it."

Margaret merely grinned and threw a piece of garlic at Sunny's fast departing back.

By the time John and the rider reached the farmyard gate, Emma, Leah, Tony and Dan were waiting for them.

As Emma expected, the man's gaze stopped when it reached Leah but the reaction was not at all what she had supposed. Instead of the intake of breath and beginnings of a smile she had come to consider normal, she saw his lips tighten and his eyes narrow for an instant before his face again became impassive. She frowned a little, in a concern she didn't yet understand. "Glad you're back, John," she greeted, "and with a visitor too."

The man on the horse raised his hat and smiled at her. "Sean Applegarth, at your service."

Emma nodded in return. "We're preparing dinner, Mr Applegarth, please come in."

"Thank you, but I'll take care of my horse first, if you don't mind."

John walked up beside him. "We're using the cattle shed until we build new stables; I'll show you."

Leah stepped towards the newcomer. "Would you like me to give you a hand ... with your horse?" she asked.

Applegarth's face remained blank. "I'll manage," he said, and then after the briefest hesitation added, "thank you all the same."

John showed Applegarth where the feed and care equipment were stored and when he had finished grooming and feeding his horse, they walked across to the house. Applegarth carried his rifle and saddlebags. The Benelli shotgun was on its sling over his right shoulder.

"Nice little commune you have here, McLean. How many of you are there?"

"Seven now, including the boy you saw. We're doing all right," John told him.

The corner of the other man's lips twitched. "If you like this sort of thing. I prefer the open road."

As they entered the house, Dan hurried to greet them. "Emma says I have to show Mr Applegarth to the guest room."

John smiled at the boy. "Thank you, Dan. You'll be more comfortable there than in the barn, Applegarth. Oh and there's plenty of hot water."

The horseman's eyebrows rose. "Enough for a bath?"

"Plenty," John repeated. "Emma said dinner should be ready in about an hour. We eat in the kitchen," he pointed in the right direction, "through there."

Applegarth nodded his approval. "Thank you. In an hour then."

John watched, as their guest followed Dan down the corridor and disappeared into the room to which he was shown. Then he headed for the gunroom to put away his rifle. As he was about to leave the room he stopped. After a moment's thought, he picked up one of the Browning pistols, loaded the magazine and slapped it into place. Then he walked to the sitting room, where he pushed it under the cushion of his chair by the fire.

He didn't know why he was so uneasy. Applegarth had been polite and hadn't done anything to cause suspicion, though his reaction to Leah had been as much of a surprise to John as it had been to Emma. He could guess at a couple of unsavoury reasons for it, but that was simply supposition and he had no evidence to support the prejudice. Nevertheless, he decided, it would do no harm to be cautious.

The dinner of steak cooked in red wine and garlic, tinned potatoes that had been sliced and fried in olive oil, and tinned peas improved with fresh wild mint Leah had discovered on one of her forays, was fit for any guest.

Applegarth sat back, took a sip from his glass of wine, the same type of Burgundy in which the steak had been cooked, and sighed contentedly. "Well, I thought I did all right for myself but after a hot bath and a meal like that, I'm no longer so sure." He bowed his head towards Margaret. "My compliments to the chef, ma'am."

Margaret glowed at the praise. "So how do you live, Mr Applegarth?" she asked.

"Sean, please," he requested. "I hunt game or sometimes take a sheep or cow. I find wild plants although I occasionally come across an isolated house or farm with something edible in the garden or fields. I take water from streams and lakes," he took another sip of wine then raised his glass, "but this is much better. Usually I build a quick shelter for the night, unless I can find a barn or bothy that is empty." He looked down, as though embarrassed, before returning his gaze to Margaret. "The only luxury I take chances for is my supply of coffee. Anything else I can do without, but if I don't have coffee in the morning, I am one very grumpy bear. I haven't been into anywhere bigger than a small village since all this started and, usually, I don't even go into houses."

John hesitated but then asked, "So where did you get the guns? There weren't many like that about, even before the deaths."

Applegarth locked eyes with him for five tension-stretched seconds before he answered quietly, "I already had those."

John's eyebrows rose but he said nothing.

Emma broke the silence. "That was a wonderful meal, Margaret, Sunny. Shall we all go through to the other room?"

"Good idea, Emma. Time to relax, I think," John agreed.

"I don't want to be rude but we're going to have an early night," Margaret told them, "if you'll excuse us, Sean, everyone?"

But even after settling in the sitting room, John did not relax. The level of the Dalwhinnie single malt Emma poured for him hardly lessened in his glass, though he joined the conversation often enough. Applegarth on the other hand seemed to drink freely and had begun to laugh loudly by the time the radio call from Sergei and Martin came through. Neither he nor John joined the others around the radio, though John made pretence of concentrating on what was happening, as he also pretended to sip at his drink.

It was Sergei's voice from the speakers. "We did not go to Edinburgh as we had thought. We went first to Fife. A community like yours lives there, eight people near a place called Kinross, on the shore of the Lake Leven but we did not find any others and they do not know of anyone else."

In the background they heard Martin correcting him. "Loch Leven, Sergei, not Lake Leven. Och, you're worse than a Sassenach."

Sergei came back on the radio. "Forgive my friend Martin, it is not a lock, it is big area of water. It is lake I think. Over." But he chuckled and they knew that he was teasing Martin.

"Are you going on to Edinburgh now, Sergei? Over," asked Emma.

"Yes, we are now outside Aberdour, but there is big smoke from direction of Edinburgh and other places to the west as well. This could not be from Glasgow. It is very strange. Over."

They continued to chat to Sergei and others for some time. Sunny asked if anyone else wanted another drink.

Applegarth stood up, shaking his head. "Thank you, Sunflower, and thank you all for your hospitality but I think I've had enough. If you will excuse me, I believe I'll get some sleep. It has been a long time since I slept in clean sheets, or in a real bed for that matter."

With a round of well-wishes he left and they soon heard his room door open and close. After the radio call John, Emma, Sunny and Leah sat talking for a while before eventually drifting off to their rooms. It was still dark when they were woken by Sunny's scream.

For a moment John stood outside his room listening. The scream ripped through the house again. Yet it came not from upstairs where Sunny and Leah slept but from the direction of the sitting room. He sprinted down the hall and whirled in through the doorway.

Applegarth was stooped, bending over the cringing form of Sunny, the top of her nightdress bunched in his left hand. John saw Leah rise from where she had been lying on the floor, behind the horseman. Applegarth pushed Sunny away, releasing his grip on her and from behind him, as he started to straighten, Leah's left hand darted down over his face. Her index and second finger hooked into his nostrils and she yanked back fiercely. At the same time, the heel of her right hand drove in hard against the side of the attacker's temple.

Applegarth roared but wrenched his face away from Leah's fingers then deliberately threw himself backwards. As he hit the floor he rolled onto his shoulders, scrunched up his legs then kicked violently upwards into Leah's abdomen. Lifted from her feet by the force of the blow she hurtled backwards and fell over the coffee table. Even as John advanced to join the fight, Applegarth curled his legs back under him, flung his body forward and leapt to his feet.

As John reached out to grab the man's shoulder, Applegarth spun towards him. His left hand flashed backwards, the fingers together and stiffened. The leading edge caught John across the throat and he staggered backwards, coughing as he tried to draw breath. Continuing his turn and stepping forward on his right foot, Applegarth drove his right hand towards John's face. His hand was cocked back, his fingers clawed and the base of his palm aimed at John's nose for a killing blow.

Through the tears of pain streaming from his eyes John saw the blow coming and recognised it. He could not avoid it completely but he lifted his head as it struck. The blow, driven by the hugely muscled arm, caught John under the cheekbone and he reeled back, his head spinning. Desperately, he dived for his chair and the pistol under the seat. He had almost reached it when three rapid blows smashed into his kidneys and a fourth hammered down between his shoulders. His vision flushed red and as he fell, darkness descended on him. Unconscious, he collapsed over the seat of the chair.

As Applegarth stepped towards the fallen man, his face a mask of murderous intent, Emma entered the room. Seeing that John was his target, she leapt onto the assailant's shoulders screaming like a wildcat. Her fingers clawed around his head searching for his eyes but he reached back, grabbed her hair and quickly bent forwards throwing her over his head. Emma landed on her feet but off balance and tumbled forwards against the wall. As Applegarth moved towards Emma, Leah regained her feet, picked up a stumpy Dalwhinnie whisky bottle and hurled it at his head.

The bottle impacted Applegarth's temple and he stumbled sideways with a curse. Straightening again he kicked the bottle away from him, towards Sunny who cowered in a corner shaking and sobbing. Applegarth glared at Leah, his new target, and pointed at her. "They should never have let you escape, you bitch, now I'll finish the job."

As he stepped forwards, Emma swung backhanded away from the mantelpiece, a candlestick grasped in her hand. But Applegarth saw it coming. He caught her wrist and dragged her in front of him. His left hand clamped over her chin and his right hand reached behind her head, ready to twist it around and forwards to break her neck.

Instinctively, Emma tucked in her chin and as the web of his hand slid into her mouth she bit down hard. At the same time she stamped down her right heel with all her might onto his instep. While Applegarth growled and fought to pull his hand away, Emma's right hand reached to her waist. Under her pyjama top her fingers closed around the handle of the kitchen knife she had taken from beneath her pillow. Drawing it from her waistband she flung off the sheath John had made for her. Swiftly she reversed the knife in her hand, then drove it edge uppermost back into her assailant's thigh. As the blade sliced deep into his flesh, she dragged it upwards.

Applegarth hissed in pain but his grip loosened and Emma wrenched herself away from him, twisting to face him as she did so. She reversed the knife once more and held it point-first toward him. With a snort of derision, he reached behind him and drew the double-edged Gerber Mk 2 fighting knife. Rising behind him, Leah now swivelled as she kicked with all her power into the back of his knee. Under the force from that shapely, toned limb and on a leg already weakened by Emma's stab and slash, the knee buckled and, as Applegarth staggered forward, Leah leapt towards him and grabbed his right wrist with both hands.

With a snarl he threw her off and stepped towards her, the Gerber raised to stab down. But the knife that speared into flesh was not his. Throwing all her weight into the blow, Emma lunged forward and drove the razor-sharp six-inch blade of her knife into the left side of his neck. As it penetrated, she twisted the knife and then slashed it backwards and out. Blood spurted from the wound, drenching Emma and fountaining over everything around them.

Applegarth dropped his knife and clamped both hands over his neck but even a surgeon could not have repaired that awful wound in time to do any good. Already his vision was failing, his focus narrowing into a tunnel of blackness centred by a bright white light, as his brain was starved of oxygen. As he sunk to his knees he tried to raise his head to speak. Emma fought to hear but his last murmur was indistinct. "You silly bitch, I was your last hope. It should have been her!"

Gradually the force of spurting blood dropped to a pulse and then a trickle and finally stopped. The outward flow of the huge dark red pool stilled, until only a reaching finger of it trickled down a dip in the polished boards, toward the hearth rug where it soaked and stained through the fibres. Emma sat down hard on the heavy wooden coffee table. Leah collapsed into a cross-legged sitting position on the floor. Sunny's sobs stopped now, as she stared in horror at the body on the floor and in almost equal horror at Leah and Emma.

Consciousness slowly returned to John and he stirred. His lower back burned and sent daggers of pain through his innards as he tried to rise. His face was stiff and ached like a bad tooth. He rolled over and shook his head to clear his vision. The tableau in front of him gradually swam into focus. He took in the body on the floor, the blood and the still dripping red blade in Emma's hand, the exhausted state of Emma and Leah, Sunflower's awed stare.

Forcing himself to his feet against a flood of pain and dizziness, John stumbled over to Emma and sat down beside her. Gently he pulled the knife from her fingers and laid it on the table. Equally as gently he guided her shaking shoulders towards him and pressed her head against his chest. He cleared his still numbed throat then asked, "Are you okay, Leah?"

Leah nodded dully then unfolded from her sitting position and went to kneel beside and hold Sunny.

"Leah," John croaked, "what the hell started all that?"

She shrugged. "Sunny heard a noise down here, it's directly under our bedroom. We came downstairs to find out what was happening. Applegarth was at the radio. I'm not sure if he was trying to call someone or damage it in some way. When I asked what he was doing he hit me and then turned on Sunny. She screamed, I went for him but he knocked me down again and then went back at Sunny. That was when you and Emma arrived."

John shook his head and gave his attention back to Emma.

Leah gradually persuaded her lover from the floor. They circled the pool of blood, keeping their eyes averted from the body and Leah steered Sunny upstairs. There she gently put her into the bed they shared, covered her with a blanket and left to have a shower.

Meanwhile, John lifted Emma and eased her back to her room. Leaving her sitting on the bed, he started water running for a bath and added a relaxing herbal mix that Leah had produced. Returning to the bedroom, he carefully helped Emma to remove her clothes, then picked his unresisting friend up in his arms and carried her to the bath. With water still running, he washed the blood from her face, hair and neck, pulled the plug to let the water drain and then replaced it for the bath to fill again. When it was nearly full John gently pressed Emma down into the foamy water, turned off the taps and left her to soak. Gathering her blood-soaked clothes from the bedroom floor on the way, he left and returned to the sitting room.

After dropping Emma's clothes on the body, John went out to fetch Margaret and Tony from their cottage. He quickly explained what had happened and then together they returned to the main house, dragged the corpse onto the ruined hearth rug and out into the yard. When they had loaded it into the back of the Land Rover, Tony and Margaret drove away. John had been unable to answer many of their questions but left them with instructions to thoroughly search Applegarth before they dumped him for the dogs. Then he returned to Emma.

She was still lying in the bath but her face was more alive and she blushed shyly as he entered. She said nothing as he took her hands, helped her to stand, then wrapped a towel around her and pulled the plug. But as he made to leave she tightened her grip around his fingers to hold him back, while she stepped out of the bath towards him. With a shrug of her shoulders the towel fell away. Stretching upwards, she slid her hand behind his head, pulled his face down towards her and pressed her mouth hard against his. When she felt him start to respond she leaned away, briefly gazed into his eyes, and then led him towards her bed.

Workers and Queens

The first thing Emma saw when she opened her eyes was John's smile. She pulled herself forward, kissed him on the lips, and then snuggled down with her head against his chest. In return he enfolded her in the comfort and security of his arms. Sunlight warmed her naked back. The scent of musk and fading memories of passion filtered into her nostrils and awakened her desire once more. Pushing away the sheets as she moved, Emma slowly kissed her way down his body.

Her mind drifted back to the night before. John was kissing her, caressing, gentle and careful. She understood his kindness and concern but this was not what she wanted now. The ghosts were gone, her desire was overwhelming and she didn't need kindness, every muscle was alive with longing for passion. She rolled him over, mounted him and impaled herself on him. He responded with equal urgency, clutching, squeezing her hips and bottom, forcing her face towards him, snatching at her lips with his. While she thrust herself repeatedly down onto him his hand dived down her belly, teasing her clitoris with his fingers in time to her own mad writhing and pummelling. Time and again she rose and fell until her thighs ached and she flung back her head, praying to the heavens for the release she desperately craved. Nothing could have denied her and wave after wave of pulsing tension began to flood through her body until, with a deep and wordless cry, she threw herself forward, her fingers digging deep into her lover's shoulders while she trembled and gasped, before collapsing on top of him in spent and glorious liberation.

Later Emma had accepted John's initiative of more gentle lovemaking, but still she could not totally relinquish control. She might have suppressed the memories of what had happened in

Aberdeen but it would take time for her to completely trust again, even with John.

Now, as he tried to twist under her morning arousal, to pleasure her as she was him, she hugged his legs so that all he could do was stroke her hair, until his hands pressed down on the back of her head, his hips arched off the bed and he moaned aloud in his orgasm. She lifted her head and grinned as he looked down at her, still panting. He bent forward to pull her up the bed but she bounced out.

"I'm going for a bath, if there's any hot water … and no, you can't join me; we have too much to do today." Emma chuckled at her lover's mock scowl then walked away. But she glanced back over her shoulder and gave a cheeky wiggle before she shut the bathroom door.

Thirty minutes later, Emma entered the kitchen to find Margaret making breakfast.

"Good morning, Emma. I was making breakfast for Tony and me. Would you like me to make some for you too?"

"No, it's okay, you're nearly finished. I'll do it while you eat or yours will get cold. John will be down in a minute."

Margaret put down the fork she had been using to scramble eggs, hugged Emma hard and kissed her cheek then went back to making breakfast.

Emma blushed. "Were we that noisy?"

Margaret answered without turning. "John asked us to do a job for him. When we got back we couldn't find him and I came to see if you were all right, but you were obviously being well taken care of."

Emma hid her face in her hands. "Oh, Margaret! I'm sorry."

"Whatever for? It's long overdue, if you don't mind me saying so, for both of you."

Tony came in through the back door. "Animals are all okay. We've got four more lambs but one dead sheep. Don't know what killed it; there's no sign of injury and it seemed fine yesterday … Morning, Emma," he added, with a smirk.

Emma blushed again. "Good morning, Tony."

John came in, bathed and clean-shaven. "Farmers around here used to have a saying 'If you keep sheep you better keep a good spade'. Sheep die," he told them. "Half the time it would take a post mortem to find out why and then you might never know what caused it. Morning, all."

Emma waggled a spoon at him from the stove, where she had replaced Margaret. "No point in trying to be discreet, John, it seems to be an open secret."

He chuckled. "Ah. Are you okay?"

Emma shrugged. "Of course. You can't hide things for long in a group this small anyway. Besides, I wouldn't want to."

John nodded. "In that case …" and wrapped his arms round her from behind and kissed her neck.

"Start that now and you'll have burnt bacon," she chided, but then added, "Oh I don't know though, it might be worth it."

John scowled. "Might?"

Dan joined them as Emma finished cooking. He went straight over to John. "Are you all right, John?"

"I'm fine thank you, Dan. How are you?"

"Mmmm, but I was worried last night. All the noise woke me up but I was too frightened to come out to find out what was happening. Leah came and let me stay with her and Sunny. I heard you moaning ever such a lot but Sunny said it was all right because Emma was looking after you."

"She did that, very well indeed. I'm a bit bruised this morning but not at all stiff."

Emma almost choked, her lips whitening as she battled the urge to laugh out loud. With a warning scowl she put John's breakfast on the table, then guided Dan towards the stove. "Come on, show me how you do scrambled eggs."

After everyone else had eaten and gone off to various jobs, Margaret put a bag on the table in front of John. "That was all Applegarth had on him, John. Not much but we brought it all."

John emptied the bag onto the table. A Kershaw Amphibian boot knife in a leather sheath, a Leatherman Wave multi tool, the sheath for the Gerber Mk2, which John had last seen lying on the floor of the sitting room, a disposable lighter, a wire saw and some nylon parachute cord, tumbled out. "Was that everything?"

"That was it," Margaret said, "Oh, except for this." From her pocket, she took a credit card-sized piece of white plastic in a protective case and handed it to John. The card bore no markings except for a black magnetic strip on one side.

John shrugged. "Well it's curious but it doesn't tell us much. I'll check his saddle bags later."

"What are you expecting to find?" Margaret asked.

John shook his head. "I really don't know. Somehow I wasn't convinced he was here by accident. We still don't know what he was doing at the radio."

After finishing his tea John went to the guest room where Applegarth's gear was stored. He unloaded the shotgun, which the dead man had left ready for use. Then he pulled the rifle from its case. To his surprise it was not an M16 but a .223 AR180B, a good rifle but not a common one. Another surprise waited in the saddlebags, a Glock model 36 semi-automatic pistol in .45 auto calibre, with three magazines and a box of ammunition. It was an effective pistol but not one for which it would have been easy to find more ammunition in the UK.

Investigating further, he found more .223 and 12 bore ammunition, including No6 shot, buckshot and rifled slugs, a spare set of clothing, various pieces of survival and camping equipment, a compass, maps, Zeiss binoculars and two army ration-packs. Nothing gave any extra information, except to confirm John's suspicion that their previous owner had been military of some sort. The maps were unmarked, he noticed. He carried it all to the gunroom and left it for the time being; other things had higher priority.

Margaret, John and Tony carried mops, buckets and cloths to the sitting room and set to cleaning away the evidence of the previous night's fight. The room smelled of whisky and blood. John recovered the Gerber Mk2 and Emma's knife and sheath, dropped the empty Dalwhinnie bottle into the rubbish bag, and then retrieved the unused Browning pistol from under his chair cushion. The pistol he put in his back pocket, the knives he set aside to clean and sharpen later. After an hour's hard work the mess was gone but they could not remove the stain from the floorboards. Instead Tony fetched a rug from one of the other rooms and covered it. Margaret opened the windows to let the morning breeze blow away the lingering smells.

Emma was in the top field planting turnip seed when John found her. Without comment she accepted the cleaned and sharpened kitchen knife and tucked it under her belt. She had been missing it all morning but had not been able to bring herself to fetch it from the sitting room, or to clean it.

John picked a packet of seed from the basket beside her, stepped across to the next row and began to plant. Before long they were joined by all the others and gradually the row of hunched figures worked along the finely tilled furrows sowing, covering, shuffling forward, sowing, covering, shuffling forward, as they went. It was with aching backs and sore roughened fingers that they eventually broke for lunch.

They sat at the edge of the field easing their muscles as they ate slices of beef and bread, accompanied by cans of beer or swigs of wine. They talked of the lambs, of the weather and their crops, of building, of brewing their own beer and wine, and the news they had heard from differing settlements the previous evening and, cautiously at first until they were sure it wasn't upsetting Emma, they talked about Applegarth.

They could have been any group of peasant farmers across the ages, across the globe, except for the guns lying beside them or holstered at their waists. Applegarth's body had been dumped in the local cemetery, in one of the open graves that had been dug for victims of the plague but never used, and quickly covered with dirt. It was Margaret's choice. Despite what he had done, or tried to do, she couldn't bear the idea of his gnawed bones lying somewhere they might have to pass.

Emma lowered the bottle of red wine from her lips and passed it back to Sunny. "What's that?" she asked, prodding at a tattoo on John's arm.

John raised his arm to look at where she was pointing. "It's my blood group, O positive. It was a craze in the regiment at one time," he explained. "One of our guys died because he lost his dog tags in an explosion and the medics didn't know what sort of blood to give him. After that a lot of us got tattooed with our blood group. Silly really but it seemed to make sense at the time."

Emma felt a rush of fondness at his embarrassment and quickly changed the subject. "You know," she said, "we're going to have to learn some songs to help us as we work."

Leah winced. "Gospel? Oh no, boss ma'am, dat is far too much de cliché for dis girl."

The others joined her laughter but eventually Emma accepted her own role and stood up. "All right, lunch is over. Back to the fields with you or it'll be cold gruel for dinner tonight."

Groaning they stood, stretched and headed back to work.

"I don't know about learning songs," John said to Emma as they returned to planting, "but we definitely need to find a seed drill, a horse-drawn one for the field crops and a hand one for the garden if we can."

"We'll keep it in mind when we're out and about. For now..." she held up her hands. "these will have to do."

Margaret left them early so that dinner might be hot, full-flavoured mutton stew rather than cold gruel but it was eaten in near exhausted silence and bed that night was for sleeping, not passion.

#

John arched his back, kneaded it at the base with his knuckles, then picked up the slice and flicked over the bacon that was sizzling in the frying pan. It was not yet six a.m., but this was a late start for them. As soon as the days lengthened they had begun to work with the natural daylight in order to conserve candles and gas cartridges. John grimaced; 'early to bed, early to rise … makes a man's back sore' was, he decided, a more appropriate saying.

Two pans sizzled on the stove, one each for eggs and bacon, and a huge kettle they had found at one of the museums had just boiled. Fresh oat bread stood on the table. They still had flour in stock but Margaret had been experimenting with the ingredients they could grow or collect for themselves. She protected their remaining flour carefully, ensuring it was dry and well sealed and pushing bay leaves into and around the containers to deter weevils and moths.

They had inter-planted the rows in their garden plot with companion plants such as rosemary, sage, garlic and other herbs plus French marigolds. It was a tactic that one of their books recommended to keep away pests or promote plant health without using chemicals. Oats had been sown in the field and they had seed for next year but no wheat, so when the last of their flour was gone it was back to traditional Scottish cooking. John thought they should have the rest of the planting done by the end of the day, next would come the job of hoeing to keep the weeds down and later, harvesting, but there would always be plenty to do in between.

He was hoping to find a chance to talk to Emma alone today. She had given no sign of what she was feeling in the aftermath of killing Applegarth and hadn't even spoken about it.

She had been ferocious in her lovemaking that night and he had been too eager for it to ask questions but afterwards she had quickly fallen into an exhausted sleep. Through the next day they were never alone, then by the time he had come out of the bath last evening she had again been fast asleep and he had gone to his own room so as not to disturb her. She crept into his bed in the early hours, cuddled up to him and then promptly went back to sleep. He left her there when he came down to make breakfast. She seemed fine but ....

Margaret usually made dinner with the help of the others in turn and she also prepared their lunch for the next day but they worked to a rota for making breakfast. The extra few minutes in bed when it was someone else's shift wasn't long but it was much appreciated. People made their own drinks, some taking real tea or coffee, some preferring Leah's herbal tea or dandelion root coffee.

John's thoughts were disturbed by the arrival of Dan, yawning and rubbing his eyes. "Morning, John."

"Good morning, Dan. Sit down, breakfast's nearly ready. What do you want to drink?"

The boy yawned again. "Tea, please."

John served up a plate of eggs and bacon and made tea for himself and Dan. The big kettle was too heavy for the lad when it was full.

"What are you doing today?" he asked

"Ermmm … feed the chickens and collect the eggs as usual. Then pull those skins through the big brass ring to soften them and then do some weeding among the plants in the garden." He stopped to swallow a forkful of bacon then asked, "Can I take my air rifle, please? I want to see if I can get those pigeons that have been eating the seedlings."

"They won't come while you're among the plants."

"They did yesterday when I was at the other end," Dan protested. "Not right down but onto the fence."

"All right then, but remember, safety always comes first and if you aren't sure of the shot …"

"Don't take it," Dan finished for him.

John smiled and nodded. He allowed Dan to keep the Meteor air rifle and ammunition in his own room but not to use them without permission. He had also instructed the lad on safety with the various rifles, pistols and shotguns they had and allowed him to fire each of them to satisfy his curiosity. He decided that soon he would teach Dan to use a .410 shotgun and perhaps give him one for Christmas. The lad was doing well. He behaved so responsibly he seemed too old for his years.

Sometimes John worried because the youngster had no one of his own age around. Perhaps that was why he had grown up so fast or perhaps it was his experiences before and since Emma met him. Whatever the reason, John was proud of him.

He was about to call the others, when Emma entered the kitchen, closely followed by Sunny and Leah.

Emma came and kissed him on the cheek. "You should have woken me," she protested.

He shrugged. "There was time enough."

A couple of minutes later, Margaret and Tony joined them.

"So what's on today?" asked Tony.

Emma dipped her bread into egg yolk, sucked it and moaned appreciatively before she swallowed, and then answered, "We should get the last of the neeps planted today, then we can move on to other things. The only other planting after that will be the oats later in the year and those we can broadcast, so it won't be so hard on our backs."

Margaret groaned. "That will be a relief."

Emma continued. "We've found a couple of possible sources for beehives. None were listed in Yellow Pages but we found a beekeeper in a local directory. Tomorrow we'll take the Land Rover and trailer and fetch back as many hives as we can. The more bees we have around for pollination the better, not to mention the honey and wax."

"I brought most of my equipment from Findhorn," Sunny explained, "so we don't need to worry about that but we could see what is available in case we need spares, or to cache at the emergency place."

"Which is something else we should do," John added. "We haven't been there for ages, deliberately so as not to attract attention to it but I think we're pretty safe in that regard these days. We should check things there are okay. I don't see any groups descending on the area looking for a place, do you?"

A general round of shaken heads and mumbled chorus of "No" confirmed their agreement.

"And then," Emma resumed, "we need to look at doing some building. We've progressed faster than I thought in some things and I think we can manage to do the building while we keep other jobs on the go. Let's talk to Sergei and Martin tonight to see if they can fit a visit into their plans."

"Who's on the radio tonight?" John asked.

Leah smirked. "I am."

John and Emma glanced at each other. Their chances of getting Sergei and Martin to visit had now improved substantially.

#

In fact, because the planting and other jobs took several more days, it was well into the following week before they could make time to look for beehives. Sergei and Martin had promised to come but were in the Borders area and agreed to join them in about two weeks. Before then the group were to collect as much as possible of the building materials, tools and equipment Martin had suggested they might need.

Despite the hard work, Emma and John found time and energy to confirm that their feelings were not confined to one mad night of post-hazard release. On the third night Emma poured out her heart and tears into John's shoulder, in a tidal surge of emotion that left her feeling scoured but cleansed. Then, on a perfect spring afternoon, the urgent jobs were done and they set out to find Sunny's bees.

"It will be good to have bees again," Sunny told them, shouting above the Land Rover's whine. "I miss them."

"Have you decided where you want to put the hives?" Emma asked.

"On the top field, a bit below the wood and just off the track. It is south facing, sheltered from the wind and well-drained. Our crops will still be the main attraction for them but the heather up there will provide flowers later in the year. We can put some rocks in that old tin bath, for the bees to sit on while they drink. We'll put the hives alongside the fence, uphill from the gate."

"Did you say you want to get four hives?" John asked.

"That would be about right for us. If we get more we can put some around the side of the farm, near the kitchen garden. If we have more honey than we need we might be able to trade some."

"How much are we likely to get?" Emma asked.

"Thirty pounds per hive, perhaps, if it is a good year. There will be wax too but not much, only about a pound per hive."

Margaret leaned across to avoid shouting. "What if we get too much honey?"

"We leave more for the bees. Up here we need to leave them thirty to forty pounds anyway, for the winter. That should save us from having to feed them and it is better than anything we could give them, but it depends how long and wet the winter is." Sunny pondered for a second. "I know we have to be careful but we should visit the house first, John, to see if we can get some extra veils and gloves, and we could use any empty jars they have."

John held up a gas mask. "As few people as possible enter the house and we wear these. There might not be anyone there, of course. We've found plenty of places that were empty. Everyone gone to the hospital, I expect."

Sunny continued, "If they are standard hives they won't be overly heavy; even if they are full of honey two of us should manage to get them onto the trailer without any problem."

Margaret leaned towards her again. "How do we prevent all the bees flying out when we move them?"

"We will block the entrance with a piece of foam. That will let air in but shut off the light."

"Won't they fly back home when we open the hives again?"

Sunny shook her head. "We are too far away for that. The rule is to move a hive less than three feet, so they don't become disoriented, or more than three miles so they don't head back to where the hive used to be. We are taking them nearly ten miles away."

They approached the detached bungalow along a gravelled drive; it's once neat swathe now speckled green with grass and weeds. The garage stood open and empty. Sheep grazed and lambs played in the field to the right of the drive. The garden to the left swirled with colour as mixed flowers swayed in the late afternoon breeze and the air vibrated with the hum of contented bees about their foraging.

Emma twisted in her seat and smiled at Sunny. "It sounds like we've come to the right place."

Sunny nodded excitedly. "We could not have chosen a better day. The bees will be calm after a good day's gathering. It won't be long now before they all head back to the hive. Then we need to wait until dusk so that they are settled before we move them. We must handle the hives very gently when we do."

John pulled up outside the garage and the four followed the path around the bungalow towards the back garden. An artist's palette could not have rivalled the riotous mix of colour and texture that greeted them. Herbs and flowers, apple trees, blackcurrant and raspberry bushes had provided for the bees', and their owners', needs from spring to winter. A vegetable patch stood almost empty except for weeds; prepared but not planted before the plague hit. On the lawn alongside the field, grass, far too long now, tried to draw a veil around a child's swing. From somewhere close a burn gurgled. And there, at the bottom of the garden, looking like a row of miniature skyscrapers, stood eight silvery-grey cedar wood hives.

As they stood entranced Margaret took a deep breath. "What a loss!"

"Aye," said John, "but what a place to have lived before they went."

Sunny sighed, and then pointed to a long extension to the bungalow. "That must be the honey house. Let's take a look."

John and Sunny put on gas masks before entering the building. They found themselves in a room that was obviously kept pristinely clean but now bore a fine layer of dust that somehow matched the comfortable, muddled untidiness. Mesh screens covered the louvered windows, inner door and raiseable skylights, leaving the building cool and airy. A stack of hive supers stood in one corner and next to it a tiered rack of frames. Blocks of wax were piled on shelves along with scraping tools, and moulds for wax and for making sheets of the foundation on which the bees built their combs.

A smoker, vaguely resembling a coffee jug but with a set of bellows where the handle should be, was placed on the floor below a white overall and veiled hat. A pair of Wellington boots stood next to it. Boxes of empty jars and lids were stacked in another corner. An electric centrifuge for spinning honey from the combs gleamed from its place by the end of a worktable.

Sunny removed her mask and nodded appreciatively. "They were well set up. Can you get the jars, wax and equipment into the Land Rover while I check the hives, please? Then we will wait for the bees to go home."

John, Margaret and Emma had finished loading the Land Rover as Sunflower returned.

"Is everything okay?" John asked.

"Yes, it's all right – well seven of the hives are anyway. One is virtually empty and infested with wax moth but the others are healthy. We should be able to get six on the trailer. I've put empty supers over the existing ones and taken the crown boards off and replaced them with travelling screens, so the bees will get plenty of air while we are on the move. I've put the tops back on for now but we will stand the hives in them for the journey."

John nodded, satisfied that the trip had been worthwhile. "I'll have a scout around the house, see if there's anything we can use. Why don't the rest of you have a look round the garden and sheds?" Replacing his mask, he headed for the back door, while the others enjoyed a stroll in the garden. Soon afterwards, he emerged from the house carrying a cardboard box and a couple of supermarket carrier bags.

Emma put her hand on his shoulder and rose on her toes to peek over the edge of the box. "What did you get?"

"Some tinned foods, candles, matches and a can of gas for refilling lighters, soap, shampoo and cleaning stuff. There's not much but there's no point in leaving it to waste."

Margaret sniffed as he removed the mask. "What's it like in there?"

"It's very clean. There's a couple in bed in one room but the house is in good order and well sealed, no sign of predation and very little smell."

Sunny pointed to the windows. "All the windows are screened. Insects will find their way in eventually but the mesh is obviously helping."

"Are we about ready to load the hives?" Emma asked.

Sunny looked over the now almost silent flower beds. "Give them half an hour to settle down and then we will start."

It was dark when they had all the hives loaded with the roofs removed and the stacking sections roped or strapped together. Sunny checked that the hives were oriented so that the frames inside were aligned with their direction of travel in the trailer. "So that they don't flap together and crush any bees," she explained.

She sprayed the travelling screens with water to give the bees something to drink and to help with cooling, and then declared that they were ready to go.

"Please drive carefully, John," she pleaded, "we don't want to shake up the hives more than we need to."

John frowned. "I'll do my best, Sunny, but the track up the hill to the top field isn't exactly smooth. That will be the only part that causes much bumping but I'll go slowly."

Then, with Sunny at the back of the Land Rover anxiously watching the hives, they returned to Knockside and the bees' new home.

Once at the top field they gently unloaded the hives. Sunny replaced the crown boards and roofs then carefully tugged the packing from the entrances. A few bees emerged inquisitively but within a few minutes the hives returned to peace.

"In the morning I'll check that everything is all right and remove the travelling screens. The bees might keep going up there to drink for a while and they've been through enough changes for now. I can manage now if you want to go on down."

"I'll give you hand," volunteered Margaret. "If I'm going to be your second on the beekeeping I want to learn all I can about it."

John and Emma headed for the Land Rover.

"We'll see you in a few minutes," called Emma. "It probably won't be long before dinner is ready."

Dinner was roast rabbit with herbs, rice and tinned peas, courtesy of chefs Tony and Dan.

"Not up to Margaret's standard I'm afraid," apologised Tony, when everyone was seated, "but there's plenty of rabbit thanks to Dan."

Leah held up her hand. "I did offer to help but they decided this was men's day in the kitchen."

As usual they chatted as they ate and drank. Sunny squeezed Leah's arm affectionately. "And what have you been up to?" Sunny asked.

"Oh, I've been on the radio. Sergei and Martin are not coming for a few more days. They're down with colds. Apparently everyone at a community they visited had it but they all recovered, so it doesn't seem too serious. They just don't want to risk passing it on."

"Very wise," agreed Emma. "Are they all right?"

Leah laughed. "They're men and they have a cold, Emma. They think they should be tucked up in bed being looked after by a nurse. Preferably one with a short skirt and an open blouse to raise their temperature even more, knowing them."

"And what are they doing instead?" Emma asked.

"I've prescribed fresh air, gentle exercise and pine needle tea, for the vitamin C," Leah told her.

Margaret nodded knowingly. "I bet they still want the nurse, to serve them the tea."

"Well they will have to take turns," Leah asserted, "and make do without the uniform. I doubt they'd find one to fit either of them anyway."

John shook his head. "Don't, Leah, the thought of that sight isn't a pretty one."

"Oh, I don't know," chuckled Margaret.

Tony glowered.

"But there was something else," added Leah more soberly. "It took them a while to find their way south of Edinburgh. The city and several other towns were in flames."

John's eyebrows rose. "After all this time and with no electricity on, that has to be deliberate."

"Maybe it's someone trying to clear out the disease and rats, like Hendrie's people were doing in Glasgow," suggested Emma.

"But who could be doing it?" asked Margaret. "It sounds extremely organised."

Leah recounted what Sergei had told her. "In a couple of the places they visited, stories of a mad preacher were circulating. They say he wanders around reciting biblical passages and calling on God to help him to complete His work in ridding the Earth of the remains of sinners and blasphemers. They even say he doesn't confine his efforts to the towns. There have been fires that have been attributed to him at some of the occupied farms."

Tony appeared startled. "What about our fire, could that have been him?"

Emma frowned and shook her head. "You know, this is how superstitions and witch hunts get started. First there's a rumour. Then it's connected with something that isn't really connected at all. Then someone finds a scapegoat. Then someone sees a way to profit from it, by blaming or condemning someone else and before you know where you are, it's like Salem or the fourteenth-century campaigns against the Jews during the plagues, all over again."

"But not in the twenty-first century, surely," protested Margaret.

"We may be living in the twenty-first century but all the time our lifestyle is getting closer to the twelfth," Emma said. "Oh I know we're not that far back yet but give it a few years, when the batteries and gas canisters and fuel and ready-made clothing are gone. We might develop solar and wind power on a small scale, enough for our own settlement's needs, but the closer people get to nature the more they realise its mystery and power. Even sun and wind power are elemental."

Without realising it her gaze had settled on Dan and the room had grown still.

"In time, when much of what we've learnt has been forgotten, people will feel the need to explain what they can't understand and when they can't … superstition, myth and magic will provide the answers; unless we preserve our learning and make sure it's passed on. We mustn't allow the Dark Ages to be our descendents' future."

Not an eye left her face, no one even breathed noisily, until Tony leant across the table towards Dan. "You better put away your rifle, pal, I think you might be going back to school."

A flurry of nervous laughter followed but when conversation started again it was quiet.

Emma stood up and again the room fell silent. "Let's get some drinks and go through to the other room. Thank you, Tony, Dan, that was a lovely meal."

"We'll join you in a minute, after we have washed up," volunteered Sunny, passing a plate to Leah.

As the rest started to leave, John took Emma's hand and gave it a small squeeze.

"What?" she asked, but he merely smiled and shook his head.

#

By the time Sergei and Martin did arrive they were fully recovered from their colds and the farm area looked more like a builder's yard. Piles of concrete blocks, timber, plastic piping, sand and bags of cement covered the ground. A mixer was pushed into one corner surrounded by wheelbarrows, shovels and water buckets. John had made two sawhorses and the rubble had been cleared from the areas where the barn and workshop had once stood. Two new generators were sited under a tarpaulin

near the barbed wire fence.

Martin faced the group. "My God you have been busy. Did you only want a barn and a workshop or are you after building a new town?"

"Well, we were thinking more of a castle, but a small one to start with," Emma told him.

"Uh, uh, and would that be Norman or Disney design, my lady?"

"We thought traditional Scottish with a touch of post-modernism."

Martin laughed. "Aye well, you'll get what I can do and you can decorate it after. How did you get this lot here, John?"

"We've still got the tail-lift truck we used to fetch wire from Lossiemouth. It was always parked down at the back of my place, so it survived the fire."

"Any problems getting the stuff?"

"No, there's plenty of builders' yards and merchants about. There's more where this came from, if we need it."

Martin shook his head. "We might need something specific but you've got plenty of the basics. We'll see as we go on."

Margaret appeared in the farm doorway. "Food! Eat it now or the pigs will get it."

"Margaret," protested Sergei. "Martin and I, we do not eat so much."

"Well, I meant the other pigs, Sergei, but if the cap fits … there's beer too if you want it, Martin."

Martin shook his head. "Beer and building don't mix. It leads to too many accidents." He glared around at the others meaningfully. "If anyone drinks on my building site before the end of the day, they end up as part of the foundations. Understood?"

The would-be workforce nodded cheerfully.

John swallowed a piece of oatcake and then addressed Martin. "How long do you think the building will take us?"

"Not too long, we aren't redoing Windsor." He glanced at Emma, grinning. "The foundations and floors are already there, that will speed things up a lot and there's no complicated plumbing or electrics. I've got a good idea of what you want from the drawings Leah made to your descriptions and it's straight forward enough. Some interesting features, like the defensive positions that project at the corner and by the gate and the other firing ports that double for ventilation but they won't add too much time. With all of us working and as long as the weather holds … it might take a month, not much longer."

"Are the two of you okay with staying that long?"

"Aye, we enjoy the travelling and sleeping out and most of the people have been friendly but it'll be good to stay put for a while."

John leaned forward conspiratorially. "Leah wouldn't have anything to do with that, would she?"

Martin laughed. "Her being here doesn't make staying any harder, that's for sure."

Emma walked over to them. "What are you two whispering about?"

"Sergei has a new network diagram for you, Emma," Martin said, dodging the truthful answer. "We have fourteen stations on the network now, including us."

"I know," she agreed. "The evening chats are getting busy."

"Because of that, Sergei is giving everybody details of an emergency frequency," Martin explained. "We, or one or two others with generators, will monitor it all day, outside of the normal chat time. That'll leave the rest of the day for people to use the main frequency for their own chat if they want to organise it. People are starting to use other frequencies too. Not everybody has the batteries or power to run the radio all day though."

"Us included," agreed John, "we're hoping to get a wind turbine. We know of a couple of local suppliers."

"Then we should build that in while we're doing the other work," suggested Martin. "It could add a couple of days but we might as well get it up while we're here. Sergei will help with the electrics."

"So what do we do first?" Emma asked.

"Start building. The walls are going to be concrete block, other than the reinforcing on the defences, so they won't take long. The roofing will take longer. I'll do the marking out and then we'll get to it."

"Will it take all of us?"

"The more we have working the quicker it will be. Why?"

"Other things still have to be done," Emma explained, "animals need to be looked after, the garden and crops tended, food gathered and cooked, but that isn't for you to bother about. We'll arrange some sort of rota. With luck the building will be done before we need to shear the sheep or mow the hay."

"I think that, for this year, we should take full advantage of all the technology we've got," John suggested. "Use the tractor and hoe and generators and anything else we have. We might not have diesel later and we won't have all this building work or, hopefully, the other problems we've faced. Same with the building, use the generators to run power tools or whatever that makes it quicker and easier. It'll still be hard enough."

Emma nodded in agreement. "That makes sense, John. All right let's do that. If we have to go back to horses and scythes next year so be it. This year has been rough enough without being any tougher on ourselves than we need to be."

During those next few weeks they worked harder than they had ever done. Even so, John wasn't sure which tired Sergei and Martin more: the work, or Leah's regular nocturnal visits. Everyone was involved in the building at some stage and the rota for looking after the animals, cooking and other domestic tasks came almost as a relief. If the work wasn't any easier, at least it taxed different muscles.

In mid June, a storm came lashing across the North Sea to drive them indoors for several days but even that did not stop them completely. In the animal shed, timber was sawn and jointed, frames made up and their reference books on wind-power designs studied intently. The storm cost them time and the loss of one of the hives they had so carefully transported but it was over in three days and they again bent to the construction. By the end of the third week in July the main building work was done.

As everyone gathered to watch Martin hammer the last nail into the huge new wooden gates, Emma arrived carrying a tray of drinks.

"Are we officially no longer a building site, Martin?" she asked.

He nodded his confirmation. "Aye, we're done apart from the wind turbine."

"Then this calls for a toast and a celebration."

That brought a rousing cheer from everyone as they took drinks from the tray.

Emma raised her glass. "To the new Knockside and to Martin and Sergei."

The toast was raised. "Martin and Sergei."

Glasses in hand, John and Emma wandered out through the gates, to look at their work from outside. Emma was in thoughtful mood as she inspected the defences, the gates and the base of the tower they had built, on which they would add the steel structure for the turbine and the new antenna Sergei had suggested for their radio.

"Remember what I was saying before we started all this, about our becoming medieval? Well the firing ports may be horizontal instead of vertical but we're still building forts. I hope we never need it again."

"Emma's castle," John mused. "All it needs is a flag." He raised his glass. "It already has its queen."

She clinked her glass against his. "And its knight." The others were now following them outside into the late afternoon sun. "And its workers, plenty of mates but not a useless drone among them," she added, smiling. "Tomorrow we seek out a wind-powered electric system, to add a little twenty-first century technology to this medieval fortress farm of ours."

Wind and Tears

Everyone in the group gave Sunny their full attention as she spoke that evening.

"I am not an expert in these things but some of the people at the Foundation were, so I will tell you what I remember from them. Setting up for wind power is not as easy as you might think. It is not simply a case of putting up a windmill with an old alternator and connecting it to a few batteries. Well, not if you want something that is going to be of real use and will last through the winter, that is."

She paused to take a sip of her tea. "We have to calculate how much energy we need for whatever uses we intend. Then in selecting a generator and tower we must take into consideration the average and maximum wind speeds at various heights where it will be set up, so that we can decide what output to select and how tall a tower. Basically, the higher you get the faster the wind speed. Because the power of the wind is cubed for each doubling of its speed, small increases in speed, and therefore in the height of the tower, make a lot of difference in the power output of the rig."

She looked around at the furrowed brows and blank faces but Margaret was nodding in understanding.

"I get that," Margaret confirmed, "the maths is fairly basic but will the various machines, at this Windtronics firm Emma found in yellow pages, be labelled with the information we need?"

Sunny shook her head. "I doubt it. At best it will be in the manuals we may find to go with them. But it is going to take some study here, and then when we see what is at the shop, to get the tower and turbine that will best suit us."

John frowned. "The maths might be basic for Margaret, but not for me. Isn't there an easy alternative, Sunny?"

"If all you want to do is charge the batteries for the radio and emergency lighting then yes. There should be complete kits that will do that. There may even be something we can use in tandem with a set of photovoltaic cells, solar panels that generate electricity, so that we have power in either calm, bright weather or on cloudy, windy days."

Martin now joined the conversation. "That sounds good, but surely people used to build this sort of thing for themselves, didn't they?"

"Yes, enthusiasts did and some commercial models existed, even back in the nineteen-thirties," Sunny answered. "The amateurs would take an alternator and a mast and make a propeller-driven turbine but without the proper electronics or mechanical drives and attenuators they were either pretty inefficient or did not last very long. If the alternator is not spun fast enough you don't generate the current you need, spin it too fast and you soon burn out the brushes. Don't ask me more for more detail than that, I'm not a mechanic or a technician. If bees generated the electricity I might be able to help more."

Emma sighed. "I think this is more complicated than any of us expected. I wish Alan was still here. We might have to trim our expectations a bit, at least for now. The important thing is to have an alternative to the generator for charging the batteries; we need to maintain radio contact. As I understand it, if we wanted to run a refrigerator or freezer from wind power then we would be most sure to get the power in the winter, when we least need refrigeration."

"That's right," agreed Sunflower. "With solar power as well we might be all right in the summer but really we would need the generator to be sure of topping up the batteries if we had a long cloudy but calm spell."

"Then I vote we keep it simple," said John. "We're doing okay as we are, and did even through the winter and spring. When we run out of gas then we use candles, if we run out of those then we'll make our own. People did all right before electricity; we can do it again."

"We can," Margaret said, "but wouldn't it be nice to switch on a light, plug in the kettle or slip a CD into the hi-fi? We can survive without but people invented electricity to make life easier and more pleasant and to achieve things that weren't possible without it. I think we should be aiming higher than bare survival, we should be trying to improve our lives, to achieve and progress."

Tony groaned at the memory. "Aye, restore the pubs and bring back football. That will be progress."

Emma thought back to the Claymore and Targe where she had first started to respond to the effects of the plague. It had been a simple act, taking a drink of whisky and leaving without paying, but it had been the start of a change in attitude that had enabled her to survive. It was less than six months ago but it had been a different life, a different world.

John gently squeezed her arm. "Are you okay, Emma? You were miles away."

She nodded. "Remembering the last time I was in a pub." She shook her head to clear it. "So, what are we going to do about electricity?"

Sunny summarised for them. "As I see it, we can either study what we need and what is available, make our choices and then build or we can erect something simple for now, with the possibility of upgrading later."

Martin gave them an extra consideration. "If you want to take time to study your options then Sergei and I should be off. We can always come back if you need a hand. If you want the simple option we'll stay until that's done and then help you to form the Knockside Electricity Company next time we're here."

"Let's take a vote," suggested Margaret.

In the end they decided that the equipment would still be there when they needed it and so they would first erect a simple set-up for battery charging while they studied further. Sunny and Margaret agreed to extend their beekeeping partnership activities to become the leading team for alternative power. The following morning they, together with Sergei and Martin, would visit Windtronics to gather equipment and more information.

They were a few minutes late logging on to the evening radio chat but when they did, it was to bad news from a small community near Jedburgh.

Katrina, the Jedburgh station operator, was speaking. "There were about a dozen of them, all wearing combat jackets and carrying military rifles. They came in three Land Rovers at about four o'clock this morning. Before we knew what was happening they had broken in the door. Ray went down the stairs with his gun and they shot him without a chance. Then they dragged the rest of us outside and ransacked the place. They took everything they wanted, did everything they wanted, shot the dog and then drove off south again."

"Didn't they say who they were? Over," someone asked.

"They didn't say a word except to order us about. Wouldn't answer any questions, wouldn't listen to what we said. They took what they came for and went. They only missed this radio because it's in a hut further up the hill from the farm." Katrina signed off with an exasperated, "over."

Tony spoke next. "Was anyone else hurt, apart from Ray? Over."

"Depends what you mean by hurt. If you mean did they leave Angela and me alone then ..." Katrina's voice choked off tearfully and the radio was silent for a few moments before she continued. "No, of course they bloody didn't. What do you expect? They knocked Phil out when he tried to stop them. I think he might have concussion."

The chat devolved into a muddle of concerned and angry speculation for a while before someone asked Katrina what her group would do now.

"We're moving north, to Galashiels," she said. "This was a good place but not any more. At least there might be some strength in numbers up there, even if we do have to join in with their church services. If anyone else is down in the borders you better be ready, it will probably be your turn next. Out."

As talk resumed, Emma put down the microphone. "Border raiders. We really are going back to the Dark Ages, aren't we?"

John sighed hard. "People are starting to get organised. Some will be like us, or the traders in Glasgow and some will be like these bandits. They couldn't have got much at that place and nobody is facing any shortages yet. They must have been out for sport and picked a soft target."

"They seemed damn well organised though," Martin observed.

Margaret straightened. "Well they wouldn't find us such easy pickings."

"There's a lot of territory and a few other communities between them and us," John agreed, "and we're probably better defended than most. Even so, it's a good reminder to us all to be careful, especially when we're out in small groups like your trip tomorrow, Margaret."

Tony plucked at Margaret's sleeve. "I'm coming too tomorrow, even if I only stand outside and keep watch while the rest of you are inside."

Margaret nodded. "All right, Tony," she agreed, "if that's okay with you, Emma? We won't be away long and the more of us that go, the quicker we'll be."

"Yes, take Tony as well. You might need him anyway if the equipment is heavy," Emma said.

The following morning they hitched the trailer to the Knockside Land Rover and with Margaret driving, Martin beside her and Tony, Sergei and Sunflower in the back, they prepared to leave. As Margaret was about to drive off Dan ran up to them.

"Can I come too, please, Margaret? It's ages since I went out anywhere." he pleaded.

Margaret looked at Emma who turned to John.

"We can't keep him confined to the farm up all the time," John reasoned, "and five others are going, more than there will be of us here."

Emma took a deep breath then nodded. "Go on then, Dan, but make sure you look after Sunny."

"I will," he promised happily, as he clambered into the back of the Land Rover.

John, Emma and Leah stood watching as the vehicle and trailer clattered along the track and disappeared from sight at the bend.

"I hope they'll be all right," Leah said.

Emma put her arm round Leah's waist and hugged her against her hip. "They'll be fine. The borders are a long way from here and plenty of them are going, and they're well armed."

"All except Sunny," Leah corrected, still staring down the track. "I fear for her sometimes. She's so strong in so many ways but she would never defend herself. If anything happened to her I would …."

Emma squeezed her again. "Don't worry, Leah, you heard – she has Dan as a bodyguard."

Leah sniffed then broke away and walked towards the house.

John watched Leah's long graceful stride carry her across the yard. "I'd hate to be the man who touched Sunny," he said. "He'd be in almost as much trouble as anyone who messed with you."

Emma reached up, kissed him then raised an eyebrow. "Or as much trouble as the woman who messed with you," she warned.

John laughed. "Then you might get in a lot of trouble, because I'm hoping you're going to mess with me quite often."

Emma's eyes opened wide. "Well, the house is almost empty and we were up rather early, we could … ermmm … go and see how much trouble we could get into with one another."

Without another word, John took her arm and guided her in the direction of the house.

#

When the Land Rover returned, the trailer was loaded but the group were strangely quiet.

"Whatever's wrong?" asked Emma. "Couldn't you find what we needed?"

Margaret's face was grim as she answered. "We got it all right, but the place, Emma." She shut her eyes for a moment, swallowed, and then continued. "For some reason a big group of people had gathered there. I don't ever want to see anything like that again. The whole place was teeming with rats and flies. We put on masks or put handkerchiefs over our mouths and snatched what we needed then got out of there as quickly as possible. Luckily the place was well-organised and labelled."

Emma shook her head in disbelief and concern. "You shouldn't have gone in at all, Margaret!"

"I know! I said we should leave it and try somewhere else but the boys were being macho, they said it wasn't as bad as Glasgow. In the end we all pitched in and got it done as fast as we could. I still feel sick and itchy."

John came back from sorting through the load in the trailer, just in time to hear Margaret's tale. "Did the rats bother you at all?"

Margaret shook her head. "No, they didn't attack us or anything but they didn't seem frightened of us either. The flies were worse, and maggots crawling all over everything. Ugh!" She shivered at the memory.

Leah had come from the house and now gave them a warning. "You should all strip, in the barn, and your clothes should be burned. Then you should wash all over in some of that animal shampoo Emma got for the cats. Even if the rats came nowhere near, you may have picked up fleas and the flies probably landed on you."

Margaret nodded vigorously. "I don't think I've been bitten but I itch all over. It might just be the thought of it."

"What about the rest of you," asked Emma, "is anyone else itching?"

"Well I wasn't," said Dan, scratching at his hair, "but I am now you've talked about it."

"Right!" Emma commanded. "Everyone into the barn. Use the old tubs we brought to use as water troughs for the animals. Get some water into them. We'll bring towels and cat shampoo and some hot water and clean clothes for you. You lot get undressed, put your clothes in those fertiliser sacks and we'll burn them. Use the stalls we put in for the horses in winter if any of you are shy."

"I'll get some spray and fumigate the Land Rover and the stuff in the trailer," John volunteered.

The newly returned windmill hunters shuffled off towards the barn. All of them were now scratching spontaneously. Emma, John and Leah hurried away to their tasks.

Soon they were running backwards and forwards with insecticide shampoo and kettles or pans of hot water and barn was reeking of splashing, pungent suds. The tops of the sacks of discarded clothes were rolled and fastened with tape before John took them away. Sergei, as usual, made a joke of it by actually climbing into one of the tubs and singing, loudly but badly, from a Russian opera as he bathed.

"Did you spray the Land Rover, John?" Emma asked.

"Aye, and the trailer too, with both insecticide and some flea spray. The bags of clothes are out back. I split a bale of straw, drenched it with petrol, piled the bags on top and put a match to it."

"Then let's hope that's done the trick. I'm really angry, John; they should never have gone into somewhere like that."

John nodded. "Well, it's done now but you're right. With luck we won't need to do anything of the sort again."

"Need to or not, none of us will!"

John watched while she strode off back to the house. Angry she may be, he thought, but it was because she was worried about them. He frowned and sighed. The memory came to him of Sheenagh's comment after Margaret had shot Terry at Lossiemouth, 'What's done is done and no undoing it,' she had said. Wise woman, he decided, as he followed Emma to the house.

#

The logo on the side of the turbine identified it as an African Wind Power model AWP 3.6. Beside it lay a pile of tubular steel piping, a large reel of cable, a stack of batteries, and various fittings. Over two days they dug holes and filled them with rocks as the foundation for the pole base and attachment points for the wire guy ropes which would secure it. Then they poured the concrete bases and fitted them with fixing bolts for the tower and guys. While the concrete was drying they dug a ditch, laid steel pipe along it and then threaded the cable through the pipe. The cable ended in the new workshop, where the deep-cycle six-volt batteries would be racked. The batteries were connected in series in pairs to provide twelve volts and each pair connected in parallel to extend the capacity of the batteries. In all they had twenty-four six-volt batteries. The turbine would produce up to one thousand watts, to charge all of the batteries simultaneously.

They screwed together the sections of the pole and bolted the footing to the concrete base. The metal bracket at the base of the pole was designed not only to secure the rig but also to allow the eighty-foot long pole to be raised or lowered, for servicing or if winds were expected to exceed the one hundred and twenty-five miles per hour it was designed to withstand. They would need to use the Land Rover's winch to haul it up, complete with the two hundred and fifty pound load at its top, including the nearly twelve-foot diameter fibreglass rotor blades.

Sunny explained the lack of an integral system for raising and lowering the turbine. "They would probably have had hand winches in the shop somewhere but I couldn't see them and we didn't want to hang around looking."

"How often are we likely to need to pull it up and down?" John asked.

Martin waved the instruction manual. "According to this, it should need inspecting and greasing once a year, other than that only in emergencies."

With the turbine, power cable, blade and tail assembly and mast finally fitted together, they connected the winch cable and prepared to erect the whole structure. Martin, Sergei and Tony each controlled one of the guy wires as Emma slipped the winch into gear and John directed the incoming winch cable onto its drum. Slowly and carefully Emma increased the winch speed and the elegant wind generator lifted into position. Margaret fastened the securing bolts while the three men each tensioned a guy and locked it in place.

When everyone was gathered around, Sunny released the brake, the tail swung the nose into the wind and, to a rousing cheer from the whole group, the blades slowly began to rotate.

"How fast a wind do we need to start generating power, Sunny?" Emma asked.

"It should cut in at six miles per hour," Sunny explained, "and keep increasing in charging rate to around twenty-five miles per hour. At eight mph it will give an output of about seventy-five kilowatt hours per month and at fourteen mph around two hundred and fifty – that is plenty for our needs. Remember how I said small increases in speed meant big increases in power?"

Emma nodded absently, fascinated and mesmerised by the grace of the powerful but unexpectedly quiet machine.

Back in the workshop, Sergei finished checking the battery connections and flipped the switch on the charging regulator. The needle of the ammeter swung and settled, showing a steady charge. As Emma entered the workshop she saw him sit down on the workbench and wipe his brow.

"Are you all right, Sergei?" she asked.

The big Russian smiled. "I am AOK, thank you, Emma. It is a very warm day and much hard work. It is time for a cool whisky I think, yes?"

"Now that we have power, you might even eventually get a cold beer when you visit," she promised, "but if you prefer a whisky, then I think you've deserved it."

Sergei stood and walked towards the door.

Emma linked her arm through his and stopped him. "Are you going to stay for a few days and have a rest now, Sergei?"

He nodded. "I think so, yes. Then we go to see some more of the borders. I think the small settlements, they need radio if there are bad people there."

Emma hugged his arm. "Well, you and Martin take care. Talk to John about some more guns. That pistol of yours won't do you much good against twelve raiders with army rifles."

Sergei and Martin left three days later. The turbine was working well and already the Knockside settlers had begun to use it to charge batteries for the radio and to power some lights in the house and a small refrigerator. Martin had also helped John to fit up some vehicle floodlights, to illuminate both the inside and outside of the farm area as needed. Margaret had provided the travellers with a supply of food for their journey and John had given each of them a military rifle and a case of ammunition to supplement Sergei's pistol and Martin's shotgun.

It was a cheerful send-off although, as always, they were sorry to see their friends go. Sergei was nursing a sore head. Considering that he had drunk over half a bottle of malt whisky the night before, that didn't surprise Emma at all.

Together John and Emma closed the big new gates and returned, arm in arm, to the house.

"Have you seen Dan this morning?" he asked her. "I thought he would have been up to see Sergei and Martin off."

Emma frowned. "I'll go and look for him. He's not even been down for breakfast yet. Maybe he went out after rabbits and didn't realise the time."

But Dan had not gone hunting. Emma found him still in bed. His eyes were shut but his face was white and his pillow soaked with sweat. As she gently shook his shoulder the boy groaned and threw his arm across his face to shield his eyes from the light.

She spun towards the door and shouted. "John, Leah, come here. Quickly!"

Feet clattered on the stairs and John burst into the room closely followed by Leah.

"What is it? What's wrong?" John demanded.

"Dan is burning up, he doesn't seem to hear or understand me at all and he keeps shuddering."

John placed the back of his hand on the boy's head then touched his pillow.

"From the amount of sweat he's lost it could be partly dehydration. Leah, will you bring a big jug of water, please? Oh, and any of your medicines that'll help to bring down fever."

Leah rushed away without a word

Sunny peeked into the room. She swallowed hard before she spoke. "I heard you talking. Is there anything I can do?"

"Could you put out a radio call on the emergency frequency please, Sunny? See if anyone knows where Fhionna is and if we can talk to her on the radio."

Then, troubled by Sunny's hoarse voice, Emma called after her, as she was about to leave. "Sunny, are you all right this morning?"

"My throat is rather sore but I feel all right other than that."

"Then after you've used the radio, will you check on Margaret and Tony, please?"

"Of course," she answered, as she left.

Leah returned a few minutes later with a large jug of water, a glass and a steaming cup on a tray. John took the glass from her and she put the jug on the cabinet beside him then offered Emma the cup. "This is a mixture of meadowsweet and peppermint; it should help him."

"Thank you, Leah. Sunny was saying she has a sore throat; how are you feeling?"

"I'm fine, but I have a very high immune rating anyway. What about you, and you, John?"

"I'm okay." He had pulled Dan into a sitting position and was slowly dribbling water into the lad's gaping mouth.

"Me too," confirmed Emma.

Leah pulled two surgical masks in sealed packets from her pocket. "Fhionna left us these on her last visit. I think we should wear them while we are tending to Dan. I should have thought of it earlier."

Emma frowned but accepted the masks, tore open the packets and both she and John put one on.

She pulled up Dan's vest, checking his body for a rash, and felt in his armpits and groin for swollen glands or any other signs she could relay to Fhionna but there didn't seem to be anything other than the fever, the fast pulse and the rapid, shallow breathing, in which she now detected a worrying gurgle.

"I'm going to see how Sunny is getting on. Is there anything else I can do?" Leah asked.

Emma shook her head. "Not for now, but thank you, Leah."

Emma walked through to the bathroom. From the rail she took a towel, soaked it in cold water, wrung it out then returned to bathe the sick boy's face and body.

As she was finishing, she heard footsteps in the hall and Sunny called from the door.

"Fhionna and James were at Galashiels but they left yesterday to see a couple further to the west. One of the men had broken his arm. The people she is going to see don't have a radio but Galashiels is sending a rider. They said it could be tonight before we hear any news though."

"Thank you, Sunny," Emma said. "How are you feeling?"

"I'm all right but Leah made me gargle with warm salt water, yuck. I'll take some honey later, much nicer."

"How are Margaret and Tony?"

"Margaret is okay. Tony doesn't feel too good but Margaret says it is a hangover and serves him right."

Emma sighed in relief. "Then apart from your sore throat it looks as if it's only Dan. Thank goodness! What's everyone doing?"

"Margaret is checking the batteries, Tony is out seeing to the animals and Leah is going through the medical books. I was about to do some weeding."

"Good. Even with one of us sick, the work has to be done. Thank you, Sunny."

John glanced up from administering the water. "Do you want to get on with something else? We can take it in turns looking after Dan."

Emma shook her head definitely. "No, there's nothing that urgent at the moment, maybe when we've got him more comfortable."

John went back to his task but the boy was taking in hardly any liquid.

"I wish we could give him this intravenously; his breathing's so difficult he's coughing it up rather than swallowing," John observed.

Emma frowned in concentration before she spoke. "We don't have the equipment for that, but we could rig up an enema. I once read about some people who were adrift in a lifeboat. They took in water that was too brackish to drink that way. It saved their lives."

"All right, however we can get fluid into him. If you tell me what we need, I'll get it while you look after him."

"Any large bottle will do but a hot water bottle would be good and a bit of soft tubing. He probably needs salt as well but I don't know how much to mix. Make it plain water for now."

John left but soon returned with two hot water bottles full of filtered water. Into the top of one of them he had pushed a rubber bung with a glass tube through it, to the outer end of which was fitted a length of plastic tubing with a clamp.

"I got the bung and tubing from the wine making kit Bob and Ellen had in the cupboard under the stairs."

"That will do fine. Help me to get him on his side."

Emma knelt beside the bed, pulled down the boy's pyjama trousers then, assisted by John, rolled him onto his right side. While Emma gently inserted the tube and released the clamp, John pushed a hole through the tab at the base of the hot water bottle then tied it, top down, to the window handle.

John smoothed back Dan's hair from his forehead. "I hope he doesn't remember this. He'd never look you in the face again."

"As long as he gets better I don't care," she said, but she couldn't hold back the tears running down her cheeks.

After a few minutes she looked up. Her voice was more under control as she asked, "You really care about Dan, don't you?"

John's eyes crinkled above the white cotton gauze mask. "I never had a son, only two daughters. I loved them every bit as much but I've enjoyed having Dan around, taking him shooting and such."

She squeezed his hand. "You will again."

John gazed into her eyes but his own were damp. "I hope so."

Emma stood up, pulled the masks from her own face and his, kissed him briefly, repositioned the masks and then returned to monitoring the flow of water from the enema.

By the time the radio call came through from Fhionna that evening, Sunny had developed a fever and was being looked after by Leah. Margaret had gone to bed complaining of a headache and pain in her chest. Tony was looking after her, though he was already sweating and showing all the signs of succumbing to the illness too.

Emma was sitting by the radio while John cared for Dan.

The speaker crackled for a second, and then Fhionna's voice broke the silence of the sitting room.

"Hello Knockside, Hello Knockside, this is Medic One. Over."

Emma snatched up the microphone. "Fhionna, this is Emma. Thank God! Where are you? Over."

"I'm back at Galashiels, I hear you have a sick boy. Over."

"Not only Dan. Sunny, Margaret and Tony are ill too. Over."

"What about the rest of you? Over."

"John, Leah and I are fine. Over."

"All right, describe the symptoms and give me any other information you might have. Over."

After Emma had completed providing as much detail as she could, the radio fell quiet for a few minutes.

"Fhionna, are you still there? Over."

"Yes, I'm still here, Emma, but I don't have much to go on. Fever, headache, sweating, noisy breathing. They obviously have a chest infection but no other signs. Are you sure nobody has a rash, spots or blisters, any glandular swelling? Over."

"Nothing that we could find. Wait a minute. Over."

John had entered the room and from the first glance at his face Emma could guess the news. Her head sagged and her body shook as the tears fell onto her hands and the microphone.

Fhionna's voice rasped from the speakers again. "Emma, are you there? Over."

John slid the microphone from Emma's unresisting fingers and raised it to his mouth. "Fhionna, this is John. Dan died about five minutes ago. Over."

No answer came for nearly a minute, then Fhionna's voice was quiet. "Oh, John, I am sorry. Look, James and I will get packed up and we will be with you as soon as possible. Over."

"No! I don't think you should, Fhionna," John protested. "We don't know what this is or what's going to happen to the rest of us. Emma, Leah and I have shown no symptoms, only those who went to that damn place for the wind generator but I still don't think you should come here. You're the only doctor we know of, you're too valuable to risk."

"John, there is no point in having a doctor around if they won't visit when people are sick. That's my job - I'm not going to be just a bone setter. Over."

John softened. "Well, at least leave it a couple of days. Let's see what happens with the adults, they might fight this off better than Dan. Over."

A short silence followed before she spoke again. "John, have you heard from Sergei or Martin? Over."

"No I haven't, not for a couple of days now. They said they were heading back to the borders. Over."

"I don't suppose they said which route they were taking?" Fhionna asked.

"No, Fhionna, I'm afraid not. Over."

"All right, we'll try calling them but it's possible they have the same illness as the rest of your group. We'll stay here tonight and then start in your direction first thing in the morning," Fhionna told him. "They have fuel here even though they rarely use vehicles any longer; they've gone over totally to horses. We'll see you tomorrow. Over."

"We'll be expecting you then. Hopefully we'll have better news by the time you arrive. Out."

But the news did not get better. The following morning neither Margaret nor Tony came to the kitchen at breakfast time. John and Emma found them in their bedroom. Margaret was lying face down on the bed. Tony was sitting in the chair beside her, his head on the bed, his fingers still clutching her hand. Margaret was cold but Tony could not have died long before.

John's fingers tightened around Emma's hand for a moment, then his face set. "You go and see how Sunny and Leah are doing. I'll get a shovel. There's no point in hanging about."

Emma saw the hard lines of his face and knew the hurt he was hiding. She reached up and kissed him once on the lips and then went to do as he had asked.

John pulled Tony's body onto the floor and straightened his limbs before rolling the young man, whom he had come respect despite his unconventional relationship with Margaret, in the coverlet from the bed. He wrapped Margaret in a sheet. Then he fetched the Land Rover and backed it up to the cottage door. He carried Tony over his shoulder to the Land Rover but he had to drag Margaret. Dan's little form was no burden at all, as he carried him from the house to the vehicle. Then John drove to the corner of the field that already contained two white crosses. He climbed out and slammed the door, hard, behind him. And then, pulling on his work gloves, he picked up the shovel and started to dig.

Emma stood at the door of Leah and Sunny's room watching, as Leah tenderly wiped her lover's face with a wet towel.

"How's she doing?" Emma asked, through the surgical mask.

Leah jerked, startled by Emma's muffled voice, but quickly regained her self-control. "She is hanging on, Emma. She's not well but Sunny's strong and she's fighting it."

"You don't look as if you slept any more than John or I did. Do you want to take a shower? I'll look after Sunny for a while if you do."

Leah sighed in gratitude. "Thank you, I'll do that. How are the others?"

Emma shook her head. "Gone. John has taken them to the field. He's digging now."

Leah closed her eyes for a moment, and then stood up. "I will have a shower. I'll only be a few minutes."

Emma crossed to the bed and sat down on the edge. She picked up the towel Leah had put aside and took over wiping the restless Sunny's face. It was as pale as moonlight through cloud, shining with droplets of perspiration. Her breathing was a fast, shallow pant. For a moment the stricken girl opened her eyes and tried to speak but she had neither the strength nor breath to form the words and her soon eyelids drooped again in surrender.

Leah returned, drying her hair with a towel.

"Thank you, Emma. Is there any change?"

"She opened her eyes once and I think she tried to say something but she was too weak."

Leah took the towel from Emma's hand and sat beside her on the bed, her own towel wrapped around her head. She met Emma's eyes but only sadness showed there now. All memory of the playful invitation Emma had seen so often before was gone.

"I'll stay with her now," Leah said.

Emma got up to leave. "Call me if you need anything," she offered.

Leah bowed her head in thanks. "I will."

Wearily Emma plodded out to the field, to help John. The hole was six feet long, five feet wide and already about three feet deep in the soft deeply worked ground.

John paused from digging, to watch as Emma approached, but didn't speak.

"I think it will need to hold a fourth soon," Emma told him.

John nodded. "I expected it would. When I'm done I'll cover them with a tarpaulin and leave it open."

Emma pulled a shovel from the back of the Land Rover, jumped down into the hole alongside John and began to dig. They had dug about another foot deeper when they struck rock.

John sighed and shook his head. "That will have to do. It's deep enough."

He boosted her out of the hole and together they carried the bodies from the Land Rover and lowered them in. John jumped down to arrange them more neatly then climbed out again. The tarpaulin they expected to find in the vehicle was missing, so instead they shovelled a layer of earth over the cloth-wrapped remains of their friends and then left them until they would be joined by another.

As they entered the house, their spines were chilled by a wail that should only have been torn from the throat of a demon in torment.

Together they leapt up the stairs and down the corridor to where the scream had now been replaced by a high-pitched undulating sob. Leah sat cradling Sunny's head tightly against her. Her body rocked in time with the tortured cries. For the first time either of them had seen, tears rolled down Leah's cheeks in a steady stream. Abruptly, her body stilled and her eyes swivelled to them, wide with the madness of grief. Her arm stretched out towards them, her finger pointing in condemnation.

"You! This is your fault. You and your damned Western need for power. She need never have died if not for you!"

Emma's face collapsed in grief and disbelief at the assault. "Leah! You don't …"

But she never got to finish what she would say. Letting Sunny's head fall to the bed, Leah's hand flashed under the pillows and she spun back, her Browning nine-millimetre pistol clasped in her hands. In the same movement she thumbed off the safety catch and raised it to point at Emma.

John leapt forward knocking Emma aside as he launched himself towards Leah. The pistol roared twice and kicked upwards in Leah's hands. John's hands slapped to his head, as a cry of anguish burst from his throat. Yet momentum still carried his body and he collided heavily with the maddened woman, knocking her backwards onto the bed and collapsing on top of her to pin her down with his motionless dead weight. As Leah struggled to free herself, Emma ran. She hurtled down the stairs and into her room. Snatching the always-loaded, sawn-off AYA twelve bore from beside the bed, she turned and ran again, but this time towards where her fallen partner lay.

Slamming herself against the wall outside Leah's room Emma breathed in hard then whirled into the doorway. The shotgun flashed to her shoulder as her eyes desperately sought her target. Leah was there but the pistol was beside her not in her hands. Instead she sat on the bed, her back against the headboard, Sunny's head cradled in her lap.

John's still form lay on the floor.

Emma lowered the shotgun muzzles slightly as she tried to work out what was happening. Panting from the strain and the running, she eventually mustered the breath to whisper, "Leah, what have you done?"

Slowly Leah's eyes rose. They were directed towards Emma and yet not at her, as if focused somewhere far beyond. Deep within her subconscious, a mental switch, implanted by the conditioning of her terrorist tutors, had been thrown. Her will was no longer her own. Her voice was strange, deep, almost chanting.

"I am the needle. I cast the shadow. From the light of my nation arose the weapons of God to strike down the infidel. From my village I alone survived the test that was to provide the weapons. From me they formed the shield to protect our people." One hand now rose to point at Emma's trembling body.

"But you and your kind were your own undoing, and ours. My teachers expected you to die in your thousands or hundreds of thousands but your weak and feeble bodies died in billions. And in your perversion you caused even the weapons of God to change into swords of evil. Our weapons mutated and killed not only the billions of you who deserved to die but even our own people. Now only I, and a few of you, are left. Your soldier Applegarth found me and knew me but you destroyed him. You saved me, not knowing that my only reason for being here was to find out how many like you remain and how I might finish you all. I killed that little whore Morag and the old fool Alan and would have done another if you hadn't returned after I set the fire. I would have killed you all eventually and then moved on to seek out more."

Her gaze dropped to Sunny and her hand drifted down to wipe away the blonde hair, long since washed clear of its purple and silver dyes, from the pale but peaceful face.

"Of you all, only Sunny was worth saving. Only she was pure and good enough."

Now the glazed mask fell from Leah's eyes and they glared in hatred again as they fixed on Emma. Her lips curled back. "And you destroyed that. I thought you too might be worth saving, Emma, but no, you are no better than the rest." Her hand swept down, snatched up the pistol and raised it to aim at Emma.

But before she could fire, Leah's face collapsed in shock, her eyes and mouth open wide. Her body slammed back against the headboard then slumped sideways, a dark red stain smearing the pale material as she fell.

Emma did not register and could never remember the roar of the shotgun firing, nor its recoil in her hands. She had not even realised it when the muzzles had crept upwards in response to Leah's admission of murdering Morag and Alan. Her gaze was fixed and uncomprehending, while she stared at Leah's lifeless, staring eyes. Slowly she lowered the gun. Shaking with the terror of what she was sure she would find, she staggered forward and bent to feel for a pulse at John's wrist. She had heard Leah's shot, had seen John clasp his head. Even now she could not bear to lift his face for fear of what she might see. Her trembling fingers detected no throbbing sign of life, only the sticky wetness of blood pooling below him.

Numbly she turned and walked from the room. As her footsteps echoed down the long wooden corridor only one thought reverberated in her grief and shock filled brain. John was gone. Everyone was gone. Once again, she was alone.

Postscript

As Fhionna steered the Range Rover onto the track leading to Knockside, she immediately sensed something was wrong. The headlights cutting through the early morning gloom showed that the cattle grid was lowered in place and the gate left open.

James came back from the intercom fastened to the gatepost. "There's no reply, shall we go up?" he asked.

Fhionna nodded, her forehead deeply furrowed in concern, while James climbed into the passenger seat. As they rounded the bend below the farm she pressed harder on the accelerator. The next grid by the barbed wire fence was also down and the massive new wooden gates at the entrance to the farmyard were wide open.

The heavy tyres ground to a halt in the yard. It all looked different since the last time she had visited, new buildings enclosed two sides and beyond she could see the slowly rotating propeller of the wind turbine.

Sliding from her seat she slammed the Range Rover door behind her and called out. "Emma? John? Is there anybody there?"

The only reply was from the echo of her voice.

Fhionna grabbed her bag from the back of the vehicle, and then she and James hurried towards the door of the main house. Inside she called again. Again she heard no reply. They checked the kitchen, the sitting room, and then started on the bedrooms. Eventually, upstairs, they found Sunny and Leah's room and the macabre tableau it contained. Knowing from a glance that there was no point in checking Sunny or Leah, Fhionna knelt beside John and began to examine him. The back of his shirt was soaked with blood from a hole in his left shoulder.

Carefully she pulled away the material to examine what was obviously a bullet wound and, as the material tore away a sealing clot, a tiny flow of blood pulsed out. Swiftly she checked his neck and found what Emma's trembling touch had missed, a faint and slow but regular beat.

Glancing up at James, she smiled with relief.

"He's alive but not by much. Help me to get him up. We'll take him to the infirmary room, all the medical supplies are there and there's too much risk of infection in here."

#

Many miles away to the west, Emma rolled over in her sleeping bag. The Thermarest insulation mat kept her from the cold of the Land Rover's floor but it was cramped here in the back. She sat up and stared out of the window at the grey, rain-swept sky and heather-clad hills around her. Glumly she rested her chin on her knees as she hugged them. She didn't know where she was and she didn't really care.

Then from outside came a scraping sound at the side of the vehicle. Snatching up the AYA from where it lay beside her, she twisted towards the noise. The big brown eye of a red deer stag peered back at her through the side window. It broke from rubbing its antlers against the side of the Land Rover, and then, with a snort and a toss of its head, it wandered off.

Emma reapplied the safety catch and put the shotgun down. Even when you think you have nothing to live for, she mused, the instinct for self-preservation is still there. Taking a deep breath she struggled out of the sleeping bag she had taken from the shop in Forres, so many months ago. She didn't know where she was and she didn't know where she was going but she knew she couldn't stay here. Should she return to Knockside, she wondered? Fhionna and James were going there, so she wouldn't be alone. But then she would have to deal with the reality of burying John, and of seeing Leah's body again. She shuddered and screwed her eyes tightly shut. There was no point in going back. Everything she had worked for and come to love was gone.

It was time to move on.

#

Two days later, John opened his eyes, to find Fhionna smiling down at him.

"Hello, you lucky man," she greeted, and then gently placed her hand on his chest as he tried to raise himself. "No, don't try to move, my stitching is good but it will be some time before you're ready for that; you've lost a lot of blood. You have a broken collarbone, which I've set, some rather creative restructuring of your shoulder muscles, if I do say so myself, and a bullet crease on your scalp, which will heal itself."

She placed a glass of water to his lips and he sucked, with difficulty at first and then greedily as the cooling liquid flushed the stickiness from his mouth. Fhionna withdrew the glass.

"Take it slowly," she chided.

Working his tongue into usefulness he croaked one word. "Emma?"

Fhionna shook her head. "She wasn't here when we arrived. The Land Rover is gone and all the gates were open." Again she stopped him from trying to rise. "You're going nowhere. You can tell me what happened later. Rest now. You're just lucky that tattoo on your arm told us you are the same blood type as James, otherwise you wouldn't be here at all."

Again he fought to form a word and again it was a question. "Leah?"

Fhionna sighed but gave in to his desperately inquiring expression. “Leah is dead. She had a massive shotgun wound to the chest. James and I buried her and Sunny with the others. We found them by where you’d put Morag and Alan.”

John nodded, closed his eyes and lay back. Leah was dead, the Land Rover was gone, that meant Emma was alive. Wherever she had gone, he would find her.

End

Disclaimer

None of the characters in this book are intended to represent any single person I know, living or dead. Their characters and appearance are amalgams of the multitude I have met in many places and at many times. If you know me and think you recognise something of yourself in one of my characters, and it is something you like, then I definitely got that from you. If it is something you don't like, how could you imagine I would think of you in that way?

Many of the places referred to in the book are real and I know them well. Just remember the circumstances under which they are viewed in the book and that they may therefore seem different from how you now know them.

This is a work of fiction. The action within it mainly takes place after the end of society, as we know it. I do not and would not recommend or condone it as acceptable for anyone to act out any of the activities that take place that would under normal circumstances be unlawful.

Other books

If you have enjoyed this novel be sure to look out for the sequels by the same author.

Coming soon:

Slow the Shadow Creeps

Fast the Shadows Fall

For more information on these books and related topics please visit: www.tfns.co.uk

About the author

Son of a Scottish mother and Yorkshire father, David Eric Crossley was raised in Yorkshire. After a number of unsatisfying jobs, he joined the forces in 1970 and was a soldier for over 20 years.

Qualified as an instructor in Nuclear Biological and Chemical Warfare, Combat Survival, Weapons, Tactics, Urban and Counter-revolutionary Warfare, Explosives, Advanced First Aid, Light Rescue and Firefighting, among other things, and an experienced sniper and forward observation officer, he served in Africa, Asia, the Gulf, Central and South America and Europe. He has experienced the reality and aftermath of war and served in Aid to the Civil Powers operations after two major floods, a hurricane and an earthquake.

After leaving the forces, David settled in Scotland. He has worked as a training consultant, was Training Manager Scotland for the British Red Cross for 4 years including training overseas service and emergency response volunteers, and ran his own training company. He now works as an independent IT training consultant and lives near Glasgow with his wife, Patricia, but still has a cottage in Moray, where most of the action in There Falls No Shadow takes place.

David has been writing professionally since the 1980s and has had over 80 magazine articles and short stories published in outdoors, survival, military, business and general interest magazines. There Falls No Shadow is his first novel in the Shadows series.

You can contact David at:

TFNSbooks@decrossley.co.uk

Printed in Great Britain
by Amazon

77766985R00169